SO NOT MY THING

SO NOT MY THING

MELANIE JACOBSON

Srishti
PUBLISHERS & DISTRIBUTORS

Srishti Publishers & Distributors
A unit of AJR Publishing LLP
212A, Peacock Lane
Shahpur Jat, New Delhi – 110 049

editorial@srishtipublishers.com

First published in India by
Srishti Publishers & Distributors in 2024

10 9 8 7 6 5 4 3 2 1

This is a work of fiction. The characters, places, organisations and events described in this book are either a work of the author's imagination or have been used fictitiously. Any resemblance to people, living or dead, places, events, communities or organisations is purely coincidental.

Printed and bound in India

CHAPTER ONE

I NEEDED the perfect revenge outfit to wear for an ex who never knew he'd been in a relationship with me. Something that would draw no attention to me in our upcoming meeting but would look amazing if he noticed me anyway.

That was what happened when the universe decided to make you the butt of a cosmic joke.

Which it had. In spades.

I settled on a black suit with a slim-cut blazer and a pencil skirt paired with black slingback heels instead of the flats I often wore. The tasteful pearl earrings and necklace my grandmother had given me when I graduated from LSU four years ago finished the look.

Chloe, my roommate, would tell me if I'd gotten my look right. I stepped into the hallway to find her door open to her empty bedroom, the rest of the apartment quiet. She was already at Miss Mary's restaurant downstairs, then. Good. Two opinions were better than one.

I picked up my laptop bag—a light-blue leather satchel—and checked myself out in the mirror over the living room sofa.

Blown out hair, subtle lipstick, understated but elegant outfit and accessories.

"On point," I told my reflection. I wished I felt as confident inside as she looked outside.

I took the stairs down to the ground floor then slipped through the back entrance of Mary's Place, the breakfast café that had taken up residence on the bottom floor of our family's building in the Bywater for my whole life and most of my dad's. I nodded at Jerome in the kitchen, well into breakfast prep. Miss Mary's grandson was a huge Black man, built like an oak and steady as one too. He shot me his usual shy smile and went back to whisking eggs.

In the dining room, the weekday regulars sat in their usual spots, about a third of the forty tables filled. Normal for a Tuesday. And just as normal was finding Chloe sitting with Miss Mary at the matriarch's favorite table in the back of the restaurant, each with a mug of coffee in front of them, the half-full pot beside Miss Mary.

"Morning, Ellie," she said as I stooped down to drop a kiss on her wrinkled brown cheek. "Am I pouring this to go, or will you be joining us like a civilized person?"

"To go, Miss Mary." I was already slipping my traveler tumbler from my bag. "I'm so sorry, but I have a big meeting today, and I need to get in early to prep." When she took the tumbler from me, I held out my arms and did a slow turn. "Can I get outfit approval?"

"You look sharp," she said. "But a soft kind of sharp. Like you're about to pick somebody's pocket but make them feel glad you chose them. What look you going for?"

"A soft kind of sharp," I answered.

"Nailed it." Chloe ran a glance down me over the rim of her mug. She was dressed for work at the newspaper, but her blue eyes blinked slowly, the caffeine clearly not in her system yet. "Almost makes me think I should take up yoga if it'll give me a butt like that."

"I think that might have more to do with some really expensive tailoring." I smoothed down the back of my skirt even though I knew it didn't have a single wrinkle in it. It was a fidget. I couldn't fidget during the meeting today. "Do I look hot but also like I'm not trying to look hot? Like you would only know I was hot if you were paying attention? But also I might be easy to not pay attention to if you weren't trying to pay attention?"

Miss Mary and Chloe exchanged a look. "Maybe she's having a stroke," Chloe said helpfully. Her eyes were brighter; the coffee was doing its work.

"I'm not having a stroke. Just trying to strike a certain…tone."

"You look good," Miss Mary said with the same finality she used for informing customers what they were getting for breakfast if they took too long to order.

It was reassuring, actually. If Miss Mary said it, it must be true.

"And not like a try-hard," Chloe added, which clinched it for me. "What are you trying hard for but trying to look like you're not trying hard for?"

"It's nothing," I said.

"'Nothing' doesn't have you fussing over your clothes and going into work an hour early," Miss Mary noted. "Try again."

"It's…we have a big client coming in today, and I want to make a good impression. That's all."

"A good impression but also no impression," Chloe said. "It's a mystery wrapped in an enigma."

Miss Mary chuckled into her coffee mug.

"I like it better when you're not completely awake," I told Chloe.

"You know how to make it stop. Tell us what's up." She studied me with interest now. That was bad news because Chloe was an aspiring investigative journalist, and once her curiosity was in play, she could be relentless.

There was no way I was ready to tell them about Miles Crowe. They'd both understand immediately, Miss Mary especially. She'd had a front row seat to the whole disaster all those years ago, and she'd wiped my fourteen-year-old tears almost as often as my mom had. Chloe and I had met in college, after the worst of it, but there was no way *not* to know the story unless you'd lived under a rock for a decade. She'd understand why I hated Miles Crowe with a white-hot passion I didn't even reserve for mice, and I *hated* mice.

I hated Miles Crowe more than poison ivy, itchy socks, the stink of the French Quarter on the hottest day of summer, people who didn't use turn signals, "namaste" puns on yoga tank tops, chigger bites, and the thick crust of smashed lovebugs I had to scrub off my car's fender every Saturday in the spring.

Combined.

But somehow, he had ended up on my calendar this morning anyway.

I had half a mind to run over to Miss Lila's shop in the French Quarter for a charm to ward off the bad juju coming for me. She said the stuff in the store was junk for tourists because *real* voodoo was too sacred for them, but I sort of wanted the comfort of a charm anyway.

Just a little gris-gris to hang over the doorway. Or maybe some sage to smudge. *Something* to stop the inevitability of Miles Crowe reappearing in my life.

I'd been quiet too long, and now I had Chloe and Miss Mary's undivided attention. Time for evasive maneuvers. "Are the chicken biscuits ready?" I asked Miss Mary.

"You know it, honey. Jerome's got them boxed and ready for you. Must be a big meeting if you need to bring in catering." The interrogation wasn't over as she reached for the coffee pot.

"My boss is pulling out all the stops, so you know that means breakfast from Mary's Place."

"Course it does," she said, unmoved by my flattery. She had the best chicken biscuits in New Orleans, and she knew it. "Thank her for the order, but I still don't like her running you as ragged as she does."

"You sound like my mom," I said, accepting my full tumbler of coffee.

"We both get to claim you. I figure I raised you..." she studied me like she was calculating, "about twenty-five percent, and your mama did the rest."

"True that." I took a sip of the hot chicory coffee and smiled. "She still doesn't make coffee as good as yours."

"Nobody can." Miss Mary spoke with the calm certainty of gospel truth. "But I sure wish Jerome would learn. I'm not going to be around forever."

"You going somewhere?" I asked, pausing before taking another sip.

Chloe blinked at Miss Mary. "Is something wrong? Are you sick?"

Miss Mary looked from one to the other of us like we were crazy. I'd seen the same look so many times from her in my life that I relaxed and took another sip of my coffee.

"Nothing is wrong with me," she said. "I just shouldn't be the only person in my life who can make a decent cup of coffee."

"Fair enough," I said.

I glanced down at my watch. It was pretty, a tortoiseshell band with a gold-plated face that I'd picked up at the Banana Republic outlet. But one day, it would be a slim gold Rolex, the gift Brenda, our lead broker, gave to each agent when they listed their first ten properties. I had less than a year to hit that number if I wanted to do it in record time for our brokerage.

To be clear, I didn't care about Rolexes. But I cared that winning one from Brenda meant I was on my way to my dreams.

If it weren't for those big goals, I'd have called in sick today or found anywhere else to be except the office when Miles Crowe came for the big pitch Brenda had put together. But she wanted all hands on deck, a demonstration of the full resources she would bring to bear in finding Miles Crowe the best commercial real estate in the city. And that meant every agent there, smiling, oohing and aahing over his second-rate celebrity self and Brenda's presentation.

As soon as his name had come up, I'd stayed out of the office discussions, but we had an open floor plan, and I couldn't help hearing the details even though I didn't care about them. Apparently, now that Hollywood had lost interest in him, Miles was returning home to open a jazz club where he could perform every night and people *had* to listen to him because he owned the place.

What a tool. He hadn't changed in twelve years.

And since I had to look like a supportive team player, I'd sit quietly at the conference table as far from Miles Crowe as possible and get through this morning with my dignity intact.

That would be the biggest victory of all since it was my dignity he'd stolen all those years ago.

"I'm going to get the chicken biscuits from Jerome, then head out," I said. "Thank you for the coffee, Miss Mary."

"Any time."

It was our usual routine. I knew she'd have coffee waiting for me whenever I came down for the day, and if I took too long coming down, she sent one of the servers up to leave some in front of my door. When I'd moved into the apartment over the café after graduation, I'd tried to convince her she didn't need to do anything special for me just because my parents owned the building.

She'd fixed me with a stare that shut me right up. "I've been making coffee for the upstairs tenants no matter who they were since I've been running my place. You ain't special. Or else y'all all special. One of the two."

But that didn't mean I would take it for granted. My mom would be appalled if I ever neglected a thank you.

Jerome helped me load the flat of biscuits into the trunk of my Mercedes, which sounded fancier than it was. It was the cheapest model available, and I'd bought it used when someone had returned it after a three-year lease. Even then, I'd had to take out a loan. I didn't even *want* a luxury car, but you had to project success to commercial real estate clients. A Mercedes—even a boring one—could do that for you.

Our office was Downtown—the Central Business District—a fifteen-minute drive from my apartment. I spent it listening to the *Gladiator* soundtrack because it always sanded down the spikes of my anxiety. I needed to walk into the meeting appearing as calm, cool, and collected as possible.

It was the exact opposite of the way Miles Crowe had last seen me, but I'd changed enough in twelve years that he shouldn't recognize me. I didn't want him to see even a trace of the gawky teenage girl he'd humiliated publicly on national television.

That girl—Gabi Jones—had been a frizzy-haired, scrawny, zitty, brace-faced, glasses-wearing, tear-stained high school freshman.

Graduating from puberty, Lasik, hair serums, gym-time, and careful study of fashion trends had turned me into Elle Jones, a sophisticated 26-year-old with a confident smile and a slight air of mystery.

I hoped, anyway.

It was the image I'd cultivated since college.

I pulled into Crescent City Property Investments, retrieved Miss Mary's biscuits, and rode the elevator up to our offices on the fifth floor. It was the premier boutique agency for New Orleans commercial real estate, the biggest of the little guys.

Because I brought my family's historic Bywater building with me as a client, I could have gotten on with one of the major national brokerages, but I hadn't wanted that. I'd wanted to be somewhere with roots in the community, and that meant Crescent.

The reception desk sat empty, but Brenda was already in her office, the only private office on our floor. She had a very literal open-door policy, and this morning was no different as she typed furiously at her keyboard.

"Hey," I said, popping my head in.

"You're early."

"Wanted to make sure I got the chicken biscuit sandwiches here in time. Need any help setting up?"

"I think it's okay, but let's go look."

I followed her to the conference room. Through the windows, I could see she'd already placed a linen folder embossed with the company logo at every seat. Each folder contained slick brochures, net sheets, and disclosures for the locations she'd be highlighting in her presentation.

I set down the biscuits on the table designated for refreshments. High-end paper goods sat in neat stacks and waited only for the coffee and other small bites to be delivered by a local café.

While Brenda fussed with the alignment of the napkin display, I made my most crucial decision of the morning: I picked my seat.

The whole office would be in the meeting except for the receptionist, Jay. Miles Crowe was bringing his business manager, so that meant eight people at the table, with him sitting beside Brenda at its head. I needed to be on the same side of the table with one person between Miles and me and one person between me and the screen. Optimum invisibility.

I dropped my laptop bag in the chair and browsed through the folder, but I knew the specs for each property by heart. Brenda had zeroed in on properties for the jazz club here in the business district but closer to the hotels and high-end restaurants. I got it. The business district had a sophisticated vibe and not too many music venues. But they were expensive leases, and while that made sense for Crescent's bottom line, it wasn't the way I would have gone.

In fact, if it were anyone but Miles Crowe opening the club, I'd say that he should be looking in the Bywater. But I didn't want Miles Crowe in my neighborhood. I didn't even want him in my city.

"Hey, y'all." One of the other agents, Dave, popped his head in. "We lookin' good?"

"We're looking good," Brenda confirmed. "Let me run through this presentation with you one more time before the client gets here."

Dave and I obediently took our seats and listened as Brenda did her spiel, other agents checking in with a wave as they arrived. She was an old pro, and the only feedback I could have offered was to pick different properties. So I kept my mouth shut other than to compliment her.

When the pastry delivery from the café came, Brenda turned her attention to fussing over the display. I checked my not-a-Rolex-yet to see that we had ten minutes before Miles Crowe was due to arrive.

Yeah, right. I'd bet my—future—Rolex he would be late. He was a notorious diva which was why a lot of his career had fizzled. He'd made buckets of money for a few years there, but his tantrums had become so legendary that he hadn't been worth the trouble to hire anymore.

Or so I'd heard through office gossip. I'd made a point not to follow his career.

By ten minutes *after* 9:00, my future Rolex was safe. No Miles, and one very twitchy Brenda.

By the twenty-minute mark, I was beginning to wonder if I'd stressed myself out over his visit for nothing. By the thirty-minute mark, I relaxed enough to slip into the conference room and serve myself some coffee. *Someone* needed to enjoy it before it went stale.

You know what? Might as well get some food too. My stomach got weird when I was nervous, so I hadn't bothered eating this morning, but there was no reason not to now. I'd leave the chicken biscuits for the rest of the office since I could have them whenever I wanted, but I opened the pastry box from the other café to browse. It had about four different Danish plus beignets.

Mmmmm, beignets. I picked up one of the perfect puffed, deep-fried squares of dough. Normally, they were a terrible choice for any kind of formal setting because the coating of powdered sugar had a tendency to get everywhere, just like with funnel cake. But since Miles the Diva wasn't coming, I didn't care.

I scooped one up and treated myself.

Mmmm. I closed my eyes to savor it. I knew exactly what went into a beignet. Just flour, oil, butter, and the sugar, really. But somehow, they were magic, and this was a good one.

Surely you know what happened next. Surely.

Yeah.

Suddenly every head in the office turned toward the door, and almost like puppets jerked up by their strings, they all rose and headed toward me in the conference room while Brenda went to greet with a smile the man who had ruined half my life.

CHAPTER TWO

I BARELY HAD time to study Miles Crowe before he and his manager were trailing Brenda into the conference room, Miles already extending his hand to each of us for a shake.

He was still hot.

Shoot.

I didn't have time to set down my dainty dessert plate with the remnants of powdered sugar on it before he was turning to me, but that ended up working to my benefit. When he held out his hand to me for a shake, I gave him a polite smile and a nod toward the plate, like, "See? Hands full."

He shot me a quizzical look, and I froze for a second. Had he recognized me? We'd never met in person, but my face had been everywhere on the internet for years, and it was possible.

But he didn't say anything before turning toward the next person, so I dropped my plate into the trash can and walked to my seat. Walking had never felt more complicated. I wanted to strike the perfect balance between casual and purposeful. Instead, I kept fighting the urge to hunch and scurry.

I forced my shoulders back until I caught Dave's eyes widen and realized that my subtle power stance looked more like I was sticking out my boobs. I dropped my shoulders faster than a Mardi Gras necklace could hit the ground at a parade and slid into my seat to watch Miles work the rest of the room.

"I thought people were supposed to look shorter in real life than they do on TV," Donna, the office manager, said quietly from her seat next to mine, "but he looks taller."

"I guess." Her comment gave me a reason to study him for a few seconds while Dave took his turn getting his handshake. Miles had filled out since he was a teenager, growing into the promise his broad shoulders had shown on his skinny frame back then. He was still on the lanky side with a build more like a runner than a gym rat. Although…he wore a fitted black sport coat, and the plain white T-shirt beneath it hinted that he made time for the gym. His distressed jeans and worn black Converse saved him from looking like a douchey frat-bro and more like a low-key star. Back then, his thick, dark hair had a tendency to flop and curl. Now it was cut with some length on top—not enough to spill over everywhere—and a close fade on the side.

"Well, let's get started, shall we?" Brenda said, leading him and his manager to the seats on either side of her at the head of the table.

"Sorry we're late," Miles said. "We were—"

"Don't worry about it," Brenda was already waving away the rest of his words. "You'll find Crescent is a very laidback environment."

Donna kicked my foot beneath the table. It would be fair to say we were somewhat flexible, but I didn't think Brenda had ever had a single laidback moment in her life. She was hard-charging energy, all the time.

"In the folders in front of you, you'll find the spec sheets for the three properties we think will serve you best, but I'll put them up on the main screen while we take a virtual tour."

That was Donna's cue to start the presentation while Brenda rose to narrate from our end of the table. Dave sat across from me, and as he turned from Miles's end toward the screen, his gaze swept over me then paused, his eyes widening a tiny bit again.

I glanced down to make sure that my boobs weren't somehow sticking out without my knowledge and gave a small gasp. Donna glanced over and immediately gave me a sympathetic look.

I could add "a metric ton of sugar" to my power suit accessories. There was a sprinkling of it all over my lapels, down to the first two buttons, stark against the black fabric.

No, sprinkling was kind. It was a sugar apocalypse all up on my bosoms.

No wonder Miles Crowe had looked at me in confusion. He must be wondering how a toddler got invited to the grownup table.

Why didn't you tell me? I mouthed to Donna.

I just saw it, she mouthed back. She handed me the napkin under her coffee, and I took it, but I didn't bother wiping at the sugar. Anyone with beignet practice knows that the sugar only smears when you rub at it, like erasers pushing chalk dust on a dirty board. There was no way to fix this until I could get to the bathroom and dissolve it with water, but I couldn't walk out in the middle of Brenda's presentation.

I tried to pay attention to what she said, but I knew the properties inside and out. They weren't sites I would have picked. They would all work as a club space, but none had the vibe I would want if I were opening a jazz club. But the three properties she was presenting were double profitable for the firm because, as the listing agent, Brenda would earn a double commission.

Who knew? Maybe these were exactly the kinds of polished places Miles was looking for. I snuck a glance down at him to gauge his reaction. His dark blue eyes were crinkled like he was listening intently, but I couldn't tell one way or the other what he thought.

Brenda brought her presentation to a close. "I think you'll agree that each of these properties has unique advantages. It just depends on what you want to prioritize."

"That second one looks good," Miles's business manager, Aaron, said.

"The one near the Sonesta." Brenda nodded. "It would be an excellent option."

"You'd share parking with the hotel," Dave added. This is what we were here for. To jump in and hype the properties.

"Parking is a huge deal in the city," Donna added. "Subleasing rights from the hotel is one of the easiest ways to solve that."

Other agents jumped in as well, each repeating features they liked about the property. I kept quiet because they had it handled.

"I don't know if it's the right vibe," Miles finally said, after hearing them all out. It gave me a jolt to hear him use the same word I'd been thinking. "I think I need something…scruffier." His voice had deepened since high school, but it still had a round, mellow tone to it, like if I could taste his words, I'd pick up a faint trace of honey.

Not that I was thinking about that.

"You can certainly adapt the interiors to reflect your aesthetic," Brenda reassured him. "Let's take a look at Poydras Street again." And she was off and running on why the first property would be perfect.

I kept my eyes on my folder and prayed that the other agents would help a tiny bit less so this meeting could end faster.

"Elle?"

I glanced up when Brenda called my name to find everyone looking at me expectantly, and warmth spread from the back of my neck to my cheeks. I hated the way my skin prickled. "I'm sorry?"

"Miles asked what you thought of these properties."

I looked down the table to where he sat.

He smiled. "You haven't said much. I wondered if you had a different opinion."

I didn't hesitate. "Brenda knows this market better than anyone."

He gave a slow nod. "Thanks."

"How about if we schedule some onsite visits?" Brenda asked.

"Yeah, sure." Miles didn't seem too excited about the idea, but his manager pulled out his phone like he was checking his schedule.

"Great. We'll let the rest of these folks get back to their other clients while we set something up. Thanks for your help, team."

We all rose as she admonished us to be sure to grab some of the refreshments. I held my satchel across my chest as I made my way out, trying to angle my body so that Miles saw even less of me before I left.

I dropped it at my desk and beelined for the restroom. I'd almost made it when Brenda called my name from the conference room door.

"Elle, can you come join us, please?"

I half-turned. "Yeah, in a second." I had to get this powdered sugar off first.

"We don't want to keep Miles waiting." Her voice was firm and a touch cool.

I hesitated, debating whether I should leave the sugar as it was or try to brush it off.

Brush if off, I decided. At least they would realize I knew it was there.

I made a few ineffective swipes at it as I headed toward the conference room, smudging it as badly as I expected to. "Sorry about this," I said, looking down at the mess so I wouldn't have to meet Miles's eyes.

"Been there," he said, and I glanced up at the note of humor in his tone. "Not sure who even orders beignets for a business meeting anyway."

"I did," Brenda said even more stiffly than she'd called my name.

Crap. I didn't want to get on her bad side. "My fault for eating them. I should have known I didn't have the skills to outsmart a beignet."

"You sure this is the agent you want?" Aaron asked.

"Ignore him," Miles said.

"Um, what?" I wasn't totally sure I'd heard Aaron right.

Brenda offered me a professional smile. "Seems Miles would prefer to work with you on finding the right property for his club."

"Oh." I quit brushing at my boobs and let my hands fall to my sides. "That's not the way to go here. Like I said in the meeting, Brenda knows this market better than anyone. You'll be in excellent hands with her." I gave him the same professional smile Brenda had just given me.

"It's true," Brenda confirmed. "Not to put too fine a point on it, but I've been at this for twenty years, and I'm happy to help you find the perfect location."

"I need to…" I gave a vague wave toward my sugar situation. "Good luck with your search." I hurried to the bathroom, wondering if anyone would notice if I hid in there the whole day.

The mirror revealed a hot mess, darker dots where the sugar had landed trailed by smears where I'd tried to wipe them off. Pathetic.

I dabbed it away with seventeen billion wet paper towels. At least it dissolved with water and the black fabric didn't show the wet spots.

I eyed my reflection again, wondering how she'd betrayed me after such a promising start this morning. My lipstick had worn off a little, but the rest of my makeup looked okay, and my hair was still behaving at least. I had to straighten it every other day with a flat iron to keep it under control because it was neither straight nor curly on its own, and the New Orleans humidity translated the in-betweenness into some epic frizz. But the dark brown strands were behaving themselves.

"Too bad you ruined it with your sugar shenanigans," I told my reflection. She stuck her tongue out at me.

I dawdled to give Miles plenty of time to clear out, but when I walked out to my desk five minutes later, he was leaning against it, scrolling through his phone while Aaron stood off to the side, talking too loudly on his.

I shot a look at Brenda's office, but she'd shut her door and was staring intently at her computer screen.

"Can I help you?" I asked, approaching Miles the way I would a skunk in my alley.

"Brenda agreed that you're the better agent for me," he said, sliding his phone into his back pocket. He straightened and studied me, like he was evaluating everything from the cut of my suit to the shine of my watch. It wasn't in a creepy way, but I still didn't like it.

"She said that?" I glanced at her office again, and this time she was watching me. She gave me a slight nod.

"Yeah."

"Did she say why?"

"I think you'll probably have a better sense of what I want."

"Why would you think that?" I'd given him literally no signs that I wanted to work with him or that I cared about his stupid club.

"Instinct. I don't think you liked those properties either. So how does this work? We just drop by some places?"

I did not want this client. Not even for a healthy commission. But Brenda was probably already offended that he'd dumped her for me, and if I turned him down, it would only embarrass her more. She'd been too good of a mentor for me to do that.

"Happy to help," I said to Miles with a bland expression. "We'll check out some places. I'll schedule walk-throughs on the three properties we presented you with today."

A slight crease wrinkled his forehead. "But I don't like those."

That was exactly why I was showing them to him. He could fire me and find himself another broker. I'd even recommend Ginger, one of the other agents, to show him properties in the French Quarter. That might be more his "vibe." But I didn't owe Miles anything, and I wasn't about to play into his entitled rock star garbage by trying hard to please him. "You may feel differently when you're in the space. It'll at least help me pinpoint better what you do and don't want."

"Here's my number," Aaron said, extending a business card. "Text me and we'll schedule it."

"It's okay, Aaron." Miles plucked a business card from the holder on my desk. "Elle Jones," he read. "I'll text you later and work it out."

"Sure. Sounds great." My tone was barely polite.

He tucked the card into his back pocket and gave me a nod. "Talk to you soon."

Then he and Aaron sauntered out.

I watched them go, more frustrated than I could remember being in forever. The last time I'd been this annoyed, my lab partner hadn't done his part for our final project, and I ended up with a B+ in the class.

"Well, that was interesting," Dave drawled.

"That was not my choice."

"Obviously. Why not?"

And that right there was the problem: no one in this office knew that I was one of the first viral GIFs to ever "break the internet." They'd probably sent the GIF of me having a public meltdown over Miles a dozen times to friends over the years in texts and Facebook threads. No one recognized me anymore. Or that the world's most-used meme for rejection was my face next to his.

Nor would they ever know.

"I guess I just don't like high maintenance clients," I said.

Donna blinked at me. "That's not true. You held Michelle Perrin's hand through her absurd property search and never lost your cool."

Michelle Perrin was a fast-rising culinary star who'd wanted to ride the momentum of her fame after almost winning her season of *Chef Supreme*. I'd helped her find the perfect spot for her bistro in the Bywater. But she'd easily been the most demanding client I'd ever had.

"He didn't seem that high maintenance," Dave added, completely unhelpfully. "Kind of more down to earth than I expected for a rock star."

"Except for arriving almost an hour late and hating everything we showed him, you mean?"

"Is this going to be a problem?"

I turned to find Brenda behind me. "No, not at all. Also, I'm really sorry about that. I swear to you that I didn't try to poach him."

Her air of coolness evaporated as she gave a small sigh. "I know. Why don't you step into my office?"

I followed her back to her desk feeling more relieved than worried. Brenda had always been a fair boss, and I was glad for a chance to explain myself. Except I had no explanation as to why Miles had insisted on me as his agent. There'd been no hint of recognition on his face when we spoke.

"I know you didn't poach him," she said as I settled into my seat. "I could feel my age working against me, and it made me defensive."

"Your age? You're so young." There was no way she was even fifty yet.

"Yeah, but he sees me as a different generation. He'd probably be more interested in me as an agent if he were opening an antique shop or something." She rolled her eyes, and I couldn't decide if it was at Miles or herself.

"It doesn't matter. He'll be a great client for us to boast about, and you've got strong instincts. Knock him out with some stellar properties. I trust you. I just wanted you to know I'm not upset with you. A win for you is a win for all of us."

"Thanks for understanding," I said. "But honestly, I'd be happy to hand him off to someone else. I'm pretty busy trying to help another client look for a boutique space."

"You can do both. He's made his decision, and the client gets what the client wants."

Miles wouldn't. I'd find a way to make him someone else's headache without him firing the firm all together.

"All right," I said, standing again. "I guess I'd better go set up some showings."

And figure out how to get him off my client list. There was no way Miles Crowe would ever be worth the trouble.

CHAPTER THREE

I WAS a frustrated mess when I slammed the door to my apartment shortly after five that afternoon.

When Chloe didn't immediately demand to know what was wrong, I realized she probably hadn't made it home from work yet.

I stripped off my suit and threw the jacket in the corner. It was going to have to be dry-cleaned before I wore it again.

If only they could dry-clean my memory, and they could remove the section where I met Miles Crowe for the first time and I was covered in beignet dust.

I flopped onto my bed and stared at the ceiling.

I mean, *seriously*?

There had been only one objective this morning: fly completely under Miles Crowe's radar, then never see him again. Instead, I'd stood out in the worst possible way, and now I had an appointment with him tomorrow.

"Hey, universe? You suck."

The universe didn't answer.

I put on joggers and a tank top and went downstairs to the café for sympathy. Jerome was almost done wiping down the kitchen, all except for the counter where Miss Mary worked on the bread dough she would leave to rise overnight for sandwiches the next day. Then they'd lock up, and Jerome would drive her home.

"Hey, sugar," Miss Mary said, glancing up as the kitchen door closed behind me. "You hungry? I can whip up an omelet for you."

"No, that's okay, I'll do it. Want one?" I walked into the commercial fridge and grabbed the ingredients I needed.

"No. Douglas has some red beans and rice waiting for me." Miss Mary punched the dough, her face relaxed. Maybe I needed some dough to punch.

"Lucky. I guess you'll be having red beans and rice for dinner too, Jerome?"

"You know it," he said, grinning at me as he filled the mop bucket.

The back door to the kitchen opened, and Chloe walked in, sniffing the air. "Omelet?"

"Yeah," Miss Mary said. "Whip one up for Chloe too."

"Yes, ma'am. Grab two more eggs," I told Chloe, and she slipped into the cold storage to obey.

She handed them to me and grabbed another mop to help Jerome. "Everybody had a good day?"

"Can't complain," Miss Mary said. "Good lunch rush. Even ran out of chicken salad."

Jerome nodded, a man of few words as usual.

When I didn't say anything, Chloe paused her mopping. "Ellie?"

This was such an old routine for all of us that I wouldn't get away with silence. But I didn't want to talk about the day from hell. "It was fine."

"Uh oh," said Jerome, pausing with his own mop.

"What? It was fine." I cracked another egg.

"Uh huh," Miss Mary said. "That's the kind of 'fine' I give Mr. Douglas when he doesn't get the yard cut."

"Bad client," Chloe guessed.

"Stupid tenant?" Miss Mary guessed, giving her dough another whack.

"Too much work?" Jerome guessed.

There was no use in trying to avoid it. They'd get it out of me now or five minutes from now. I minced my onion the way Miss Mary had taught me but with extra hard thwacks. "Miles Crowe," I muttered. I thunked a cast iron skillet onto the cooktop hard enough to make Jerome wince.

"You're kidding," said Miss Mary.

"Dang," said Chloe.

"Who?" asked Jerome.

"That dude who won *Starstruck* a while back?" Chloe said. "You would have been young. It was a big deal when we were in high school."

"Can't be that big of a deal if I never heard of him." Jerome went back to mopping.

"You see that?" Miss Mary said. "Jerome doesn't know. It's not a big deal."

"I don't know what?" he asked, stopping again.

Chloe and Miss Mary exchanged looks.

"One of y'all going to tell me?" He'd lost interest in mopping.

I sighed. "You know that meme that goes around with a guy on one side saying, 'So not my thing,' and the other side says 'Rejected' over a crying girl?"

"Yeah…?"

"That's me."

He blinked. "Nah."

"Believe it," Miss Mary said.

"Y'all messing with me?"

Chloe shook her head. I murdered some peppers, seeds flying.

Jerome dug his phone out of his pocket and tapped it a few times, looking from the screen to me. "This is you?" He turned the screen toward me, as if that picture hadn't been burned into my brain for twelve years.

Chloe swatted his hand down. "It's her."

"Bruh." He looked at me with wide eyes.

It was such a perfect way to sum up the situation that I had to laugh. "Yeah. Bruh."

"I don't think I ever met a walking meme." He studied me like he'd never seen me before. "How did that even happen?"

"How did I have a childhood crush turned against me and ruin my life for years?" I hated that I still felt a flicker of the shame that had drowned me the day Miles had gone on *Live with Laura*.

"Well, yeah." He ducked his head like he realized how much deeper his question went than he meant it to go. "You don't have to answer that." He went back to scrubbing the floor like he was trying to dig through it with the mop.

"It's okay," I said. "I shouldn't have said it so snotty."

"Want me to tell the story?" Chloe asked.

"Might as well." I moved on to slicing up a mushroom and tried to make my brain go somewhere besides the kitchen while Chloe served up the worst disaster of my life for Jerome's consumption.

"I met Elle halfway through college, and by then, she'd already done her Cinderella makeover, so people didn't realize who she was the minute they saw her. But one night when I texted her the meme because I didn't know it was her, she busted out crying and told me the story."

"Thanks," I said, my tone as dry as a pork rub. "That makes me sound way less pathetic."

"To be fair, I probably would have too," Chloe said. "So Elle here was born Gabrielle Jones and used to go by Gabi."

"Yeah, that's what Dylan still calls her sometimes," Jerome said.

"Right. So you've heard our Ellie singing when she's cleaning up back here and she thinks no one's listening?"

He grinned. "That I have."

My cheeks heated. "Get on with the story."

"Our Gabi-now-Ellie had quite a set of pipes. She was in high school show choir as a *freshman.* Nobody makes show choir as a freshman."

"You ought to sing louder," Miss Mary said. "I've been missing it."

I waved like I was dispersing her words. I didn't sing in public anymore.

"Anyway," Chloe continued. "She saw Miles there and fell madly in love, and—"

"Stop." I sighed and threw the veggies into the hot skillet. "We had a regional show choir competition. Miles Crowe was there. He was a junior, and he had a solo. My very dumb fourteen-year-old self was immediately heart-eyes for him. Like, imagine the most unironic use of that emoji, and that was me. Which would have been fine. I probably would have dreamed of seeing him again the next year then gotten over it. But then he went on *Starstruck*, and the top four finalists do hometown performances. And suddenly, the normal celebrity crush some teen girls get went into overdrive because this one seemed so *possible*. Like, he lived in the next town over, my cousin knew his best friend, and I was so sure I would meet him for real."

"It's all she talked about for two months straight when she found out he was on," Miss Mary said.

"I was ridiculous," I agreed. "But I got tickets to his hometown performance at the fairgrounds. My cousin even got us passes so we could be down at the front of the crowd. The producers love having teenage girls in the front. Watch any of the dance or singing competitions on TV. You'll see."

"I believe you," Jerome said.

"Anyway, when it was Miles Crowe's turn, they cut to him live, and he was so good." I sounded like I was admitting that against my will. But he was. I couldn't deny that. "So I..."

"Had the meltdown," Chloe finished.

"Yeah. Full snot-nosed, ugly-cry, fangirl meltdown during his performance. The camera panned to me three or four times. Some producer in a booth was loving it."

"Going viral was a new thing back then," Chloe said. "And memes weren't much of a thing yet either, but our girl here was *everywhere.*"

"Yeah. It was bad. Reporters would wait on the sidewalk outside of my school and interview every single kid walking off campus to see if they knew me. I had invitations to go on every show. All the major late-night shows. Every major morning news show. My mom wouldn't let me do any of the late-night ones because she didn't trust them not to be mean to me, but she said yes to *Live with Laura*, of course."

"Duh," Chloe said. Laura was a former local TV newswoman who'd made it big in Hollywood.

"So I go on Laura's show, she's super nice about everything, and she gives me a bunch of *Starstruck* swag including a signed poster of Miles Crowe." I'd burned that after his own appearance on her show. "Two weeks later, he wins the whole thing and does *Live with Laura*. By then I was already a GIF that you sent to show you were really excited about something."

"That must've been weird," Jerome says.

"Yes and no? Social media was still pretty new, so I had no idea how big it would get and keep getting. Anyway, Laura asks him if he thinks my 'moment' helped drive up the votes to help him win, and he's like, sure, yeah. And then..."

At this point, I didn't want to tell the story anymore, so I turned back to the skillet, giving it a shake. Stupid onions, making my eyes sting.

"That boy did her wrong," Miss Mary said. "Laura asked him if he had a message for his number one fan, and he said she seemed like a sweet kid but she so wasn't his thing."

"Dang." Jerome shook his head.

"Made us all so mad," Miss Mary continued. "But I wish you wouldn't have quit music, Ellie. I miss it. She used to write her own stuff and put it on YouTube," she explained to Jerome.

Chloe's eyes widened. "I didn't know that. How come I didn't know that?"

I shrugged. "That was then. Lots of teen girls go through that phase. If it's not songs, it's bad poetry. I deleted my channel." I still sometimes worked my feelings out in lyric form in a notebook, but I hadn't put any of it to music in ten years, at least. "I outgrew it."

"Did you, though?" Miss Mary asked. "Seems like it still sticks with you sometimes. Like when you stop singing the second you know someone is listening."

"Any rejection you get when you're fourteen is going to stick with you," I said. "But I could have let this go if I hadn't become *the* meme for rejection after that. Like, that clip had ten million views on YouTube by the time I graduated from high school. I haven't even looked at it since then." I shook the pan to get the veggies moving and glimpsed Chloe pointing up with her thumb to indicate to Jerome that the views had gone even higher.

Whatever. I didn't want to know. I broke the last two eggs into a bowl, single-handed like Miss Mary taught me, and scrambled them, the fork making an angry hiss as it scraped at the bowl over and over again. I could imagine how much higher the views had climbed based on the number of times I ran into my own face on the internet. Dylan had even brought me a Trivial Pursuit card once where I was an answer in the Entertainment category.

Apparently, America had been bored when I'd had my moment.

"I'm sorry that happened, Ellie," Jerome said quietly.

"Yeah, me too. So now that the facts are fresh in everyone's minds, maybe you'll all believe I did *not* choose Miles Crowe as a client."

"So how did it happen?" Chloe asked. "Did he recognize you? Was he trying to make up for being a jackass back then?"

"He didn't seem like he did," I said. "And he didn't explain why he wanted me to be his agent. Brenda ended up being pretty cool about it, but I tried eighty-seven ways to get out of it, and he was basically like, 'Nah, this is what I want,' so that's not super awesome."

"What are you going to do?" Miss Mary asked. "Be the best real estate agent ever?"

I stopped whisking for a moment to stare at her. "Do you even know me?"

Chloe grinned. "You're going to make his life miserable until he fires you?"

"No. Good guess, though. That was my first plan."

"What, then?" Jerome asked.

"I'm going to find him the worst possible property for what he wants to do and negotiate the most expensive possible lease for the longest term possible." It was the plan I'd decided on as I drove home.

Jerome sucked his teeth. "That's cold."

Miss Mary came over and gave me a hug. I waited for her to talk me out of it, but instead she said, "Good girl."

And that made Chloe laugh all the way through the perfect omelet I plated for her.

CHAPTER FOUR

I PACED INSIDE of the empty space on Julia Street. I'd arrived ten minutes early for my appointment with Miles because I was always early for appointments. I loathed tardiness, and I was already annoyed knowing that Miles would be late today like he'd been at the office.

If he was more than five minutes late, I would text him that I was leaving and he could book another appointment. Even better if he booked it with someone else.

I checked my outfit to make sure it looked good on the extremely slim chance he did show up. Gray pinstriped trousers with a wide leg, fitted white top, stacked red heels to keep it interesting. Hair in a low ponytail, simple silver pendant necklace with a fleur-de-lis charm.

Pace. Pace. Pace. Walking back and forth inside the front door wasn't enough to burn off my nervous energy. And there definitely wasn't enough in the boring beige walls and acoustic ceiling tile behind me to keep my mind busy.

What if Miles had recognized me yesterday? What if that was why he'd chosen me?

Worse, what if he didn't recognize me yesterday but did today?

I didn't want to deal with either scenario. I absolutely did not want him to see *Gabi* Jones. Only the most distantly polite version of *Elle* Jones possible. I wanted a third scenario to be true: Miles hadn't recognized me yesterday, wouldn't today, and would be bored enough with my services that he'd pick another agent or firm.

Maybe running through my affirmations would help. Normally, I focused on business, repeating the outcome I wanted, or naming my goals. Stuff like, "I will close this deal." Or "I will make my second quarter goals." Simple ideas that I repeated until they felt inevitable. I'd listened to a metric ton of self-help and sales psychology books that said to do this, and so far, I was meeting all my goals. It basically boiled down to, "Here's how to talk yourself into believing you can do it."

But yesterday, I'd pulled up an old podcast from when I'd first started at Crescent City Properties. I'd been so intimidated about whether a barely-out-of-college grad could break into New Orleans commercial real estate that I'd had to begin with an even simpler affirmation about basic self-confidence. *Act like you're as successful as you want to be until you* are *as successful as you want to be.*

Today I'd have to take it even further: *Act like you were never the teenage girl this man humiliated on national television. Act like you have always been the picture of grace and composure.*

"You are a…duck," I said aloud. One of our sales seminars had used that metaphor, the idea that your feet might be paddling furiously beneath the water, but to the client, you look serene. "You are a *swan*," I said next. Even more graceful. Why not? I lengthened my neck like a ballerina.

When Miles showed up, I'd be the picture of composure. Subdued, elegant.

I glanced down at my watch. It was nine o'clock exactly, and there was no Miles walking through the door.

What I would *not* do was wait forty-five minutes for him the way the whole office had on Tuesday.

He had exactly five minutes before I walked out and texted him to reschedule.

When the minute hand hit the five, I pulled out my phone and started the text as I headed out the door.

Sorry you couldn't make it. I'm punctual and expect my clients to be as well. Please notify me next time you have a conflict.

There. That should tick him off enough to fire me and go find someone else to cater to his whims.

I pressed send right as I hit the sidewalk and a male voice called, "Whoa!" and hot coffee drenched my chest as I smacked into something hard.

"I'm so sorry," the voice said as I gasped.

Miles. It was Miles. I'd plowed right into him, and somehow, he was holding two dripping coffee cups and a huge brown stain was spreading across my pristine white shirt.

"Oh, man, seriously, I'm so sorry," he repeated. "Did it burn you? Are you okay?"

The coffee was seeping through to my skin, and I plucked the fabric away from my body. "It wasn't hot enough to burn me."

His phone dinged and he checked his Apple watch. "Uh, that's from you, canceling on me."

I refused to feel awkward about it. "Didn't think you were going to make it."

"And now I bet you wish I hadn't. Let's go get you dried off," he said.

"It's fine. I've got napkins in my car and a shirt I can change into. Why don't you look around the space while I clean myself up?"

I didn't wait for an answer as I continued down the block to my car. I grabbed some napkins and dug into my gym bag where I'd thrown in a black tank top this morning. It was made of Lycra with white racing stripes down the side, but at least it wasn't soaked in bean juice.

I walked into the corner Starbucks and caught the barista's eye, holding up my black tank and pointing to my shirt.

"Four seven one six," he called, giving me the bathroom code.

I ducked in and stripped my shirt off. There were no paper towels, only an air dryer at the worst possible height for drying my boobs. Next, I dabbed at my damp skin with toilet paper. It disintegrated in my hands and left balled up white tissue lint behind.

"I hate everything."

Saying it didn't dry my skin any faster.

Great. Looked like I was getting an early quad workout. I positioned myself in the most awkward possible squat beneath the hand dryer, then kept waving my hands to keep the air going until my chest was mostly dry and the toilet paper lint was gone.

I straightened, my thighs protesting, yanked on my gym top, and tried hard not to storm out, leaving a tip for the barista before I deposited my ruined shirt in my car and headed back to Miles and the property.

"Calm, cool, collected," I chanted on the trip back up the street. "Calm, cool, collected." I said it at least fifty times before I reached the door, and even though I didn't feel remotely collected, I had at least talked myself into faking some calm. I took a deep breath, skirted the coffee puddle on the sidewalk, and walked in.

Miles turned as soon as the door opened. "Elle, hey. Sorry about that. I'll get your shirt cleaned, no problem." Today he wore jeans and a short sleeve black shirt that looked tailored to perfection. Without the jacket he'd worn in the office, it was obvious that he put in his gym time.

"I don't think the coffee will come out." I turned to scan the space, the epitome of professionalism. "It's fine. I've got other shirts."

"Then I'll replace it. Let me make it up to you. Can you text me your size?"

There was a time when having Miles Crowe's personal number would have meant *everything* to me. Fourteen-year-old Gabi could both imagine Miles asking her to marry him in a huge romantic ceremony where he sang a song he'd written for her and also could never have imagined a moment in which he'd be offering to buy her a new shirt.

Elle did not care about either of these things. *Calm, cool, collected. Get this guy to drop you.*

"That's not necessary," I told him. "Let's talk about the property."

He studied me for a second, hesitating. His shirt made his eyes bluer. I refused to look away, but I wanted to. He cleared his throat. "I think you might still be mad, and I get it. I was late, and I ruined your shirt. I feel so bad. Like, terrible."

He sounded…sincere? Well, he should. Not that it mattered. He wouldn't be my headache much longer. I needed to redirect this meeting and get it over with so I could go home and change.

You are grace personified, I reminded myself as self-consciousness over my gym top crept in. I did the swan thing with my neck, reclaiming my composure.

"Oh no, did it burn your neck?" he asked.

I quit stretching my neck and fought a blush. "No, it's fine. Look, if we're going to work together, you're going to have to be on time. I have other clients and responsibilities." There. That should tick him right off.

"Understood. I'm so sorry about this morning. I stopped to get us the coffee at this place around the corner, and I had no idea it would take so long.

I didn't even bring Aaron today because he runs late constantly, and I still didn't make it on time. I feel terrible," he repeated. "For Tuesday too. Couldn't get Aaron out of the door."

"Then fire him," I said because I found myself almost believing his apology. "If he can't keep an appointment, you should find a manager who can."

"Fair, except he's my cousin, so I can't." He sighed. "I'll figure out how to make this up to you, but in the meantime, we're here, right? Might as well talk about the space."

Might as well use the time to convince him I was the wrong agent for him without actually saying I didn't want to work with him. If I did, he might ask why, and that would open up a discussion I refused to have with Miles Crowe, ever.

"Sure, let's talk about the property," I said. "As you can see, it's the most spacious one Brenda identified for you. Did you get a chance to explore it while I cleaned up?"

He nodded once, slowly. "Yeah. It's definitely enough room, but I already knew from the presentation that this wasn't going to be right. I was hoping for some new properties to consider."

"These are the best ones in Downtown, and it's most efficient to start by figuring out what does and doesn't work for you and calibrate from here."

"I guess that makes sense." He sent a quick glance around the room. "I don't know how to explain this, but places give me a vibe. I know," he said with a wince, like he thought I was about to interrupt him. "It sounds like I've been in California too long."

"Not really. People talk about places having a vibe all the time."

"Right. Uh, I don't think I mean it the way most people mean it."

I was curious in spite of myself. "What do you mean then?"

"It's like…I can kind of feel the soul of a place? I don't know." He shoved his hand through his hair like he was frustrated with himself for his lack of words. "I know what song I would write about a place I'm in. That's the only way I can explain it."

"What song would this place get?"

"It wouldn't. That's the problem. It's a great space for something else. Maybe a FedEx or something, but this place has *no* soul."

I didn't want to tell him that I knew exactly what he meant. Tourists always beelined for the French Quarter without ever realizing that the true gem was *next* to the Quarter. In the Bywater, we had Royal Street and all the rest too, but once they crossed Esplanade into the Marigny and on to the Bywater, the streets were alive with locals who were escaping the neon clatter of the crowded Quarter. On *their* side of Esplanade, it was full of bachelorette parties and moms escaping their kids for the weekend, everyone drunk and sloppy in the streets at night.

On *my* side, it was happy chatter, friends calling to each other, lively conversations between sidewalk tables, the music of locals spilling from the doorways of lowkey bars. And none of it disrupted by drunken shrieks and the rude things men called to women, trying to entice them to do a little flashing and earn plastic Mardi Gras beads, year-round.

"It sounds stupid, I know," Miles said, and I realized I'd been quiet too long.

"No. It doesn't. The Central Business District, as advertised, is pretty corporate."

"Should we go look at the other two properties, then? Because this one is so not my thing."

My breath caught, and my mind blanked as I struggled for words. He might as well have stabbed me for how hard those words hit me, the *Live with Laura* words. The meme words. *So not my thing.*

He *did* know it was me.

"You okay? Sorry, that was a bad joke. When I was an idiot kid, I…you know what? Never mind. Don't know why I resurrected that."

So…he *didn't* know it was me in that meme with him?

I gave him a long look, weighing and measuring. He didn't seem to be watching me for any kind of reaction to see how his joke had landed. I hadn't seen a single flash of recognition in his face the whole time we'd been in here, no fishing to suggest that he knew who I was. Who I'd *been*. And what's more, he'd called his words a bad joke and avoided a chance to bring up his own fame.

I ran through the evidence of the morning. He'd only been five minutes late because he was getting me coffee, he'd apologized for spilling it, offered to buy me a new shirt, and had the instinct to know this building lacked soul.

Maybe Miles was more grounded than I thought. He wasn't Bywater-cool, but a lot of jazz clubs thrived in the French Quarter.

"Let's not look at the other two places," I said, making an announcement before I even fully realized I'd made a decision. "In fact, let me look at some different properties I'm thinking of in the Quarter."

"Great, let's go."

"I didn't mean now." I swept a hand down to indicate my workout shirt. "I need to change."

"Oh, right." He looked sheepish. "Me too, I guess." He plucked at his shirt, and it stuck to him slightly.

"You spilled on yourself too?"

"Kind of a lot," he admitted.

"You didn't say anything." I would have expected a rock star to pitch a fit. Then I took a short breath and offered an apology. "I'm sorry. The coffee spill was my fault."

He shrugged. "Not really. I bet if I'd been on time, it wouldn't have happened. Anyway, not a big deal, but I wouldn't mind drying off."

"I'll text you with some appointments for tomorrow. Sound okay?"

"Sounds great. Looking forward to it. I'd better, uh…" He gestured toward the door.

I followed him out and locked up behind us.

"I'm this way." He jerked his head in the opposite direction from where I needed to go.

"I'm the other way. Drive safe. I'll be in touch tomorrow."

He nodded and headed up the street.

I watched him go until he was long out of sight. "Looking forward to it," he'd said. He'd sounded like he meant it.

Weirdly, I kind of did too.

CHAPTER FIVE

I SETTLED in at my desk the next morning and texted Miles that I wanted to check on the properties before I brought him to see them and set an appointment with him for Monday. I spent time on LoopNet checking out the spaces available and found some strong possibilities. None of them was perfect, but with a little imagination, each could be adapted to become a jazz club.

The rents would add up to a nice commission too. In fact, if Miles took any of these…

I opened my calculator app and ran the numbers.

"Well, well, well," I said, leaning back in my chair.

"What's up?" Dave asked from his desk a few feet from mine.

"Just realized that if my client takes any of the properties I'm going to show him, I'll meet my quarterly goal."

"Niiiiice." That was from Donna who sat a few feet in the opposite direction. "You are en fuego this year."

"I'm all about that life," I said and laughed when Dave mimed making it rain with cash.

"So you don't mind having Miles Crowe now?" he asked.

"I don't know." He hadn't recognized me. He hadn't been the diva I'd expected him to be. And getting him into a French Quarter property would make Brenda happy and make me look good. And of course, the math said it would be worthwhile.

And did I really want to give Crescent City Properties a black eye by forcing him to drop me?

"I need to head out and do some research." I gathered up my bag and waved to Brenda on the way out. One of the things I liked best about my job was that because I was a commission-only independent agent, I didn't have to report to anyone about how I spent my time. We often had to head out for client meetings and property checks. If I wanted to waste my time by not being productive, I was only hurting me. But I wasn't a time-waster. I protected my Sundays fiercely, but the other six days of the week, I was hustling. Why let Miles stop me now?

I parked on Chartres and walked to the Quarter, sitting on a bench in Jackson Square to listen to the young men busking for money while I considered possible sites for Miles's club. It was late spring, the perfect time for tourists to come to New Orleans, and plenty of them milled around the square or stopped to listen.

I was sure a lot of the tourists wondered if they might be seeing the next Trombone Shorty or Kermit Ruffins, but most of them didn't have an ear to discern the good stuff from the great.

These kids were good, though. Most of the ones who played down here were. They had to be to hustle for money in a city full of so much talent. One drummed on an upturned plastic five-gallon bucket, the percussion of choice for street musicians. Another one was on trumpet, and the third played melodica, a quirky combination of harmonica and keyboard. They were doing a cut from the soundtrack of a Pixar film that had been scored by Jon Batiste himself, a native son who had done the city proud.

Eventually, I turned my attention to the streets leading from the square into other parts of the Quarter, mentally running down each one and considering the vibe. I got what Miles had meant by that. You could get a vibe from a building or a block or a whole city. The Quarter had a personality distinctly different from the Bywater, but even the Quarter's individual streets had a different feel from each other.

Bourbon Street was out of the question. It was as commercial in its own way as the actual business district was, but with a grittier coating and a pervasive cigar-and-spilled-beer smell. It was always the most packed once tourist season started hopping during Mardi Gras, and locals stayed away. I might not respect Miles's pop career much, but he wasn't opening a pop club, which *would* work perfectly on Bourbon.

A jazz club…Royal Street was okay. Mostly antique stores, and Chartres was mainly historic townhomes with wrought iron balconies and plantation shutters. But St. Philips was a possibility. Or even Governor Nicholls.

Then again, Miles had come up through *Starstruck*, so he might like how commercial Bourbon was. It definitely had name recognition going for it, and it might appeal to him.

I rose and walked to the different properties I was considering. You could drive in the Quarter, but it was hardly worth it between the potholes and the drunk tourists always staggering into the street. I wasn't sure which was more annoying. I took pictures and made notes at each vacant site before calling it a day.

I swung by BB King's Blues Club on the way back to my car and stopped to consider it. I couldn't even remember the last time I'd gone out and heard live music, which was stupid considering I was surrounded by it most evenings.

I hurried to my car and drove home, smiling when I spotted Chloe's red sedan in its parking spot behind our building.

"Yo!" I called as I stepped into our place.

"Yo," she called faintly from her bedroom.

I knocked on the door, then leaned against the doorframe. She was lying on her back with her eyes closed. "We're going out tonight," I informed her.

She blinked and propped herself up on her elbows. "I thought you said we're going out tonight."

I grinned at her. "I did."

She sat all the way up. "So you're going to put Workaholic Elle to bed at nine and let Fun Ellie come out to play?"

"Don't make me regret it."

She whooped. "No way! This is going to be awesome. What are we doing?"

"I realized it's been forever since I've heard live music. If I want to find the right property for Miles, I have to get a sense of the different possible layouts he could work with. I want to see how other clubs use their spaces."

Her shoulders slumped slightly. "So it's still work."

"Only kind of. I could have looked this all up online. I figured it wouldn't hurt to do the research with a whiskey in one hand and a live band doing the background music."

"Yes! Correct! Let's do this! When and where?"

I shrugged. "How about dinner and music at Snug Harbor, then see what we're in the mood for?"

"Ooh, I haven't been there in a while. I heard they added a blackened drum fish to the menu. I've been wanting to try it."

I gave her a wry smile. "So you're saying it's kind of a work night for you too?"

Chloe moonlighted as a food critic on a blog she called The Kitchen Saint. No one knew who she was—even the editor—because she insisted that keeping her identity secret was essential to writing honest reviews. I was literally the only person who knew it was Chloe, and that's only because I'd walked past her open laptop once when she was composing a blog post.

"My food reviews are not work. They are love."

I snorted. "Tell it to whoever gets your three-star reviews. Don't think it feels like love to them."

"Then they should make better food." She bounced from the bed. "I'm going to shower. I'll be ready before seven with a couple of whiskey sours for us to pre-game."

I rolled my eyes. Chloe would do her best to get me into trouble tonight, but that was nothing new. Come tomorrow morning, I might have a slight hangover, but I'd also have a better sense of what to show Miles so I could seal the deal and make my quarterly goal. He'd be so impressed with my understanding of the kind of space he needed, he'd be ready to sign on the dotted line by the end of business on Monday.

CHAPTER SIX

"I DON'T KNOW," Miles said, frowning at the final space I'd booked for us to view.

The bare walls and serviceable floor tile didn't hint at greatness, it was true. But he wasn't even *trying* to take it seriously, and it made me feel kind of…stabby. It was late Monday afternoon and an unseasonably hot day. Maybe the humidity was making me cranky because none of the properties had their air conditioning on. Or maybe it was the fact that he was dismissing the last property I had to show him without considering the possibilities of *any* of the properties.

"What don't you know?" I asked. "It's the right size, it has a generous kitchen, it's a high-traffic location, and the price is good. I only showed you those other two so you'd see how awesome this one is."

"A little sales psychology, huh?"

I didn't like his tone. It sounded judgy. "Why do you say it like that?"

"Like what?"

"Like I'm trying to sell you a used car I know will break down tomorrow."

Miles ran his hand through his hair, a nervous habit I'd seen a few times today. A couple of pieces stuck up, and I wanted to reach over and smooth them back into place. "Sorry. That's not what I meant. It's just…" He looked around the wide, empty space, the walls painted dark red, the stained acoustic tiles in the ceiling. "What do *you* like about this space?"

I mustered my most cheerful sales voice, a tone that sounded like a cheerleader making a business pitch. Perky, perky, perky. "It's got great dimensions for seating. The stage could go there." I pointed to an area along the side wall. "You don't want to face your audience toward the kitchen, so putting them crossways from it lets your wait staff slip in and out unobtrusively. Your bar would go over there." I pointed in the opposite corner. "Make it extra-long for more seating. Honestly, it's a great set up. Ideal, even."

He nodded. "I hear what you're saying. And I grew up coming to the Quarter and listening at doors until I'd get chased away. I love the history of it. You can feel it in the building."

"It has a good vibe, right?"

"It does."

"But?"

He rubbed his hand over his face. "But this block doesn't."

"Do you want to be on Bourbon?" I asked. "You saw the only property available right now that's suitable for what you want to do, but you didn't like it."

"I don't want to be on Bourbon. That's not it either."

I studied him closely, the frustration clearly etched into the faint lines around his eyes, even though he was trying hard to be patient with me. Fussy clients were the norm in commercial real estate. They planned to open a business, and location was everything. Sometimes they were just picky because they had totally unrealistic expectations. But some clients were fussy because they were passionate about their vision, and I was beginning to realize that Miles was the second type.

"Why did you want me to be your agent?" I asked. I clearly wasn't showing him the properties he wanted—hadn't even tried to the first time. But he'd been persistent about it.

"It was your face in that meeting. With your boss?" He added the last part like I wouldn't remember the only meeting we'd both been in. "Anyway, that's why."

"I'm not sure I get it. What about my face?"

Miles hesitated. "I don't know. Everyone else at that table was acting like she'd presented me with the three greatest properties ever to become available in New Orleans, and you looked…polite."

"Um, is that bad? Aren't I supposed to look polite?"

He flashed me a tiny smile. "I really don't know how to explain without sounding like every cliché of a celebrity jackass you've ever heard. Wait," he said, his cheeks turning slightly pink. "I'm assuming you know who I am, but it's not like Brenda said anything in that meeting."

A short laugh escaped me. "Are you about to say, 'Do you know who I am?' Because..." The pink grew darker. "Oh, man, you were." This time it made me laugh even harder.

"I didn't mean it like *that*."

I tried a stuck-up rock star voice. "Do you know who I am?" Then I lost it again.

"Was that supposed to be me?" He was smiling a little more now. "That's not how I sound."

"You're right." I squelched another giggle. "You didn't say the actual words. Go ahead, say them so I can judge for myself."

He heaved a sigh. "We're not going to get anywhere until I do, are we?"

I only grinned at him.

"Do you know who I am?"

His voice was quiet, not rock star at all, and it wasn't funny anymore.

I cocked my head and studied him. "Yes, Miles Crowe, former winner of *Starstruck*. I know who you are."

"And some other stuff," he mumbled.

"Other stuff?"

"Besides *Starstruck*. Never mind. I'm only bringing up the famous thing because people tend to...fawn."

"Fawn?" I repeated like an idiot parrot. But I couldn't help it. This whole conversation was surprising me.

"Yeah, it means to like...pander?" He winced. "Which means to—"

"I know what fawn and pander mean."

"Right. Well, so that happens. A lot. And you didn't do either of those things when I came in, which is kind of refreshing. But more importantly, they were all being super-salesy about properties that were a bad fit, and you sat there looking..."

"Polite," I finished.

"Less than enthusiastic about me or the properties. As if you didn't think they were a great fit, and I wondered if you had other ideas. But—" and he broke off again.

"But what?"

He waved his hand. "Nothing."

"May as well finish the sentence." I was genuinely curious to hear what he'd been about to say.

"Maybe I haven't done a good job of explaining what kind of place I'm looking for."

I had a feeling that wasn't what had been at the tip of his tongue. I suspected he was going to say that I was now being as salesy as the rest of the office had been last week. And he was right.

"Salesy" was not me. I did well with my clients because I listened to them and bridged the gap between their vision and reality. Sometimes I heard and saw things in their wish lists that they didn't even recognize, finding properties that allowed them to surpass even what they'd hoped for.

I had done very little listening with Miles. I'd come in assuming I knew what he would be like, assuming I knew what kind of club a fading rock star would want: a shrine to his former glory. But if that were true, Miles would have been asking for flashy locations, trying to get in near the Hard Rock or House of Blues. Instead, the more similar a property was to those places, the less he liked it.

He'd chosen me expecting me to be the opposite of those things, and instead I'd been exactly those things. I didn't like the way it looked on me.

I took a deep breath. "Miles Crowe, it's possible I have done you wrong. Let's walk over to the one place tourists and locals can agree on and figure this out."

He quirked an eyebrow at me. "Café du Monde?"

"Café du Monde." It was a New Orleans landmark on the edge of Jackson Square, a bustling open-air café serving world-famous beignets.

"Bold move after the Sugar Incident of Last Tuesday."

"A gentleman wouldn't bring that up."

"Never claimed to be a gentleman. But full disclosure, I only mentioned it because I haven't figured out how to eat beignets without making a mess, and I just want you to remember I'm not the only one."

I smiled a little. "We can go somewhere else. Get some eggs Benedict or something that won't make a mess."

"No way. You don't promise a man beignets then swap them for eggs. Café du Monde it is."

We walked in silence to the café, but it wasn't uncomfortable. We were only a block away, and though Miles kept his sunglasses on despite the slightly gray day, he turned his head constantly, like he was taking in all the people and sights.

"You want to order or grab a table?" I asked when we reached the café.

He hesitated. "Maybe I better grab the table."

I nodded and headed for the counter to place my order. When I turned with a platter of beignets, I spotted him in the corner furthest from the street against the low iron fence that hemmed in the café dining area. A couple of women stood next to the table talking to him. He had his arms folded across his chest while he leaned back in his chair, holding himself very still, like he was waiting out a coiled rattlesnake.

I picked my way through the tables quickly and set the plate down with a clatter on the laminate top. "I got them, honey," I said. These women were around my age, and one twirled her hair while the other leaned toward him, flashing a hint of cleavage.

I wouldn't have cared if Miles was flirting back, but at the moment, he seemed more like he wanted to melt into the concrete.

"Thanks, babe," he said, reaching for the lifesaver I'd thrown him.

"Is this your girlfriend?" the shorter, blonde girl asked.

"Fiancée," I corrected as I sat down, and Miles choked on his coffee.

"Really?" asked the taller friend, a brunette who eyed me skeptically. "Where's your ring?"

"It's huge," I said. "I don't like wearing it out for everyday stuff even though it's insured."

Miles reached across the table and threaded his fingers through mine, running his thumb over my knuckles. "Can't wait until I see my wedding band on your finger every morning for the rest of our lives."

The blonde gave a happy sigh. "That's so sweet. Congratulations, y'all."

The brunette's face had gone slightly sour. "Yeah. Congrats."

"Can we get a picture with y'all?" The blonde was already pulling out her phone and turning to angle it for a selfie.

"Sure," Miles said, and leaned toward me.

"I'll take it for you," I said, standing and taking her phone. The last thing I wanted was to be in a picture with Miles Crowe, so I took one of them and handed her phone back. "So nice to meet y'all. Enjoy New Orleans. Bye." It was such a clear dismissal that I felt rude in spite of the polite words, but they made me uneasy, and I wanted them gone.

The second they turned to leave, Miles gave a small sigh. "Thanks for that."

"No problem. Must happen all the time."

"Less than you think," he said. "People don't expect to see a celebrity, so a lot of times they don't recognize me in passing. Or sometimes they do this thing where they think they know me, so they nod or say hi, and I have a feeling it doesn't sink in until later why they recognized me."

"Got it." For the whole rest of high school after the *Live with Laura* thing, my greatest fear had been being recognized by strangers. And it happened. A lot. At school, of course. But even in the grocery store or at the skating rink with friends. People used to ask me for selfies a lot. *Can you do the face like the meme?* And they'd want me to sit there either crying like I had during Miles's hometown performance, or worse, make the stupid goober face I'd made on *Laura*, the one that had actually gone into the meme for maximum hilarity against Miles's mildly disgusted face and the words, "So not my thing."

Miles picked up a beignet and bit into it. "Mmm." He grabbed a napkin and shook it out before handing it to me. "Here. You know, for your sugar bib."

I rolled my eyes at him. "Check yourself before you wreck yourself, buddy."

He glanced down at his shirt, a dark blue button up with short sleeves and pearl snaps. Sugar was drifting down as we spoke, speckling it. He set his beignet down and tucked the napkin into his own collar instead. "Told you. And I don't care. Because dang, I forgot the perfection of their beignets." He took another bite so enthusiastic, it sent a puff of sugar in the air and made me laugh.

"Fine. I'll take the hit." I picked up my beignet and leaned over my plate, trying to bite it so the sugar would sprinkle down there instead, but when I leaned back, my light green top was dusted with it anyway. "What the heck?"

Miles grinned. "That's what you get for making fun of me."

"I haven't made fun of you," I protested.

"Yeah, you have. You do it with your eyes constantly."

I narrowed said eyes at him for a second, then slipped on my sunglasses.

"Doesn't matter," he grinned. "You give off strong judgy vibes. I'll still be able to feel them. By the way, this is a good time for you to tell me how you done me wrong."

"I did say that, didn't I?"

"Yeah. So let's talk about that."

I set down my beignet and picked at one of its corners. "I normally do a much better job of listening to my clients. I haven't really done that for you." He sat quietly, like he was waiting for me to finish the thought. "In my defense, I sort of inherited you."

"How would you have approached this property search if I'd started with you on day one?"

"Hey, Miles. I'm Elle. Why don't you tell me what you're looking for, and I'll go out and find it for you?"

He leaned forward. "Well, Elle, I'm looking to open a jazz club to nurture the next generation of talent."

"And you want to build on your fanbase. I imagine it's pretty big in New Orleans, so you'll want a place with a fair amount of space for them to come see you perform."

He was shaking his head before I finished the sentence. "Elle? This goes better when you ask questions instead of making assumptions."

It was the first time I'd seen him even close to annoyed, and I wanted to snap back, but I wouldn't do that to any other client, so instead I bit back my retort. "Fair enough. You're saying you don't want a large space?"

"I'm saying it sounds like you think I'm building myself a theater so I have a captive audience. I won't trade on my name to get people in the door. I've had my fill of performing. I'm over it. That's not what this place is for."

It was another zig where I'd expected him to zag.

I swallowed and started over again. "Hi, Miles. I'm Elle. I understand you want to open a jazz club. I went to look at some this weekend to get a feel for their layout and vibe, so I have a sense of the market. But why don't you tell me more about your vision?"

He gave me a smile of thanks. "I don't know how much you know about my history…" He hesitated, like he was waiting for me to fill in the gaps.

"I know some. Tell me more."

He nodded and took a deep breath, like he was looking for the best way to explain things. "I got famous on *Starstruck*. It was a good experience, and I'm grateful because it gave me opportunities I wouldn't have had otherwise. But at the same time, it took away others."

I tensed. I hoped he wasn't about to launch into a poor-little-famous-boy spiel.

Instead, he paused again, thinking, then continued. "The main problem is that when I was sixteen, I wasn't sure who I was as an artist yet, so the industry decided for me. I did what the show producers told me and later, the record label. I became a product. A very slick, packaged product. It meant singing the songs they bought from other songwriters. It meant dressing and acting the way they told me to."

He shifted in his seat, and it felt like his mind was a world away. "I started figuring myself out in my early twenties like I think most people do. And I realized that at my core, I wasn't who the label was trying to tell the world I was. I wanted to explore different kinds of music, do my own thing. They weren't happy about it, and I acted out. Trashed hotel rooms. Took the stage late. Bailed on PR events. It got harder to get bookings. I didn't care. I wanted out. So once I did the final album on my contract, I didn't renew with them. Did my own thing for a while, but…" His expression darkened.

"Did your fans follow you?"

He shook his head. "No, not really. I got pigeon-holed early on by forces outside of my control, and I don't think anyone was ready to see me differently." He picked up another beignet and downed it, brushing absently at the sugar and making a bigger mess than I had at the office. "It's okay. I've had lots of therapy in the last two years. I can make my music for myself, and it doesn't matter if only a handful of people like it. Or even find it. My dad is an accountant, and he still helps me manage my finances. I did a rock star job and I got rock star paychecks. I live kind of low-key, so I'll never spend what I've earned. I don't have to chase money."

He blinked and turned his head to focus on me. "Sorry. I only mean that I can afford for this to be a passion project. I don't need to make money from it, but it would be nice not to lose money on it either. The most important thing is to create a place where musicians can come and be themselves, whether they're starting out or reinventing their sound. I wish I'd had a space like that for me. New Orleans shaped me as an artist, and I want to give back."

A self-conscious smile appeared. "Sorry again," he said.

"For what?"

"I monologued. Didn't mean to take you hostage with my angst."

"It's okay." I meant it. I hadn't expected anything that he'd said, and I didn't know what he meant about wishing he could be a different kind of artist. After so many years of avoiding his name and music, I'd be doing a deep dive on the internet to find out what he'd been up to for the last several years.

"Anyway," he continued, "I'm pretty allergic to a corporate vibe, and we probably feel the same about the French Quarter."

That had me blinking. "What do you mean?" I'd gone pretty far out of my way not to show my distaste for Bourbon Street.

"Not to make it weird, but you've got a lot of tells. You should never play poker."

The idea of him paying such close attention to me made me want to squirm in my chair. "I liked all the properties I showed you."

He took off his sunglasses and studied me for a few seconds, his blue eyes narrowing slightly. His eyelashes were longer than I would expect on a guy, and I wondered if they were why his eyes looked so blue. "If you were opening a club yourself, would you want any of those spots?"

"Most people would," I said.

"That's not what I asked."

I was well aware of that. "What didn't you like about them?"

"I love the history of the Quarter. I do. But Bourbon Street in particular has become kind of Vegas-fied. It's packed with party crowds and neon lights and hustlers. And it's beginning to feel more and more corporate, which triggers my allergy. People go to Bourbon Street for the experience; they want their music fast and brassy, but it's not the space for people who have quieter things to say. I want a place that does both."

I didn't even know what to say to that because he'd echoed my feelings for Bourbon Street so closely. He was seeing right into me, and it made me feel exposed.

"Elle?" He looked uncertain, like he wasn't sure if he was supposed to keep talking or wait for me, and even though his hair wasn't long enough anymore to flop into his eyes like it had on the show, he pushed it aside anyway in a quick, nervous swipe.

I cleared my throat. "I understand."

"Yeah?" His tone was hopeful.

"Yeah. And I'm sorry I didn't do a better job of asking what you need.

How would you feel about going back to my office, starting over one more time, and getting it right?"

He gave me a wide, genuine smile that made my stomach flip the way it had the first time I'd seen him perform at the show choir competition. I suspected few people got to see that unguarded smile. "I'd love that, Elle."

I stood and brushed the last of the sugar off me. "Let's go then, rock star. Time to do this for real."

CHAPTER SEVEN

MILES OFFERED to drive us both over to the office, and since I'd walked to the Quarter from my apartment, I agreed. I was curious about what he drove, anyway.

A classic Mustang convertible, it turned out. "My brother Dylan loves old Mustangs," I told him. "This is in gorgeous condition." It had a pristine leather interior and vintage burgundy paint.

"Thanks. It's a 1965. I restored it myself."

"You're a car guy, huh?" I asked as I climbed in.

"Yeah. Definitely one of the worst things about me."

That made me laugh. "My brother is a gearhead. I'm used to it."

He shut his door and fastened his seatbelt. "Sounds like he and I should talk. Radio okay?"

"Sure."

He tuned it to the local public radio station and its daily jazz lunch program. He looked so good in the driver's seat, one arm resting casually on the door, the other keeping a loose grip on the wheel, just waiting to be a poster or album cover. But I probably would have been attracted to Daffy Duck if he were behind the wheel of a classic Mustang.

I kept the conversation light on the way to the office, mostly talking about the Saints and the weather, two topics every New Orleans native could discuss at length.

At the office, Jay the receptionist did a double-take behind his desk when we walked in but otherwise kept his cool, and the handful of agents who were in smiled but stayed lowkey. Dave gave a simple, "Nice to see you again, man," then grabbed an extra chair and settled it between our desks.

I waved Miles into it. "Have a seat and let's put together a game plan. I'm going to start with a search of available restaurant spaces since you'll be serving dinner. You have a chef in mind?"

He shook his head. "No, but the problem won't be trying to find one. It'll be narrowing down too many great choices."

I smiled. "True. One of the best things about living here."

Miles patted his flat stomach. "I've eaten at five-star restaurants around the world, and there's nothing that beats a muffuletta from—"

"Central Grocery," I said at the same time Dave said, "DiMartino's."

Dave and I grinned at each other.

"We've been having this argument since he started working here," I explained to Miles. "Dave doesn't know because he's from Baton Rouge, and I had to explain what a muffuletta was."

"In my defense, nothing about the word 'muffuletta' suggests Italian charcuterie sandwiches. But I've got Louisiana tastebuds same as you, and I'm telling you, it's DiMartino's," Dave said.

Miles had sunk down in his chair, looking as relaxed as I would in my own living room. He tilted his head and squinted at Dave. "How can that be true when Central invented them?"

I held up my hand for a fist bump, which Miles delivered. "Stop talking, Dave. I'll ask you if I want to know where to get the best crawfish, but I've got muffulettas on lock." I turned my screen so Miles could see it and showed him the map with properties fitting his parameters. "What do think about the Marigny?"

He straightened so he could see the screen. "I think I'm interested, that's what. There are some great clubs in there."

"I like this space." I clicked on a former restaurant. It had good bones and a setup that could work for a club, but it was on the smaller side. "You can see from the outside that it's a different vibe from Bourbon Street."

Miles leaned forward to study the picture of the property nestled among three other businesses in a colorful row of shops. "More organic," he said. "I like it. But how big is it?"

We went through the specs, plus looked at two other properties, each of which he liked better than anything I'd shown him up to this point.

"We're getting closer," he said. "I'm still not sure any of those is exactly right, but I guess it's like you said: maybe when I go see them, I'll know for sure either way."

"You don't want to be in the Bywater?" Dave asked. "It's the next up-and-coming arts district."

"Really?" Miles looked surprised by this, and I tried not to shoot Dave murder glares. "Bywater was still rough when I was growing up."

"It's gentrifying," Dave said. "I assumed Elle must have already shown you some properties there because she's our Bywater specialist. Grew up there, even."

Yeah, and it made me protective as hell of it. *Shut up, Dave*. But I only smiled and said, "Let's take a look at these Marigny properties tomorrow, and go from there, yeah? I'll make some calls."

"Sounds good."

I rose and took a step toward the door. "We'll find something great." It was Miles's signal to leave so I could settle down to work.

"Uh, I drove you here. Am I stranding you?"

"Not at all. I'll bribe one of the other agents to give me a ride home." I needed him out of my space. I'd been resentful and keyed up every time he'd been around until lunch today. Something had shifted, and I wasn't sure what I thought of him now, but I knew I needed some distance to pin it down. "I'll walk you out."

"Great, because I have something for you."

What could he possibly have? I followed him out to the parking lot, guessing the whole time. An autographed head-shot? A CD of his latest album no one had heard of? Were CDs even a thing now?

Instead, he reached into his backseat and handed me a charcoal gray shopping bag with the store name embossed in gold. "Thought I'd try to replace the shirt I ruined. You can return it if it's the wrong size or something."

"You got me a Billy Reid shirt?" It was the most expensive boutique in New Orleans.

"My mom said that was the best place to go, and this one looks like yours from the other day."

I rustled through the tissue and pulled out a white shirt, which was, in fact, very similar to my ruined one—if my ruined one had been made of cashmere and not cotton and had cost five times as much.

It called to me. I very much wanted to keep it. I wasn't sure I'd ever owned a three-hundred-dollar shirt before. But I folded it and put it back in the bag. "I can't accept this."

"It's the right size. I'm good at stuff like that." He said it with a hint of a smile, the first whiff of cockiness I'd seen from him.

Why was that sexy? Ugh.

"No, I meant this is too much. I'll stop by Banana Republic and get a new shirt, but it was nice of you to think of me."

He leaned against the car and folded his arms across his chest, then sighed. "There's never a way not to sound like a douchebag, but if it makes you feel any better, this is both nothing and the least I can do."

What would it be like for a three-hundred-dollar shirt to be "nothing"?

I dropped the bag down to my side since he wasn't going to take it. "All right, then. Thank you. That was thoughtful. And so was the coffee you were trying to give me yesterday."

"You're welcome. I'll wait for a text about appointments tomorrow?"

"Yeah. I'll set up some stuff and let you know."

"Sounds good, but can you make it before lunch?"

I tilted my head to study him. I wouldn't have expected a request for early slots. "Anybody ever tell you those aren't rock star hours?"

He smiled. "Yeah. Aaron, constantly. That's why I leave him behind on half the business stuff I do. Too hard to get him up in the morning. But my afternoon is tied up, so before noon would be good."

I promised to see what I could do and walked back toward the building as he got into his car. I'd definitely be booking some appointments in the Marigny. But I'd also be doing a deep dive into the Miles Crowe of the last five years. Because the guy I'd spent time with today was nothing like what I'd expected.

Donna drove me home to an empty apartment, Chloe either not back from work or off reviewing a restaurant.

I changed into yoga clothes and turned on my favorite YouTube instructor, working through some poses to try to clear my mind. I'd spent too much time in my head even as a kid, and after I'd gone viral, I'd practically lived there. Second-guessing every expression on my face in case a classmate snapped a picture of me and added it to their meme cache. Rethinking every word I spoke before it came out of my mouth. For the first time in my life, I'd been glad our school required uniforms so that I didn't have to overthink which outfits would draw the least attention.

My anxiety had gotten so bad by my senior year that my parents had found me a therapist, Sara, and we'd spent a lot of time getting me out of my head. That meant being fully present in my body, and she'd encouraged me to look into yoga.

I'd kept up a near-daily practice ever since.

But right now, as I moved into some arm balance poses, I couldn't concentrate, falling over twice as much as usual. My head wanted to go investigate Miles Crowe and didn't care at all what my body was trying to do.

I gave up and sat instead, pulling my laptop closer so I could do a Google search of my old nemesis for the first time in eight years. That had been my favorite method of cyberstalking him until Therapist Sara had suggested I quit.

The first search result on YouTube was his hometown performance where I could enjoy my snotty sob face if I wanted to revisit hell, but I skipped it because no thanks.

Most of the top results were his *Starstruck* performances followed by a few videos from the string of hits he'd had after leaving the show. That had been in the early days of *Starstruck*, when winners went on to big careers after the show. It didn't happen anymore.

On the third page of results, I found links to videos he'd released in the last few years, and the tone shift was clear even in the thumbnails. The bright colors and slick production values from his pop videos had given way to moodier lighting. A couple of them were even shot in black and white, and he didn't look like he'd been dressed and styled by Cinna for the Capitol Games. Simple clothes, no elaborate sets.

I clicked on the first link. It had almost 500,000 views. A lot—until you compared it to his earlier videos with over a hundred million hits.

It was a song called "All I Want." It was a far more stripped-down performance, the focus on his voice and the piano. The video alternated between scenes of him singing and clips of him with a pretty actor who had the fresh face of a girl-next-door type rather than a supermodel. They did couple-y things like walk on a beach, cuddle on a couch drinking coffee, and hug while leaning against his Mustang.

That car really did look good.

So did Miles.

He sang about wanting to see and be seen completely.

I let it play to the next one, a song called "Right Now," the lyrics about stringing together perfect moments of happiness.

And then I kept letting them play until it was two hours later, my back sore from hunching over my laptop, and I'd gone through every song of his last three albums.

Chloe's key rattled in the door, and I slammed the laptop shut on reflex as she stepped into the living room.

She paused, her hand still on the doorknob, and eyed me. "What are you—you know what? Never mind. I don't even want to know."

"I was doing some client research."

"Uh huh. I've never done research that made me slam my laptop closed when someone else came in."

I didn't know why I didn't want to cop to what I'd been doing. Maybe because it felt dangerously close to my fourteen-year-old self watching every interview and performance Miles ever did on repeat. I wasn't sure what else to say until my stomach growled. "I'm hungry. You eat yet?"

"Yep. Swung by a new place in the business district for dinner. That's why I'm late getting home."

"And how's it going to fare on The Kitchen Saint?"

"It'll live to flambé another day. How did it go with Miles today?"

"Maybe…okay? Miles 2.0 is a definite upgrade."

"That's good." She set her purse beside the sofa and curled up on it. "Want to do my yoga for me? I'm too tired."

"I've fallen off my firefly pose fifteen times today, so no. You'll have to fall off your own poses."

"So you're not suffering irreversible psychological harm from dealing with Miles Crowe?"

"No. In fact, check this out." I scurried into my room and came back with the Billy Reid bag. "Look what he got me."

She made grabby hands and snatched it from me, lifting out the cashmere shirt. "Oh, nice. But why?"

"Remember I told you he spilled coffee all over me the other day? This is him replacing it."

She dug out the price tag. "For three hundred dollars? Dang. Can you ask him to spill some coffee on me?"

I nestled into the other end of the couch. "He's different from what I expected."

"I mean, he'd have to be, right? You can't be obsessed with someone then have them live up to your expectations. It doesn't happen."

"I was only obsessed with him for like four months until the meme. Then it was more like a deep hatred."

"But now you've met the enemy and found his humanity?"

"Something like that." I had the uncomfortable feeling that if I'd only known Miles through his last three albums, I might have been really drawn to him as my grownup self. "His newer music is interesting. Strong John Mayer vibes."

"But younger and sexier?"

"I didn't say that."

She shrugged. "Didn't have to. I Googled him myself a few days ago when you told us he'd turned up like a bad penny. Agree on the sexy John Mayer sound. But also agree with myself that he's sexier."

"I don't know about that." I was lying. He was objectively sexy. But falling for his smile and his soulful eyes was a mistake that had ruined my life once, and I wasn't going there. "What I know is that he's grown up since he was sixteen."

"Yeah, he has." She waggled her eyebrows.

I rolled my eyes. "I mean emotionally. I've had clients with a fraction of his money act ten times more pretentious. He's low-key. I didn't expect it."

"So you're saying it's not going to suck to work with him on this club?"

"I'm saying I'll live."

"Hallelujah. Let's toast that with wine and a *Clueless* re-watch."

"You don't get tired of that movie?"

"Nope. It's like potato chips. Nobody gets tired of potato chips. *Clueless* is potato chips for the brain."

We settled in to watch Cher and Dionne do their thing, but my mind kept running through Miles's music. One song played on a loop, one titled "Longing for Home," a mid-tempo ballad about finding your place. The chorus said, "Shouldn't have left, it's all such a mess/Want to go back, I can only confess/Do I crave a real place or just a quiet mind/I think I've been looking for a home I can't find."

I was never going to be a Miles Crowe fangirl again.

I wasn't going to stream his music or scrawl his name in notebooks or stalk his social media.

But that last part—finding a home—*that* I would do for him.

CHAPTER EIGHT

"I LOVE THE VIBE."

I turned to smile at Miles, who had stopped several feet behind me in the middle of the sidewalk. "Of the sky? The concrete?" I teased.

"All of the Bywater. This is it. My place is here. I know it."

"It's pretty great," I agreed. We were standing on Dauphine, the "busiest" street in Bywater, "busy" being relative. Like most of the streets in the neighborhood, it was mostly lined with houses and a café or corner grocery tucked in here and there.

"I can't believe how much it's changed since I lived here. Well, since I lived in Metairie. Back then, it was rougher."

"Things change." *People too*, I wanted to add. *I did. Maybe you did.*

"You said you grew up here?"

I walked back to join him. "Yes and no. I grew up in Kenner, but my family has owned property here since before I was born."

He narrowed his eyes at me. "So you've known this whole time how cool the Bywater is and didn't show it to me?"

I shrugged. "Not everyone gets it. And not everybody deserves it."

"What does that mean?"

"It means that I don't take every client to look at Bywater properties. Pretty much everyone in the Bywater is protective of it. We don't like corporate clients coming in. Homegrown or get out."

"You're saying I'm lucky you agreed to show it to me? I passed some kind of test?"

"Not yet. You're still taking it."

"Tell me how to get an A."

"You already have it, or you don't. I'll know soon enough." I slid my hands into the pockets of my yellow poplin shirtdress and ambled down the street, not waiting to see if he'd keep up. I knew he would.

He jogged to catch up. "This is more stressful than my *Starstruck* audition."

I'd learned how to keep my thoughts off my face, so I offered him a bland smile. "I'm a much tougher judge too."

He groaned. "I'm going to fail."

I glanced over at him. "We're going to walk, and you tell me what you think about the vibe of each block."

"Boomers and zoomers," he said on the next block. On one corner, a large condo complex was going up, scaffolding around the outside. Directly across the street, an old burned out brick house stood, doors boarded up, the roof falling in.

"Harsh," I said. "And I don't agree, but I see it."

"I can't believe it's still like this all over the city," he said. "I mean, less in the French Quarter, but still pretty much everywhere else."

I rolled my eyes. "I know. Some news show ran a story last month about how New Orleans has recovered from Katrina, and Chloe and I both threw pillows at the TV." It had been an outsider's perspective. Yes, new development was going up, but these weren't locals. So many long-term residents, especially Black ones, had been displaced after the hurricane to Texas, Georgia, North Carolina and beyond. Government relief funds earmarked to help people rebuild disappeared in bureaucratic inefficiency, and it was too hard to come back and start from scratch.

We kept walking, and I nodded at a house painted in eye-popping shades of purple and green. "I have to warn you that one of the most irritating things about the Bywater is the Airbnbs. They're everywhere. That's one. A lot of the people who could rebuild after Katrina went that route. And I get it. So many people depend on that income. And on the upside, they maintain the properties really well. But it also means you get less community here. Every block has a party house or two with guests who don't care about the noise they're making and leave in two days."

"That sucks, but…"

I picked up his unfinished thought. "You're right. For you, that might be good. Your club will give them something else to do."

"I promise I'll be a really good Bywater resident. I'll be part of the community. Work with the schools. Join the neighborhood situation. I swear."

I made a noncommittal sound. "We'll see. We'll keep walking, you keep talking."

He found analogies to explain each block. One he compared to a Louis Armstrong song. Another he compared to a Mississippi riverboat, a third he compared to a classic Lincoln car.

He wasn't wrong about any of them. When we got to Louisa and Burgundy, I stopped and turned east. "You passed."

"I passed? I passed!" He picked me up in a hug that pulled me up to my tiptoes then released me, and I wobbled for a second, every nerve ending where he had touched me suddenly on fire. He didn't seem wobbly at all as he executed some footwork straight out of one of his old pop videos.

Danger, danger. This isn't how agents and clients act. "Don't make me take it back." My voice came out breathier than I meant it to, and I took a few more steps away, still feeling like I was made of electricity. A few people had slowed to look at us, one of them staring from Miles to me and back again, frowning.

My skin prickled in places he hadn't touched. Behind my knees. The back of my neck. It was like I had a thousand pairs of eyes on me, and I felt them each like a point of contact. I hated being seen. I started walking again.

He didn't. "The hug? If you have to. Come and get it." I turned and he held his arms out wide, but I blushed and stayed where I was even though I knew he was only trying to make me laugh.

"I meant don't make me take back Bywater privileges."

He rearranged his face into a ridiculous mournful expression. "No, ma'am. What now?"

"Now we show you the first property I'm thinking about."

"Yes!" That got an arm pump.

"Don't do that. You look like a middle-aged dad at a Pelicans game."

He dropped his arm to his side. "You are a tough audience. What are the acceptable forms of celebration?"

"I don't know. Not those." Not those because it made people look at us, and I hated when people looked at me.

He gave a low whistle. "You know, *Rolling Stone* hated my first album, and even they weren't as tough an audience as you."

"Who, me?" I pressed my hand to my chest and gave him a sunny smile. "I don't know what you mean. I'm easy like Sunday morning." The second I saw the glint in his eye, I wanted to snatch the words back. "I mean like the old Motown—"

"Uh-uh." He wagged a finger at me. "I heard it, and you shouldn't confess that kind of stuff on public streets."

"Oh, shut up." I fought the smile tugging at my lips, but I could tell I wasn't fooling him. "Let's go look at this old restaurant." We walked another half block to the address, and I let him inside. "I'll show you what I'm thinking," I said, leading him toward the center. I walked him through the possibilities for the stage, bar, and kitchen service. We toured the kitchen space and returned to the dining area. "What do you think?"

"I like it." There was a hesitation in his voice.

"But you don't love it?"

He shook his head. "I'm about to sound high maintenance, I know. This is the first place I could truly imagine working for the Turnaround, but I'm not totally sure."

"The Turnaround?" It was the first time I'd heard him say it. "Is that what you're calling it?"

"Yeah. You like it?"

"I do, actually." It felt kind of perfect. "Is it a metaphor?"

"Yeah. In jazz, the turnaround is a passage at the end of a section that leads to the next section. Feels like my life right now."

It suited him and his club.

"So I like this space." He turned to survey it again in a slow circle. "But do you have any other places we could look at before I decide?"

"A couple more. Let's walk over to Gallier." There was a spot three blocks down from Mary's Place that I thought he might like.

"Sounds good."

We turned onto Dauphine, and he seemed content to take in the buildings. Rows of brightly colored houses alternated with small shops and cafés. I made sure we were on the opposite side of the street from Mary's Place. There was no way he would know that I lived right above the restaurant, but even though it made no sense, I didn't want him walking in front of my house. The idea made me feel weird, like inviting a client into my living room. I wanted to keep business separate from my personal life.

We moved at his pace, stopping when he did to study window displays or pet a dog over a white picket fence in front of a bright teal house.

It would have been a great plan, except when we reached the block with my building, my stomach growled. Loudly. So loudly that Miles whipped his head toward me with wide eyes. "Miss Jones, we need to feed you."

"It's fine. I can eat when we're done." My stomach revved like a farm tractor.

"Sorry, that's going to ruin my concentration." Miles shot me a crooked smile. "That place looks good. Let's get some food in you."

He waved at Miss Mary's, of course. Why wouldn't he? Why wouldn't he invite himself to the one place I wanted to keep strictly Miles-free? *It wasn't enough to let him into the neighborhood?* I demanded of the universe.

I tried to distract him. "Seriously, don't worry. My stomach doesn't know what it's talking about. Ignore it. Let's look at the next place." *Why didn't you go down Burgundy, you huge dummy?*

"To be honest, I'm pretty hungry myself," he said. "Does this place have bad reviews or something?"

No. Just an owner who knows who you are and is going to ask me a million questions later about why we're together. "No, it's great."

"Good. Hard to find bad food in this town. Let's go." And he crossed the street.

I froze for about three seconds, trying to think if there was any way to derail him without turning this into more of a *thing*, but I couldn't come up with a reason, so I hurried to catch up.

"Hey, Ellie," Nora, the hostess, said as I walked in. "You can go ahead and take your usual spot."

Miles's eyebrows went up. "Your *usual* spot?"

"Booth in the back corner." I led him to it and slid in.

"So not only do you like it here, you like it well enough to have a usual spot." He rubbed his chin like he was Sherlock Holmes. "You probably have a regular dish too, don't you?"

Like an actor in a sitcom, Kendra, one of Miss Mary's granddaughters, turned up at the table and deposited two glasses of iced tea. "Your usual, Ellie?"

Miles grinned.

"Yes, please."

Kendra turned to Miles. "Do you need a menu?"

He shook his head. "No. I want whatever Ellie is having."

It jolted me to hear him say Ellie instead of Elle.

"How do you feel about seafood and spice?" I asked him.

He scoffed. "Bring it on."

Kendra's forehead furrowed a bit. "I don't think—"

"You heard the man," I interrupted. She shot me an "are you sure" look. I gave Kendra a bland smile.

She tucked her notebook into her pocket and headed for the kitchen.

I took a drink of my tea, but Miles ignored his, and I felt the weight of his stare even though I didn't return it. I set the glass down and risked a glance. He looked like he was studying me, trying to read something on my face.

"You don't want me here," he said. It wasn't a question.

"It's fine. I just eat here a lot. Thought it might be better to get a look at the other properties." Cue my stomach growling. I rolled my eyes. I hated it when my life became a sitcom.

"Sure," he said. "You like it so much that everyone knows you by name, exactly where you like to sit, and what you order, and you definitely didn't want me here. Interesting." He tried to sound dramatic and detective-y, but there was a tightness around his eyes.

"Boring," I countered. "There's no mystery here."

"Oh, but there is, Ellie. There is."

I was about to make a change of subject about as smooth as a burp in church when the kitchen doors swung open and Miss Mary came out.

"Hey, honey," she said, changing course from her usual table to come and see me. "I knew you were here when the order came in. Oh," she stopped in surprise. "You have…company."

That slight pause was the exact moment she recognized Miles. I braced myself for her to say something.

All she said was, "Welcome. I'm Mary."

"Miles." He held his hand out for a shake.

"You're a brave man, getting Ellie's order."

"I'm getting scared."

She laughed her rich, warm laugh. "She's about to make a man out of you."

"Miss Mary!" I pressed my hands to my cheeks.

"I meant in the put-hair-on-your-chest way," Miss Mary said, grinning. "What did you think I meant?"

"That's not an improvement," I muttered. Especially not if Miles was imagining *me* now with hair on *my* chest. Or even thinking about my chest at all. Oh, man. I pressed my cheeks harder. *Make it stop.*

"I'll leave y'all to enjoy your brunch. Holler if you need anything. I'll be over there doing my books." She drifted to her spot at the back table.

"You okay there?" Miles's crooked half-smile peeked at me.

"Fine." I took a sip of my iced tea so I could hide behind the glass for a moment. "Trying to decide if I want to die or just kill everyone."

"Why do I feel like I'm about to become the butt of a joke?"

"Just remember you did this to yourself."

"Can't wait. I think?" He glanced around the café. "This is a great place. How'd you find it? Yelp?"

"No. Can't trust Yelp. That's all out-of-towners. I live near here."

"Yeah? That's cool. Close by?"

Right over your head. "Yeah. Pretty close."

We chatted for a few more minutes about the Bywater until Kendra came back with two plates and set them down. "Here y'all go."

Miles looked down at his plate. "Omelet? I was expecting something scarier."

"Son, you better worry," Kendra said. "Her tastebuds aren't human."

I gave Miles an innocent smile. "Better bring some hot sauce for him, in case."

Kendra almost choked on her laugh as she walked away.

"Can I ask what I'm about to bite into?"

I scoffed exactly like he had before he claimed to love seafood and spice. "Nope." Miss Mary's kitchen had been making me this omelet since I was a teenager. It had grilled shrimp, pork tasso, grilled onions, and some cheddar, all beneath a Creole tomato sauce that first Miss Mary and now Jerome doctored especially for me. Extra hot sauce with Thai chilis.

I took a bite and savored the heat from the first chili hitting my tongue. It was a delicious kind of pain, and I loved it the way adrenaline junkies loved skydiving.

Miles took his first bite too, his expression curious, then almost deflated as he chewed.

"What's the matter? You don't like it?" I asked.

"No, it's good. Good flavor. It's just—" He broke off and a strange look washed over his face. His eyes widened and he gave a short cough. "Oh. That's got some kick."

"Little bit." I took another bite and he reached toward his iced tea.

"That's—" But he couldn't finish, coughing and taking a large drink instead.

Kendra let him suffer through a couple more bites before she swept in and switched his plate out for a different omelet. "We call her order the Death Omelet, and it's an off-menu item only this crazy one eats. Nobody else can stomach it. This right here is a regular Cajun omelet for people with human tastebuds."

"Thank you," Miles said, relief dripping from every word even as his eyes watered.

I smiled and ate another forkful.

"You're scary."

I took another bite. "It clears the sinuses. My pawpaw drinks a tablespoon of cayenne in a cup of water every morning, and he's almost 100 years old."

He shook his head. "Another bite of that thing would put me on the floor. Or six feet under it."

So far, this was going okay. No one had made a big deal of Miles being here even though Miss Mary clearly knew who he was. If anyone else knew, they hadn't let on. We ate in peace for a couple minutes as he asked questions about the other Bywater properties I planned to take him to.

"The next place is on Royal and Clouet. Bigger than the first. Not sure if it's too big for you, but you could definitely pack more people in."

"I'd love a space this size," he said, glancing around then smiling as Miss Mary came over to join us.

She scooted in next to me, a cup of coffee in front of her. "This size for what?"

"A jazz club I want to open. This is very close to the size and layout I want. Stage there," he pointed to the side, "bar on the opposite side, great kitchen access, perfect amount of space. You got anything like that on the slate?"

I shook my head. "Not exactly, but some that'll work. I'll keep these dimensions in mind while I look for more spaces if you don't like the ones we go see after we eat."

"Miss Mary!" a voice called from the door. A voice that made my stomach burn like ten chili peppers. A voice that immediately turned this whole scene into a slow-motion disaster. I turned to Miss Mary, eyes wide, begging for help.

"Dylan!" she called back and shot me a *look* as she started to slide from the booth to head him off, I hoped.

"There you are," he said, already striding toward us before she could get all the way out. He stooped to hug her and kiss her cheek as she stood. "Hey, brat," he said over Miss Mary's head. Then his eyes swept over Miles, and he froze, his jaw dropping. "No way."

Miles put on the same smile he'd worn at Café du Monde when his fans had found him there, a tight smile that said it was trying to be polite. I wondered if he had any idea how pained he looked.

And how wrong he was about why Dylan was shocked to see him.

"Hey, man. How's it going?" Miles held out his hand for a shake.

Dylan took it. "I'm doing just fine. How are *you*?" he asked me, a big, stupid grin on his face.

"Great." I tried to shoot daggers from my eyes, daggers that would kill him before he said anything else. "Go away, Dylan."

"Nah. I'm going to stand here taking this in for a minute."

"Knock it off, boy." Miss Mary pinched his side—hard, judging from his wince—but it didn't wipe the grin off his face.

"I mean, I've lived with a meme, but this is the first time I've seen one come to life." He looked at Miles. "Could you make my day and say the *thing*?"

Miles looked confused. "Sorry, say what thing?"

"You know. *She's so not my thing*. And make that same face."

Miles gave him a polite smile. "That was a long time ago, man."

Dylan snorted. "It's every day for Gabi."

I closed my eyes and froze, wishing Dylan would disappear. Or I could disappear. Or Miles. I'd take any one of those options if it meant this conversation could die right now.

"Gabi?" Miles repeated, sounding even more confused.

"Gabi. Ellie," Dylan corrected himself. "My sister. Your brunch date. *Her*." He pointed at me as if Miles might not realize he had another human being sitting in front of him.

Miles still looked confused.

"You don't know," Dylan said, understanding dawning on his face. "Oh, dang, Gab. You didn't tell him?"

"Tell me what?" Now Miles sounded frustrated.

"Go away, Dylan." I added a glare for good measure.

"Go get something from the kitchen," Miss Mary ordered him, trying to help.

"Like what?"

"Find something," she said between gritted teeth. "Anything."

"What's going on here?" Miles asked.

"Come with me, my man," Dylan said, beckoning to Miles. Miss Mary tried to grab Dylan's shirt and snatch him back, but he danced out of reach.

"It's okay," I said, resigned, and she hesitated, looking toward me. "Let him go."

"You coming?" Dylan called to Miles, heading away from the kitchen toward the hall leading to the restrooms instead.

Miles shot me a look that asked if he should.

"Go ahead." I felt a slight nausea, but what Dylan was about to show Miles had always been inevitable.

Miles climbed out of the booth and followed Dylan around the corner. The second they disappeared from sight, I headed for the front door.

"You good?" Miss Mary called after me.

I waved behind me, not wanting her to see the humiliated tears waiting to fall. "Add it to my tab, Miss Mary. I'll drop a tip by for Kendra before she cashes out."

I sped outside and around to the back stairs, took them two at a time to my apartment, shoved my face in a sofa pillow, and screamed.

Freaking Dylan.

My brother was not a mean guy. But it hadn't been easy coming up a grade behind me in school as the brother of one of the most popular memes in internet history. He'd been annoyed with my Miles Crowe obsession through the whole *Starstruck* season, bemused when I lived in a state of hysteria for the week before his hometown show, and flatly irritated when I'd had a week of being viral for my meltdown. There had been no playbook for what to do when the average person suddenly became famous overnight for doing something that didn't deserve fame.

It had been disruptive, especially for Dylan. The whole situation had turned him sour for a few years. Publicly, he defended me. Privately, he resented me for having made such an idiot of myself.

I got it. I did.

But there was no excuse for him to drag Miles down that hallway. I knew exactly what he'd brought him to see: Miss Mary had lined it with pictures of her family working in the café over the years, and she had a picture of me manning the hostess stand. I was fifteen, still in my frizzy hair/glass-es/braces/acne phase.

I imagined Dylan pointing to the girl in that picture and saying, "*That's* Elle," and Miles's face as recognition sunk in.

I rolled onto my back and clutched the pillow to my chest, staring at the ceiling. The tears that had threatened downstairs hadn't fallen, but a dark and ugly feeling sat in my chest. Shame, maybe. I'd worked so hard to outgrow those awkward years, but it was impossible to put it behind me when that meme wouldn't die.

I'd even deactivated my Facebook account a couple of years ago because I was so sick of seeing the meme used in comment threads. Now I mostly used social media for business reasons and kept a locked-down Instagram for my friends.

It still wasn't enough to keep that meme from haunting me, but it had quieted the ghost in the last few years.

What would Miles think when he made the connection? He owed me the biggest apology in the world, but I hadn't wanted it if it meant him realizing it was *me* he owed it to.

CHAPTER NINE

I SURFACED from sleep to a sound it took me a moment to place.

My doorbell? No one had rung it in the two years I'd been living here.

I blinked in the morning sunlight a few times and waited. A few seconds later, I heard it again, muffled but loud enough to wake me up.

"Go away." But whoever it was wouldn't be able to hear me. I struggled upright and groped along my nightstand until I found my glasses and checked my phone. It was after nine, but it wasn't like I had to show up at the office if I didn't want to.

I'd washed away the embarrassment of yesterday with a cool shower, thrown my wet hair into the bun half-slipping down my head now, and fallen asleep watching *The Bachelor*.

The doorbell rang *again*.

"Coming!" I shouted, mostly because I was annoyed. It wasn't like they could hear that either.

I pulled the elastic out of my hair and shuffled toward the front door.

"Gabrielle Jones?" Miles called.

I froze with my hand on the doorknob. I didn't feel like seeing Miles Crowe. The only thing on my to-do list for work today had been handing him off to one of the other agents.

"Ellie? Miss Mary says you didn't come down for coffee this morning, and that means you haven't left yet."

"Miss Mary doesn't know everything," I grumbled.

"Ellie?"

"What, Miles?"

"Can you open the door?"

I eyed it. I didn't want to open the door. I didn't want to rehash the past or do anything else. Talk. Explain. Listen. Nothing.

"I'd like to apologize."

I sighed. If I were Miles, I would too. And my mom would kill me if she knew I'd lacked the grace to let him.

I unlocked the door and opened it to find him standing there in a pair of joggers and an Abita beer T-shirt. His hair stuck up in a few places, and his eyes were puffed like mine did when I stayed up too late.

His mouth dropped open the tiniest bit.

"What?" I asked.

"Nothing…I just can't believe I didn't see it before."

My hair was probably frizzing from sleeping on it damp, and with my glasses, I must look like I was cosplaying myself as that stupid meme.

I reached up to touch my hair, wondering how bad it was, but I caught myself and dropped it. *It doesn't matter*. I used a very stern voice in my brain. I wasn't sure I believed me.

"I brought you this." He handed me coffee in a to-go cup. "Miss Mary said it's how you like it, and I promise not to spill it on you."

"Miss Mary told you where to find me?" That didn't sound like her.

"No, that was your brother. He let it slip when we were talking yesterday. I came back and the table was empty, and I might have cussed because I'd wanted to apologize, and he said something like, 'Dude, she lives upstairs. Go tell her to her face.' And Miss Mary said I probably did need to say it to your face, but I'd better give you space first."

"So you waited less than a day and came at my door like a jackhammer?" But it didn't have the bite I'd meant it to. He looked almost as miserable as I'd felt during my last three years of high school.

"Yeah. Sorry. I was worried if I didn't catch you at home, I might not get the chance. And I really, really owe you."

I stepped back. "All right. You can come in. But I'm going to need to wake up more before we have this conversation. Sit and drink your coffee, and I'm going to go change out of my pajamas and wash my face."

The bathroom mirror revealed a worse situation than I could have imagined. Hair frizzing everywhere, mascara I hadn't gotten off in the shower slightly smudged beneath my eyes, glasses missing one arm because I couldn't be bothered to order a new pair.

I turned the faucet on blast before whispering to the hot mess in the mirror, "Not awesome."

I did a very fast version of my morning routine but skipped makeup because who was I kidding after I'd opened the door looking my worst? I pulled my hair into a tight, low ponytail since I didn't have twenty minutes to straighten it, then slipped on a knit shirtdress and slid on some Vans. It was my Saturday-morning-errands outfit, but I didn't have time to conjure up Work Elle with Miles waiting on my couch.

I picked up my coffee and sipped it on the way out to the living room, needing the caffeine injection more than I needed oxygen.

He was still there, his hands clasped loosely in his lap, studying the carpet. He scrambled to his feet. "Hey."

"Let's walk." The idea of trying to sit across from him made me itchy inside. I'd rather be moving and have a dozen other things to look at besides him.

"Sure, yeah. That sounds good."

He followed me out of my apartment and down the stairs without saying a word.

I wasn't sure what to say either, but by the time we reached the sidewalk out front, we were tipping from awkward to excruciating.

He shoved his hands into his front pockets. "Believe it or not, I've been wanting to apologize to you for ten years."

I nod. "That's not bad for an opening. But you suck at math. It was twelve years ago." It was a weak joke, and I wasn't even sure why I was trying to make him more comfortable. The apology was definitely owed.

"Yeah, but it took me a couple of years to grow up enough to figure out that I owed it to you. And I'm sorry, Ellie. So sorry. I was a young, dumb kid, and I had no idea that I was about to turn us into a meme. But I did know that rejection is brutal, especially a public one, and there were a million better ways I could have answered that question."

"Name ten." I'd definitely thought of a million other ways he could have handled it too.

"I'm sorry?"

"Give me ten different ways you could have said that." I wanted to know if he'd really dwelled on it through the years as much as I had.

"Um, okay." He was quiet for a moment. "I hadn't gotten very much media training at that point. Now I know the art of deflection. I could have said, 'I love my fans.' Or smiled and been like, 'Aw, what a sweetheart.' I could have said, 'It means a lot to me that she loves my music.' Or, 'It's a good thing she doesn't know what a dork I am.' I could have—"

"Okay." I held up my hand to stem the flow of words. "I believe you." He really had thought about it.

"You sure? Because I've got over 999,000 more to go." He kicked at a small piece of loose concrete as we passed it.

"I'm sure. You've thought about it. That's what I wanted to know."

"To be fair, it's only every time I see it. Which is constantly."

We walked past a few shops in silence. It was an okay silence. Not comfortable, exactly, but I didn't feel an overwhelming need to break it.

"What are you thinking about?" he asked after a couple of minutes.

"About how differently the last twelve years would have gone if you had said any of those things instead." He winced, but I wasn't sorry. The cost had been real, and I didn't have to make him feel better about it.

"Sounds like it was pretty savage."

"Yeah."

"Would you tell me about it?"

I wasn't sure how to feel about that request. No, I didn't want to talk about it. Once Chloe had put herself in charge of my makeover in college, I'd started living the life I wanted for myself. But after all the years of being angry with Miles before that, did I want to pass up the opportunity to let him see it through my eyes?

"I know I don't have the right to ask," he continued when I'd paused too long. "But I was so mad about it for so long that it took years before I calmed down enough to ask how it might have affected you."

"Whoa, wait." I stopped in front of a bright orange house with equally bright green trim and shutters. "What did *you* have to be mad about?"

He waved his hand like he was trying to erase his words. "It doesn't matter. I was trying to say that I'd like to know what it was like for you so I can give you another apology, one specifically for the fallout."

It *did* matter, and I would come back to it, but I decided to answer the question. "I don't know if I can ever separate my high school experience from the *Starstruck* experience."

"No kidding." His lips gave a small twist, and I felt a pang of stupidity.

"Right. I guess yours was tied to it too." I sighed. Might as well get this over with. "I was a freshman when all of that went down. Kind of awkward. Homely, overly emotional. I mean, that's how I ended up viral the first time."

"Overly emotional? You're saying you didn't only have meltdowns over me? Wow. Keeping my ego in check. Thanks, Ellie."

I appreciated that he was trying to joke about it, but I wanted him to see the whole picture. "It definitely wasn't just you. I cried at everything. Puppies. Tampon commercials. Saints wins. I was kind of doomed, honestly. Literally every single strong emotion I felt popped out through my eyes."

I'd been glad at first when the video went viral. It made the chance of Miles noticing me way better. I'd walked around in a lovestruck haze, not caring that at least half the kids at school who'd seen the video were jerks about it and made repulsive crying faces at me in the hall.

But after Miles did the *Laura* show, even the nice kids kept their distance. I'd been alone in my misery, trying to process the hurt. The betrayal. The shame.

"Sounds like you were a sensitive kid," he said. "And I don't mean that as an insult."

"Yeah." I stared at the small park we were passing without seeing it, trying to find the words to explain the experience without getting lost in the memories. "I didn't have coping skills yet. Even when people were nice to me, I wasn't sure if they were laughing at me behind my back. I dropped out of a lot of stuff." I'd stayed in show choir after my teacher went over my head to my parents, but I'd stayed safely in the chorus, turning him down when he'd offered me the senior solo. *I know your voice hasn't dried up, Gabi.* That was what he'd said when he'd tried to talk me into it.

But it had.

"Talking to you about this is weird," I said. "I always thought if I had a chance to meet you in person, I'd run you over with my car or something."

"Want to go get it?"

"Not anymore." I started us down the road again, angling toward the river. "You've ruined that by being sort of decent."

He went quiet, and I let him think. I did too, about something my grandmother had told me when I graduated from college. *Nothing keeps us down, Elle. Nothing but ourselves.*

"How are we even here, having this conversation?" I asked with a slight smile. "I went so far out of my way to be invisible when you came to Crescent Properties that first day."

"Not possible." The way he said it made me blush. It wasn't a practiced line, just a quiet observation.

"Anyway, I went out of my way to avoid any mention of you after the *Laura* thing. If you came on the radio, I changed it. If you were in an award show, I didn't watch it. I didn't follow any celebrity gossip because I didn't want to hear your name. I got good at it, so I guess in my mind, you've been frozen in time. Just a sixteen-year-old punk kid."

"I grew up. I promise."

He had. Nicely. It was hard not to notice how well he'd aged, the way he'd grown into his body. But I knew he meant emotionally.

"I'm figuring that out," I said. "I was thinking about some advice my grandma gave me once. She had a complication after my mom was born, a stroke that paralyzed half her face. She said she used to wish it hadn't happened, but then slowly, she realized that the experience had made her stronger. She said if I was lucky, that's what hard things would do for me too. That they'll define me no matter what, but I could decide how.'"

"So you quit letting it define you?"

"As much." I gave him a smile. "Now that you've suddenly popped up in my life as my client, I need to wrestle with defining my *reaction* to it."

"How's that going?"

We passed a tin oyster shack with the restaurant name sprayed right on the building. "Maybe my old self can be mad at your old self, and we can leave it all in the past."

He nudged me with his shoulder. It was probably supposed to comfort me, but instead it sent heat flooding through that whole side of my body. "Glad to hear it."

I needed a reason to put some distance between us, so I turned around and walked backwards. "My turn for a question."

"Shoot."

"What did you mean when you said that I'd be surprised by how much the meme had defined you even more than the show?"

He hesitated, shoving his hands back into his pockets. "We just made friends. I don't want to mess it up by answering."

"If telling me the truth is going to put our friendship at risk, it's not much of a friendship. Break it now or break it later."

We reached the end of Piety Street where it ran into Chartres, and I turned back around.

"What's that?" Miles asked, pointing ahead of us.

"A bridge to the river. It's a nice trail."

"Walk it with me?"

We crossed the bridge and watched the muddy Mississippi come into view. A train sat idle on the tracks beneath the bridge. The only sound was the light slap of the river against its banks, but it was soft. Even though the bridge wasn't high, the breeze off the water was stronger here, and it tried to tug some of my hair loose from its rubber band.

He led us to one of the benches along the path.

"I'll start by saying that nothing I'm about to explain in any way excuses my sixteen-year-old jerk self."

"Understood." I leaned forward slightly, anxious for the explanation.

"Second, it was less the meme and more your viral video that…" he trailed off.

"Are you self-editing? Pulling punches? Don't. Just talk. I promise to stay right here."

He nodded and did that nervous thing where he pushed his hair out of the way even though it didn't flop anymore. "That video made my career in some ways and broke it in others. I've always had complicated feelings about it."

"How could it do both?" It was surreal to think my teenage angst could do either.

"It turned me into dollar signs in the record executives' eyes. A lot of times on these shows, the winner gets a recording contract, but the record company never invests in the marketing and publicity that will get the winner's career off the ground. They say, 'You won a million-dollar recording contract,' but all it means is they subtract the cost of your studio times the producer, and the songwriters from that advance, then they do all kinds of shady accounting to explain where the rest of it went. If you're lucky, they send you to state fairs or casinos to play shows, but they're not trying to book you on high-profile gigs."

"I didn't know that," I said. "I heard the 'million dollar' part and assumed you guys got it all."

"We see almost none of it. But if we're very lucky, the record company sees a commercial future for us, like One Direction. Which is what happened to me. Because of you. They saw your meltdown and thought, 'We may have something here.' Anyway, they brought in big name producers and booked me to open on some big tours, and you know the rest."

"I don't," I said. "Remember my Miles Crowe media blackout?"

He shook his head, a small smile on his lips. "I never thought the one person in America who knows almost nothing about me would be the girl who shot me to fame, but…it's kind of nice."

"So you got big?"

"Yeah. I mean, I couldn't sell out football stadiums even at my peak, but I sold out a few basketball arenas. Multi-platinum records. Merch. Endorsements. I got all of that."

"But it's not what you wanted?"

He stood and walked across the path to the grass to watch me from the other side. "It was, for a couple of years. But by twenty, most of the friends I'd grown up with were halfway through college, and I was four years into a career I hadn't planned on. The thing was, I loved making my *own* music, not the songs the record company kept making me put out. But they'd already decided I was a teen idol, and they wanted me to stay strictly commercial."

"And you blamed my video for that?"

"I know how I sound. Ungrateful. Spoiled. But the truth is, the record company packaged me and sent me out as a product, and once I started figuring out who I was beyond that image…they weren't interested." He picked up a rock and tossed it out toward the river. "I didn't handle it well. Started getting anxiety about going on stage to do the songs they chose for me. Threw tantrums. Trashed hotel rooms. It was not awesome."

"You got shoved into your own box too." I sympathized with that more than most people.

"Not as bad as the box you were shoved in, but yes."

"Any box sucks if you want to get out of it and you can't."

"I did, eventually. I only had to give up any hope of more fame." He shot me a wry smile.

"Yeah, you'll have to rest on the millions you banked already."

"Hard knock life."

"Do they sell sympathy cards for that? 'Sorry you don't get to be a pop star anymore. Hope your millions are a comfort'? Maybe I can start a card line as a side gig."

"Real talk, I think the market is going to be small."

"Dream crusher."

He cocked his head and studied me. "You're being really chill about this."

I stood and crossed the path to stand in front of him. "I've had about twelve years to get over this, and I only wished you dead for the first eight."

He winced. "I deserve that."

"Yes. But you've done your time, so don't sweat it." I held out my hand for a shake. "Let's call a truce."

He stared at my hand then spread his arms. "I'm kind of a hugger, if you're cool with it."

I smiled and accepted the hug, marveling at how weird life was. This was how I'd dreamed it would go for all those months I'd been obsessed with young Miles Crowe, and the reality was that had it happened back then, I might have exploded into bits, overcome with excitement.

But now, stepping into his arms was…

Nice.

No, not *nice*. Nice was a hug from a friend or a cousin.

This was not that.

His body heat spread to me through the thin cotton of his shirt, and the steady thump of his heart beat beneath my ear.

He tightened his arms, and his heartbeat sped up. Could he feel mine doing the same thing? I kept my head tucked against his chest. What would happen if I tilted my chin up?

He would kiss me.

I would kiss him back.

But he was my client, and I hadn't crossed that line with a client, ever.

Then again, none of them had ever looked as sexy as Miles did when he laughed and his eyes crinkled. And I had never been pressed against any of them this way with a river breeze stirring the fine hairs at my neck and sending a shiver down my back.

We'd been standing this way too long, and the fact that I wanted to stay there set off a quiet alarm in some muffled part of my brain.

I stepped away, and it felt like trying to escape a gravitational pull, every part of me straining to be held against him again. But I hadn't worked this hard to put my past behind me only to drag it into my present now. "Truce in effect."

"So…what do we do now?" he asked.

I looked over my shoulder, back toward my beloved Bywater. "Now that I don't have to worry about blowing my secret identity, we go find you a home for the Turnaround."

CHAPTER TEN

We walked back up Plessy and cut over to Montegut to look at a property, then on to Clouet to look at another. I kept two feet between us at all times as we meandered down sidewalks or along the street whenever sidewalks disappeared. I needed the space. I couldn't escape the nagging feeling that after diving deep into his music and getting to know this grownup version of Miles, there was a buried part of me that would betray me by falling for him all over again.

I wouldn't. But I would make sure my wounded inner fangirl behaved herself too. This was a redemption story for both of us, Miles and Elle as we were now, not for the screwups we'd both been.

Back on Dauphine, Miles glanced up the street. "Want to grab some lunch? I'd love to eat something at Miss Mary's that won't try to kill me."

I shook my head. "Thanks, but I think my shame spiral has hijacked enough of my day. I need to get dressed and tackle some client stuff."

"Isn't that what you're doing now? We can call it a business lunch."

I smiled. "You're right. I guess this has been half work, but I really need to get into the office."

"It doesn't feel like work to me either. Which is weird. Normally, music is the only thing that doesn't feel like work to me."

My insides swooped a little, and I didn't like that. I didn't need Miles Crowe comparing time with me to making music.

"Thanks for the walk," I said, picking up my pace slightly to get home so I could change. "I'll look at those property specs again for the three Bywater leases. Why don't you tell me more about the vibe you want in the Turnaround, and I'll make a recommendation?"

He kept up with me but still managed to look like he was on a Sunday afternoon stroll, his energy mellow, his expression thoughtful. "I want it to feel like it's been there forever. Like it grew up inside a building, like it was always meant to be there. Exposed brick walls. Wooden tables and chairs. Leather booth seats. Dark, warm colors. Brass trim on the fixtures. The kind of place where everything is well-made but not so fancy that you can't relax and enjoy yourself.

"I want it to feel like the bar you always go to when you want to be with your friends but you don't want to make a big production out of things. I want the whole thing to be about the music. The people who make it. The people who love it. I want good food that has the soul of jazz. I want wait staff who know people by name. I want to nurture local talent and become a destination for industry scouts while *still* being a place where no one is treated as more special than anyone else."

"Is that all?" I asked.

"Tall order, right?"

"Yeah. But I kind of love it." We'd reached Miss Mary's, so I stopped and put a hand on his arm. "We'll find it. Give me some time to think through it, talk to a few contacts about what's possible, then I'll get back to you."

He glanced down at my hand on his arm, and I let it drop, not sure why I'd reached out in the first place. Maybe I'd been trying to punctuate my point.

"You sure you don't want to grab some lunch?" he asked.

"Nah, I have this diva client with wild dreams, and I need to get on it."

"He sounds like a jerk."

"He's all right."

"Okay, then, Miss Jones. I'll wait to hear from you."

He waved and headed around the corner to the café parking. I watched him go, wondering if I was imagining a slight drop in the slope of his shoulders. Had I made a mistake not taking him up on lunch? The truth was that I didn't have anything pressing to do. I'd told him that because I had a desperate need for space again.

I pushed open the door to Miss Mary's, the lunch rush in full effect, most of the tables occupied. I caught Nora's eye, and she nodded at me, shorthand to grab any open table I wanted. I took Miss Mary's at the back, knowing she wouldn't mind.

Kendra called out, "Shrimp salad?" as she passed by to the kitchen, and I gave her a thumbs up then settled into work, pulling out my phone and scrolling through the emails that had piled up on my morning off.

Well, not off, really, as Miles had reminded me. But he was right: it hadn't felt like work.

Kendra set my food in front of me a few minutes later and hurried off to her other tables, and I scrolled through my phone, answering more emails, putting new dates into my calendar.

Halfway through my salad, Chloe texted. *Want to try Redbird tonight?*

Are you writing a review? That was where Dylan worked, and Chloe pulled no punches. I didn't want to get caught in the middle if she didn't like the food, even if Dylan wasn't the head chef. Not that he even knew Chloe was the Kitchen Saint. But I'd still feel divided loyalties.

No. I'll go some other time to review. You can hang out with me and relax. Dylan is safe.

Chloe and Dylan didn't super love each other, so it was a decent offer from Chloe. And going out *did* sound fun. *I'm in*, I texted.

I set down my phone to pick up my fork, but I hesitated, thinking again about Miles's slumped shoulders. His *possibly* slumped shoulders. I couldn't shake the feeling that he was a little lonely…? It didn't make sense. Maybe I'd watched one too many romcoms about successful men who have everything except real connections.

It wouldn't be a big deal to have Miles come eat with us tonight. One-on-one non-work time wasn't a great idea, but with Chloe as a buffer, it should be okay. If I was right, it would make Miles feel better. If I was wrong, he could just say no.

I sent a text before I could talk myself out of it. *Roommate and I are going to try my brother's restaurant tonight. Want to come?*

He didn't respond until I was finishing my salad. *Sure, sounds good. Is it cool if Aaron comes?*

I wrinkled my nose. I hadn't liked his business manager much when they'd visited the office. And why was he bringing him anyway? Was he trying to balance it out so it would be like a double date? Or was he pulling Aaron in front of him like a shield to scream, "This is a business relationship"?

Ugh. Why did this have to be so complicated?

Sure. Meet you there at 7. That should make it clear that he wasn't coming to pick me up like it was a date, if that was what he was worried about. I texted the address and dropped my phone on the table, irritated that I was getting so wrapped up in my head.

"Something wrong?" Miss Mary asked, pulling out her chair.

"No."

"Did I see you out on the sidewalk with Miles Crowe?"

"Yeah."

"And how did that go? He seemed pretty shook when he put it all together yesterday. He apologize?"

"He did. I think we even declared a permanent truce."

"Am I allowed to like him now?" she asked, eyeing me closely to check for signs I really was okay.

"You are. Turns out he's a nice guy."

"Good. Because I do like him. Figures he would have grown up as much as you have over the last dozen years. You really are fine?"

"I really am. It's weird that after hating him intensely for this long, now we're cool. What am I supposed to use as an outlet for my rage?"

"Do you have anything left to be rageful about?"

"No. It's confusing. This is the worst superhero backstory ever. What am I supposed to seek justice for now?"

"I don't know if I can help you with that, but I might be able to give you a big, new problem to keep you busy." Miss Mary rubbed at an imaginary spot on the table and didn't quite meet my eyes. It was strange since she was one of the most straightforward people I knew.

"Are you about to hit me up for a huge infrastructure bill? A water heater that needs replacing? Newly discovered asbestos?" My tone was joking, but my gut clenched as I waited for whatever she was finding hard to say.

"Harold came home last week and announced his retirement," she said. "This is going to be his last semester."

"That's amazing! You must be so excited." Mr. Douglas—what I'd called him my whole life—was actually Dr. Harold Douglas to the classes full of environmental science students he'd taught at the University of New Orleans for thirty years.

"I am," she said, her smile soft.

"What's he going to do? Come hang out here with you?"

"So he can oversalt my grits? No, thank you. He'll give all my customers hypertension."

"He's only, what, mid-sixties?"

"Seventy next spring," she said.

"No way. I've always thought of you both as ageless."

"That's vampires, honey. We're humans. Tired humans." She bit at her lip for a minute. "He wants us to spend some time at our fishing camp out in Bayou Corne."

"Sounds like my dad. Good for him."

"I mean *a lot* of time," she said, watching me closely. "Like live there for a year or two. Then maybe do some traveling. Go up and see Mariah in Tennessee. Harold Junior in Baltimore."

I blinked at her, not quite able to process the idea of Miss Mary spending that much time away from the café. "You mean you're retiring?"

"I am, honey. It's time."

"Wow. Congratulations. Who's taking over?" Jerome was happy in the kitchen. He didn't like the business side of things. Kendra could do it, but it would be hard for her to balance full-time café management with finishing up school, and she had at least a year to go before she graduated from college. Maybe… "Theresa?" I guessed. She was Miss Mary's oldest daughter, Jerome's mom, and she had the personality most similar to Miss Mary's.

But Miss Mary shook her head. "I better say it plain: when I retire, Miss Mary's is done. Harold has a nice pension, and I've saved my pennies. I don't need to work, and to be honest, I don't want to anymore. I love this place, but it's been hard on me over the years." She winced and shifted in her chair. "It's about time I go get a hip replacement, then ride into the sunset with some shiny new skeleton hardware and let someone else chase a dream." She reached across the table and took my hand. "The lease agreement requires ninety days' notice, so that's what I'm giving you. I'll put it in writing, but I wanted to tell it to your face first."

One of the tears I had refused to cry last night slipped out.

"Oh, honey, don't worry. Bywater is hopping. You'll be able to find a new tenant without a problem."

"It's not that," I sniffled. "You're family. I can't imagine this place without you."

"I know. It's been weighing on my heart for a week now, but it's time.

This place has been home for most of my life, but…" She trailed off, looking almost shy.

"But what?"

"I think I'd like to write. That's part of why we want to go visit Harold Junior and Mariah. I have this idea I'd like to write some of those culinary mysteries, maybe have a spunky grandma who looks suspiciously like me catching murderers and art forgers while serving up recipes every few chapters."

My mouth fell open. "I had no idea you were a writer."

"I've always messed around, filling up journals and stuff. I even won a short story contest once," she said smiling. "Just didn't have time to work at it much. Now I'm going to make the time, see if I can cook up a story as good as my omelets."

"You're the best storyteller I know," I told her truthfully. "I can already imagine how good your mysteries will be. I'm going to buy every single one in hardback and keep them on my shelf of favorites. Then I'm going to cry while I read them because no matter how good they are, it'll mean you're not downstairs anymore."

She shook her finger at me. "Stop trying to guilt me into staying."

"I'm not. It's my way of saying I'll miss you."

"It's not like we'll never talk again. That's not what family does."

I rose and walked to stand behind her, wrapping her in a tight hug. "I love you, Miss Mary."

She patted my arm. "Same, baby."

"My parents will be shocked," I said, going back to my seat. "You're the only tenants they've had in this spot."

"Forty years is a good run, but they're only ten years or so from retirement themselves. They'll understand."

"I need to go upstairs and throw myself on my bed and wallow in my misery."

She tsked at me. "Stop that. You're not going to guilt me into staying, but that was good enough to guilt me into getting you a bowl of banana pudding."

I grinned at her.

She shook her head. "I played right into your hands, didn't I? That was some Dylan-worthy shenanigans."

"There isn't much I wouldn't do for your banana pudding, and there isn't much your banana pudding can't cure."

"True enough. I'll get you some, then we'll talk about a timeline for closing."

The words made my stomach clench again, a pang that told me exactly how bad I was going to feel when Miss Mary closed her doors for the last time. She braced herself to stand, but I waved her back down.

"I've got this. Two servings of banana pudding coming up."

We spent the next hour going through the calendar, choosing a date, and talking about how to arrange the sale of her kitchen appliances, ideally to the new tenant.

"Every single part of this makes me sad except one," I said as we were wrapping up.

"What's that?"

"Imagining you and Mr. Douglas tooling around everywhere, loving on grandbabies and fishing? That part doesn't make me sad."

"You said it." She sat back, smiling, her mind wandering off somewhere else. Maybe to their fishing camp.

"I'm going to get out of here and go schedule a photographer. I'll make sure it's after closing. I only have one condition to officially accept your intent to vacate."

"Tell me."

"Will you help me find the new tenant? Please? You know the Bywater better than anybody, and I don't want to mess up and put the wrong tenant in here."

Miles will want this place, my brain said.

Shut up, I said back. I did not need that kind of complication underfoot twelve hours a day.

"You're a pro. You'll do fine, Ellie."

"Please, Miss Mary? It won't feel right unless the new tenant has your blessing."

She gave a slow nod. "All right. I suppose it does make me feel better to have some say in who takes up after I leave."

I gave her another hug full of relief, then headed upstairs and spent the next two hours trying to answer emails while my mind tried to figure out what to wear for my "not date."

"Dear brain, you are very stupid," I announced when I had to rein it back for the dozenth time. It answered by flashing an image of a cute red top that would look good with jeans.

I groaned and shut my laptop before I could click open Miles's YouTube channel. Again.

I had a bad feeling that it wasn't Miles who needed to be reminded that this wasn't a date.

CHAPTER ELEVEN

"HE'S A JERK, and I'm ordering," Chloe announced at seven-thirty.

I couldn't disagree. Miles was late again, and even though Chloe and I had ordered drinks while we waited, I felt bad for taking up a four-top that could have earned the restaurant more money if it actually had four people at it.

"Let's do it," I said. "Let's get the lemongrass chicken tacos and a couple more Sazeracs."

"Does Miles do this a lot?" she asked as she flagged down a server.

"He did the first time we met." He'd been perfectly punctual ever since the coffee spill. But something about him standing me up tonight was extra humiliating, like having a witness to his no-show gave the situation an extra sourness. I felt dumb for telling Chloe that he'd grown up over the last twelve years.

Our tacos arrived about two minutes ahead of Miles and Aaron. I was halfway through my first one when I spotted them weaving toward our table.

"Hey," Miles said, so quietly I almost didn't hear him.

Chloe studied him while she took another bite but didn't say a word.

I wasn't sure what to say either. *Go away* felt right, except my mother had drilled manners into me too hard for me to let the words out. I settled on, "Hey."

"These our seats?" Aaron asked, already settling into a chair. The table was square with a seat on each side. He was next to Chloe and across from me.

Miles took the seat to my right. "I'm sorry. We got held up."

I shrugged. "We already ordered, but I'm sure the server can add yours on." I lifted my hand to call him over, but Miles shook his head.

"It's my bad. I'll do it."

When the server made it to our table with a tight smile on his face at the sight of two new guests, Miles handed him the menus without looking at them, but not before I saw him place a hundred-dollar bill on top as he returned them.

"Sorry we're late ordering," he said.

"No problem at all," the server said, all smiles now. "What can I get for you?"

"Two Abitas and two of your favorite dishes. We don't have food allergies, and we'll eat anything, I promise."

"I'll hook you up," the server said. "I'll be right back with your drinks."

"So you're an adventurous eater?" Chloe asked. Miles had stumbled onto the only way to improve her opinion of him.

"I am," he said. "I'll try anything. Even the Ellie special at Miss Mary's."

Chloe gave a low whistle. "How'd that go?"

"One of my few missteps," he admitted.

"You're both weak," I said.

"No, we just haven't had our tastebuds deadened by nuclear heat," she said.

Aaron had yet to say anything. He just glanced around the restaurant, then as if he'd decided it held nothing interesting, he pulled out his phone and swiped away.

Chloe shot me a look, like, *What is it with this guy*?

Miles, noticing, gave a small shake of his head, and mouthed, "Let him."

I wasn't sure what to say next. I'd learned the art of small talk over the last couple of years, ways to keep conversations going with clients when I didn't necessarily have much in common with them. But I was still annoyed enough with Miles that everything I thought about saying would sound insincere unless it was, *I'm super bugged that you're late*. But he'd already apologized. So I didn't say anything and wished desperately that he hadn't shown up at all.

Chloe stepped in. "Get caught in traffic?"

There wasn't much traffic this time of night, so the honest answer would be no. She was calling him out.

"No, some stuff came up that we had to handle."

"You could have texted," I said.

He winced. "You're right. Um, I think I didn't because I'm a rock star?"

"Is that a question?" I asked.

"Or a lame excuse?" That was Chloe.

"Can I try that again?" he asked.

He honestly looked *so* uncomfortable. I nodded. "Okay."

"I didn't text because I'm a *spoiled* rock star, and I've spent too much time in LA where people kiss up and never tell me I'm out of line, and although I'm not the reason we're late, it was definitely on me to text you, and my mother would take a switch to me if she knew I'd forgotten even the most basic manners. I'm sorry we're late, and I'm sorry I didn't text."

I lifted an eyebrow at him, then turned to Chloe. "What do we think?"

She gave a slow nod. "We can accept it. Look, Miles Crowe," she said, and his mouth twitched like he wanted to smile at her use of his full name. "My girl Ellie here is a busy woman, and time on her schedule is prime real estate. You got it?"

"I got it."

"Then we accept your apology." She took a sip of her drink and set the glass back with a thunk to punctuate her statement.

He eyed our plate of tacos. "What you got there?"

"Something only punctual people get." I took another bite. "These were Dylan's idea. He done good."

"This is your brother's place?"

"He's the sous chef. But he's been making a version of this since we were in high school."

"He's pretty much perfected them now," Chloe said thoughtfully, as she bit into another one. "Which is irritating."

"Why is that irritating?" Miles asked, and I had to fight a laugh at the way his eyes tracked the progress of each lemongrass taco to our mouths. I finally pitied him enough to push the plate his way and nod at it. He scooped one up lightning-quick, like he was worried I would change my mind and let his eyes drift half-closed as he chewed. "Simple. But maybe brilliant."

"That's why," Chloe said. "Dylan is such an enormous pain in the a—"

"Hey," I interjected. "I'm bound by blood to defend his honor." I snaked another taco from the plate. "He and Chloe don't get along."

"Because he's freaking annoying," Chloe said.

Miles looked like he was struggling to keep his expression neutral. No doubt he agreed after his run in with Dylan at Miss Mary's.

"Chloe still sees Dylan as the nineteen-year-old who crashed at our apartment one weekend in college and bugged her the whole time," I explained.

"Because he still *acts* like a nineteen-year-old. But he can cook a dang taco."

She sounded like she'd been forced to admit McDonald's makes good fries, and I laughed. "He'll be thrilled to hear that coming from you. Would you like one, Aaron?" It didn't feel right to ignore him back.

"No thanks." He didn't even look up from his phone.

Miles gave me a look that was a combination of apology and embarrassment. Chloe rolled her eyes.

I didn't care. I'd offered. I didn't owe Aaron anything else.

The server returned with the beers, and Aaron looked up long enough to take a drink and grimace. Then it was right back to his phone.

Part of me wanted to know the story with Aaron, and why, as Miles's business manager, he wasn't more involved with the location search for the Turnaround. The bigger part of me was glad I hadn't needed to deal with him so far.

Miles glanced around the restaurant, but unlike Aaron, his eyes lingered on the details. Redbird was done in rustic chic with cloth napkins and thick linen tablecloths beneath the glass tops. In higher end restaurants, they'd forgo the glass toppers, but for a casual dining spot, they were appropriate. These were things I'd learned from dining out with Chloe. Our family's dining vibe had been more Miss Mary's/Mom's cooking/whatever Dylan made for us. Chloe had introduced me to finer dining so I wouldn't feel like a fraud when I took out high-end clients.

"Isn't your brother kind of young to be the sous chef here?" Miles asked.

"Yeah. He's only twenty-five." I couldn't keep the pride out of my voice.

"*I'm* only twenty-five and you're only twenty-six," Chloe reminded me. "And we're successful too."

"But we're not at the same level in our fields that Dylan is in his. You'd have to be a section editor and I'd have to be a lead agent," I said.

"I'm not dealing with a lead agent?" Miles asked in mock horror. "I demand an upgrade."

"Any time, buddy," I said coolly.

"Kidding. Your lead agent didn't understand me. You do."

That warmed my heart more than I wanted it to. "To be honest, you're kind of small fry. Maybe I'll throw you back."

"How about if I pay for dinner? Can I still be your client?" he asked.

"Dylan will comp the whole thing," Chloe said. "You'll have to try a different bribe."

"Is there a way to eat my words instead?" Miles asked.

"I'd rather you didn't," I told him. "That way I can keep holding them over you."

Chloe held up her hand for a high five, which I gave her.

"Eat the last taco," I said, nudging the plate further toward Miles.

"I mean, if I have to." He was already reaching for it. "Looks like they do live music here sometimes?" He nodded toward a stage tucked into a corner, currently occupied by a grouping of live plants.

"Yeah. Small groups or solo acts. That's why I invited you. What do you think of a layout like this?"

He studied the stage, then turned in his chair to take in the location of the kitchen, bar, and hostess stand. "This has the right amount of space. I'm ambitious, and I can fill it." He grinned at me. "But I want to lay it out differently. Shotgun style, no wings, so you can watch the stage no matter where you're sitting."

"Makes sense." I could see what he meant. "Music isn't the main point here like it would be at your place."

"I might be changing my mind about that," he said, leaning forward again, his eyes lighting with a glint I was coming to recognize. It meant he'd had another idea about his club. "No other city in the world marries food and music like New Orleans does. Why not be a destination inside the city for both?"

"You really are ambitious," Chloe said. "Most jazz clubs are after-dinner type places that only serve appetizers. That's a risk you're talking about taking."

"Maybe. But I've learned the value of doing things my way, pursuing what I love, not what the market demands. It may not make me a ton of money, but it does make me happy." He wrinkled his nose for a second. "I sound like either a fortune cookie or a second-rate motivational speaker."

"Yeah, you do," Aaron said, speaking for the first time. All eyes turned to him. "If you're not going to take my business advice, why are you dragging me to business stuff?"

Miles rubbed his lips together for a second, like he was trying to stem the first words wanting to get out of them. "You're right. Bad idea." He dug his car keys out of his pocket and tossed them to Aaron. "Take the car. I'll grab an Uber."

Aaron didn't even bother to argue. He took the keys, stood, gave Chloe and me a curt nod, and headed out.

"What is his deal?" Chloe asked. Her tone was curious. I'd have sounded pretty angry.

"I'm sorry about him," Miles said, running his hand through his hair and mussing it. "He didn't want me to leave Los Angeles for Louisiana, and he doesn't want to trade concert revenue for club revenue."

I blinked at him. "So your business manager's priorities in no way align with yours?"

"Basically."

"Why not fire him?" Chloe asked.

"He's my cousin."

"Oh," Chloe said. In Louisiana, everyone had *that* cousin.

"Yeah. He's six years older than me, and when I broke out big on *Starstruck*, he had a business degree in marketing from Duke and he'd been working for a record label in Nashville for a year. My parents wanted someone they could trust managing my career, so they hired Aaron."

"That doesn't sound like a lot of experience," I said.

"It wasn't. But you know how it is when it's kin. And it's been fine."

I raised my eyebrow, not believing his half-hearted defense, but I didn't expect him to trash family any more than I would. "How involved is he going to be in this process?" I asked instead.

He sighed. "I don't know. I'm going to have to talk to him. I better go." He reached for his wallet as our server returned with our food, setting each plate in front of us. "Or not," he said, surveying each plate with an appreciative eye. "Someone needs to help you guys eat Aaron's."

"Not all heroes wear capes." Chloe raised her glass in a toast.

He pressed his hand to his heart in a show of mock humility. "It's the least I can do."

"I brought crab cake pasta and duck bajeaux," the server said. "It's slow roasted and served with bamboo dirty rice, candied yams, pecan gravy, pickled bamboo and black-eyed peas. I hope I picked right."

"I don't know how this could possibly be wrong," Miles answered, eyeing the food. "Does your brother always work this hard to impress you?"

I shook my head, but it was too late.

"Chef is your brother?" the server asked Chloe.

She pointed at me. "Sous chef. And her brother."

"You're Dylan's sister?" the server asked me.

"Yes. I don't usually tell him I'm here until after I've eaten," I explained to Miles. "Otherwise, he…innovates."

"That doesn't sound like a bad thing," he said.

"It wouldn't be if he was trying to make her something good," Chloe said. "But he'll put horseradish in the mashed potatoes or deep fry weird stuff and send it out. He has the soul of an eighth grader."

"You can tell him I'm here," I told the server. "He can't do anything to me now."

The server left with a smile and a promise to let Dylan know he had visitors, and we picked up our forks, liked we'd choreographed it. Chloe grinned and picked up her table knife to hold it like a conductor's baton, her hands held up in the universal sign for "hold it," then she nodded, and our forks all clinked against our plates in a musical chorus as we went after our first bites. I'd gotten a seafood platter and Chloe had chosen a pork chop with apple chutney. Miles chewed and gave a small groan.

"Wow," he murmured. "He's good."

"Agreed," Chloe said between bites. "It's annoying. I desperately want to try Aaron's crab cake, but I also desperately want to keep eating this."

"I'll take one for the team," I said, pulling Aaron's plate close enough to snitch a bite. It was as delicious as it smelled. "You're going to want to try that."

We settled into eating and occasionally offering comments on the food. "Try mine," Chloe said, tilting her plate toward me. I scooped up a forkful of pork and chutney.

"Oh, wow," I said, letting the sweetness slide over my tongue. "Try mine."

She agreed that it was good. Actually, what she said was, "That's good too, damn it."

"You want to try some of this?" Miles asked.

"Definitely." I'd been eyeing his since the server had set it down in front of him. He nudged it toward me slightly, and I tried my best to spear a piece of duck and bamboo rice and black-eyed peas, but somehow I'd lost coordination in my fingers and I couldn't keep it all on the fork.

"I got it," Miles said, scooping up a forkful and extending it toward me.

Hesitating even for a split second would have made the whole thing feel weird, so I leaned toward him and accepted the bite, something I'd done a million times with Chloe, but this felt different. Much different. As he slid the fork from my mouth, I stopped breathing for a second, the tiniest hitch at how much more intimate that felt than it ever had with anyone else. Not even with ex-boyfriends.

I was thankful I could hide behind eating as an excuse for not speaking. "You might have gotten the winner," I said when I found my voice again. "You have to try it, Chloe."

Chloe had no problem scooping up her own bite from Miles's plate. "Oh, yeah. That's the stuff."

"Hey, dummies." Dylan was walking toward our table.

"It doesn't suck," Chloe informed him. It was the best he was going to get from her and he knew it, but he had to twist the knife.

"If that's your way of saying I'm a genius, you're right. And you're welcome."

"Which of these did you actually make?" I asked.

"Did you get the lemongrass chicken tacos?" I nodded. "That's me," he said with a smirk. "And those three are Chef's, but that dish was my idea." He pointed to Miles's duck.

Chloe looked even more annoyed.

"Good job," I said.

"Thanks, sis. I've got to get back to the kitchen, but dinner is on the house. Even for you." He made a finger gun and fired it at Miles before walking off.

Miles pursed his lips like he was thinking about saying something, then flattened them again.

"What?" I asked.

He shook his head. "I know I should thank him, but—"

"But you kind of want to murder him instead?" Chloe interjected.

"That." He pointed at her, like, *Bingo*.

I smiled. "Do you have siblings?"

He nodded. "I'm the youngest of three, but none of them act like that."

"Do *you* act like that?"

He looked mildly insulted, but before he could deny it, he gave me a half-smile. "Maybe I used to."

"Kudos to you for growing out of it," Chloe said. "We're still waiting on Dylan."

We ate the rest of the food, running out of room but still determined to leave no speck behind. But when the server appeared to ask if we'd saved room for dessert, I groaned. "No."

"Not even a small one," Chloe added.

"Even I'm not that ambitious," Miles said.

The server took our plates and left a tray with dinner mints but no bill. Miles dug out his wallet. "Let me get the tip."

Chloe shot him with an imitation of Dylan's finger gun. "You bet, champ."

He tossed another hundred-dollar bill down, and as we all pushed away from the table, I had the familiar feeling of wanting to hang out longer while simultaneously needing to run away.

"Do you need a ride?" I asked, not sure what I wanted him to say.

"No, I'm good."

Disappointment chased relief.

Again.

I needed a name for this feeling. Maybe…insanity?

"I'll get an Uber. Do we have any appointments I need to know about?"

I shook my head. "I want you to look at the place on Gallier again, but how would you feel about my getting an architectural rendering of what I think it could be?"

"Yeah, sounds great." He held the door open for us. "Do we need to set up an appointment for that?"

"No, I already booked it," I said, giving him a cheeky smile, "but he'll need a few days to get to it."

"Good job." He held up his hands and looked at them. "Is this where I use ironic finger guns? I feel like it's my turn to do them, but I get stage fright over finger guns."

I fired a finger gun and clicked my tongue for extra bro factor. "I got your fingers covered, buddy."

He gave a low whistle. "Expert level."

"That and free dinners are the only perk of being Dylan's sister. We'll see you tomorrow."

I waved at him then stepped from the curb, Chloe right beside me. She waited until we were out of earshot. "You're heartless."

I shot her a confused look over the roof of the car as I dug out my keys. "What are you talking about?"

"Poor guy was obviously trying to find ways to spend time with you, but you shot down all his excuses."

"What? No." But a prickle of pleasure skittered through my stomach as I wondered if she was right.

She rolled her eyes. "Call it my reporter's instincts, or, I don't know, living on this earth as a female for twenty-five years, but he was absolutely trying to get on your schedule again."

I waved my hand like I was shooing her words away, when really, I wanted to gather them up and save them, tuck them into a jar like I used to with my favorite rocks.

I climbed into the driver's seat and shut the door harder than I needed to.

Get over this right now, I told myself as I started the car.

But I didn't dare name what the "this" was.

CHAPTER TWELVE

Miss Mary handed my phone back to me, grinning. "These photos make this place look so fancy, I want to ask for the agent's number so I can lease it myself. Except it's already my place. At least for a little longer." The photographer had come the day before in the late afternoon and stayed until the kitchen was spic and span, getting shots for the listing.

"Sarah does good work," I said. "I'm going to go list it right now, but I wanted you to see your place through her eyes. Sometimes I wonder if you see it the way the rest of us do."

She smiled around the café, which was empty except for a couple of tables near the front windows. "I know what I did here. And I know you're trying to lure me into staying, but my mind is made up. I already wrote an outline for my novel!"

"No way. That's amazing, Miss Mary. How does it end?"

"You're not one of those sneak-a-peek at the end types, are you?" she asked, her eyes narrowed. "Have I nurtured a viper in my very bosom?"

"I am. But I still read the whole book even though I know."

"I can't with you. Go do your work while I contemplate this new information about you. Think you know someone…" she muttered as she headed back toward her table.

I went up to my apartment and finished the listing. I knew the specs by heart, but it took me an hour of revising to nail down the property description.

It needed to communicate the soul of the place, to weed out the wrong tenants and draw exactly the right one in. I thought about Miles for a minute. In some ways, the dimensions were perfect for what he needed. But the idea of him literally underfoot every day didn't feel right.

Five hundred words and a nugget of my soul later, I had a description I could live with. That I even loved. Property descriptions needed to paint a picture for potential tenants, and this was my masterpiece.

This building is a piece of Bywater's soul. Built in 1906 by architect Remy Duplessis, for over a century it has served as a home to some of Bywater's most ambitious entrepreneurs. For the past four decades, it has been home to Miss Mary's Place, beloved by locals. But it's ready for its next phase, serving as a bridge between its history and its future. It needs a visionary with a respect for the past.

From there it went more into the building's architectural features, ending with the practical details about space and suggestions for use.

There was always some hungry young chef looking to make their mark on New Orleans cuisine. I hoped my words were enough to tempt one of them into the gamble. I didn't want to have to fend off one of the bigger restaurant groups looking to expand their brand.

I printed it out and ran it downstairs to Miss Mary. "What do you think?"

She read it over and grabbed a pen. "Looks good but add some adjectives. Rich history, bright future. Oh, profound respect. That'll sound good." She read it again. "So now what?"

"Now I post it and we hope for nibbles."

She nodded. "How's it going with finding a place for Miles?"

"All right. He likes a spot on Gallier."

"Is it the right spot?"

"Could be." I folded the printout and gave it a sharp crease. "It'll take a great designer, but there's potential."

"He mentioned the other day that he'd love a spot like this. That was before I even told you I was retiring." She watched me closely. "Did you think about him for this lease?"

"For two seconds. But I don't want him living under me."

"Why not? Does it bother you to have me down here?"

"Of course not." I knew where she was going with this, and I didn't want to get into it. "But you make me coffee every morning. I better go get this posted."

"I'm just saying if it doesn't matter to you about living over one tenant, shouldn't matter about living over another."

"He and I have way different history."

"*Ancient* history. Thought you guys called truce."

"We did." I glanced around the space that had looked the same for as long as I could remember it. "Anyway, can you really imagine a jazz club in here?"

She did a quick survey too. "I don't know. Maybe. I'd be open to considering it." Jerome poked his head from the kitchen and called for her. "Worth thinking about some more," she said, already heading back to see what was needed.

I went upstairs and made her edits, then hit "post" and headed out to a professional networking brunch to do some prospecting for new listings. It went well, and I had a feeling at least one of them would call to follow up, so I walked into the office with a smile on my face.

"Hey, Jay," I said, pushing through the doors.

"Hey, Elle. You have a—"

"Need a visionary?"

I turned at the sound of Miles's voice to find him walking from my desk with an expression I couldn't pin down. He didn't seem angry, exactly. More like someone was holding him on a leash and he was out at the end of it. He looked broody, like in his "Skin So Deep" video, and it was irritatingly sexy to have that focused on me.

I gave him my most professional smile. "Miles? What are you doing here?"

"Thought I'd drop in and find out how I'd failed the visionary test. Or if I'd somehow led you to believe that I don't, what was it—" he checked something on his phone—"'have a profound respect for the past'?"

Jay shot me a wide-eyed look.

Obviously, Miles had seen the listing for the café space. Obviously, he wasn't thrilled about it.

"Why don't we go sit at my desk and talk about this?" I said, leading him toward it. Except he wasn't following. I turned around to face him. "It's this way," I offered with an idiotic finger point.

"I'm too wound up to sit."

A few of the other agents were watching but trying to look like they weren't. Except for Dave, who was openly staring. I hadn't felt so exposed since…

Well, since my crying clip had gone viral.

"All right, how would you feel about a short drive and then a walk and talk?"

His jaw ground back and forth a couple of times. "That's fine. I'll drive."

Then he brushed past me and walked out the door. Or not brushed past me. He didn't even touch me, but the intensity of his energy prickled on my skin.

I turned to follow him, and Jay asked, "Wait, do you want to do that? Dude looks big mad."

"He is. But he won't hurt me. I'll be fine." I was sure of it.

"Okay, but I'm calling you in twenty minutes, and if you don't answer, I'm calling the police. These shoes are too expensive for me to be wandering on the riverbank looking for your body."

I rolled my eyes at him. "Thanks for the concern, but I'll be fine. For real."

"Twenty. Minutes."

I flashed him a thumbs up and headed down to the parking lot.

Miles was standing beside the Mustang, the passenger door open and waiting for me.

"My receptionist has asked me to confirm that getting into your car won't end with my murder."

Miles snorted. "No. At this point, you're mostly in danger of having to watch me eat sick amounts of Brennan's bread pudding while I punish you with pouting and silence. Broody musician."

I hid a smile and slipped into the seat. "I might prefer murder to pouting," I said when he shut the driver's side door and started the car. "But also, bread pudding? Aren't you supposed to snort cocaine off a model or something when you're mad?"

"No, that's rock star *partying*. I'm *brooding*."

"Right. So maybe whiskey and petulance?"

"I like bread pudding better than whiskey. But I've got loads of petulance."

We lapsed into silence on the ten-minute drive to Brennan's, although I texted Jay to let him know I would not be murdered. It was lunchtime now, and the main dining room of the iconic pink restaurant on Royal Street was nearly full when we walked in, but the hostess recognized Miles and led us to a quiet corner on the patio.

She left us with drink menus which neither of us touched.

"You're mad I didn't tell you that Miss Mary's place is coming up for lease."

"Damn straight. It's perfect."

I blinked at him. "It definitely is not."

"Why not?"

"I live there." That was an answer I could safely give him.

"So? I thought we'd called a truce."

"We did. But I live over a breakfast café. Miss Mary and the staff clear out by five. I have quiet evenings and wake up to the smell of coffee and bacon every morning. I don't want to live over a jazz club."

"You're saying your idea of a 'visionary' is someone who comes in and replaces it with something exactly like what's already there? You're only going to lease to someone who sells breakfast and lunch?"

"It's not that crazy," I told him. "When Mary leaves, there's going to be a need for a breakfast place. It would be a smart investment."

"That's an extremely narrow potential tenant base."

"It's the ideal, but I can live with a dinner place too."

"I'll serve dinner. Let me have the property."

"You'll serve dinner, then drinks, then I'll have bass pumping up through my floor past midnight. I'll have drunks in my alley and whooping at all hours. That's extremely different." It was a bulletproof argument and as compelling as the one I couldn't make aloud. *I like the idea of you being close too much to let it happen.* "And don't forget, Chloe and I aren't the only ones up there. I've got tenants in the unit across the hall too. They didn't sign up to live above a nightclub."

"That's what sound-proofing is for. The materials are incredible. You're giving me easily solvable arguments."

A server stopped by for our drink orders. When he left, Miles leaned forward and pinned me with a gaze that demanded an answer. "I want to know the real reason you won't consider me for the café space." His voice was quiet, earnest. It held a tinge of hurt.

I lied because I had to. "I want someone with Bywater roots in there. Who grew up there or grew up spending time there like I did."

"Figures." His lips twisted, and his tone was almost bitter.

"What does?"

"That I don't fit the profile perfectly." His fists clenched on top of the tablecloth. "It's been the story of my life. The music industry tried to force me into prechecked boxes, and I was miserable until I rejected their labels. Literally. And now I don't fit your boxes, so you won't even consider that I might understand the Bywater better than you think I do."

I shifted in my chair, uncomfortable with the emotion radiating off of him. He'd always been so mellow, and for the first time, I saw hints of the anger that must have led to all the tabloid stories about his tantrums and screaming matches over the years.

"Don't worry," he said, as he unclenched his fists and pressed them flat on the table. "I've had the requisite spiritual retreat to Bali, two years of therapy, and a good dose of humility since I left my label. I'm not angry. Just disappointed."

"I'm sorry," I said. Not because I was going to change my mind, but because I'd hurt him without wanting to.

"Is there anything I can do to change your mind?" he asked.

I tried a joke to break the tension. "Go back in time and grow up in the Bywater?"

"That's what it's going to take?"

"That's what it's going to take."

The server dropped off our drinks, a Coke for me and iced tea for him. He took a long sip and glanced around the restaurant.

"Have you seen the turtles?" he asked.

It would be a random question anywhere else, but it was one of the things that made Brennan's famous. The fountain had been home to over a dozen turtles give or take a few for forty years. They sunned themselves and slid with happy plops into the water from time to time. They were as well-known to city natives as the ducks in the Peabody Hotel in Memphis.

"Of course. Used to love feeding them when I was a kid."

"Same. We came here for Mother's Day brunch every year and for every special occasion. Because I'm *from* here, Ellie. These are my roots too." He leaned forward, his eyes a darker shade of blue than usual, the corners creased with worry. "How soon do you expect to fill the space?"

"I don't know. I'm willing to wait for the right tenant to come along."

"Could I ask a favor? Could you not sign a lease agreement with anyone until I've had a chance to make another pitch?"

He had a determined glint in his eye, but I had no idea what it indicated. I didn't think my gut level instincts were going to change no matter how much he offered to overpay for the square footage or how fancy his soundproofing was. It was a promise that cost me nothing.

"I can do that, but honestly, don't get too invested in the idea of that space."

"Give me a couple of weeks, and we'll talk about it again," he said. "I won't bug you about it until then."

"Sure. Does that mean you don't want me to show you any other properties?"

"Yes. I'm going to be busy the next few days, so I won't have time."

"No problem." I said the words casually, but a pang of disappointment in the pit of my stomach caught me by surprise. Miles had become a part of each day even when I didn't expect him to be. I always got an email or text from him about something. And every other day, he ended up on my schedule for a showing, or he'd appear at the café. I'd even flattered myself into wondering if some of those contacts were excuses to connect with me.

"Great. Hey, I better get you back to the office. I have some stuff I need to do."

It was as if his mind was already on whatever that stuff was and I had become part of the background. "I'll grab an Uber," I told him. "Don't worry about it."

Instead of arguing, he pulled out his phone. "I'll order it for you." He had it requested before he even finished speaking, flashing the screen at me.

"Thanks," I said.

"I'll walk you out." He threw several twenties on the table, and we hit the sidewalk below Brennan's front awning as my ride pulled up. "I'll be in touch." He was already turning in the direction of the hotel parking before I was all the way in the car.

As the door clicked closed, I had the feeling that we'd disconnected completely.

CHAPTER THIRTEEN

A WEEK WENT by without a word from Miles.

I tried not to care.

I listed two more properties and closed a deal on a third. I showed the café once to a prospect, but he wasn't too sure, and only someone who saw the magic in it deserved it, so I didn't try to close the deal.

I went on runs beside the river. I went out to eat with Chloe a few times. I kept myself as busy as I possibly could.

But I still found myself streaming Miles Crowe songs on my runs. Or checking out the spaces where Chloe and I ate to get ideas for the Turnaround.

It was stupid.

I was so stupid.

And that was exactly why I didn't follow up with Miles after a few days like I would have with any other client. If he'd decided to move on to a different company and agent, that was probably for the best. It was too confusing separating the crush I'd had forever ago from my perception of him now.

But did that stop my stomach from flipping like Brennan's Bananas Foster when his name lit up my phone on a Thursday afternoon as I was leaving work?

It did not.

I took a deep breath and answered the phone. "Hey, Miles."

"Hey, Elle." I liked it better when he called me Ellie. "Sorry I've been MIA for a minute."

Is that how we were measuring eight days now? "No problem. What can I do for you?"

"I'm wondering if you have some time tomorrow to swing by a place in Tremé. There's something I'd like to show you."

"Tremé? Sure." It was the neighborhood north of the Bywater and the birthplace of jazz. Like, that's literally where it was invented. "Did you find a property there you're interested in?" Tremé was more for adventure tourists who were into the deep history of a place rather than the party and convention crowd. It would be harder to get a new club off the ground there.

"No, not exactly. I'll send you an address. Would four o'clock tomorrow work?"

"No problem." I started the car and was reaching for my seatbelt when Miles's voice came out of my car speakers.

"Do you want this like I want this—" his voice sang.

I cranked the volume down.

"Uh, what was that?" Miles's tone was amused. Very amused. Sounding-like-he-was-trying-not-to-laugh amused.

"Nothing," I said, turning off the stereo completely.

"Really? Because it sounded like 'Need It.'"

"Huh, weird. Nope. I'm just leaving work, so let me let you go. I'll see you tomorrow."

"All right, see you tomorrow."

I clicked to disconnect then curled my hands around the steering wheel and squeaked out a strangled scream. "Seriously, car/phone/universe? Do you all hate me?"

Was that the kind of thing there was even an explanation for? The kind of thing you could even come back from?

"Call Chloe," I ordered my phone.

"Hey, Ellie," she answered.

"I'm going to die."

"Of?" She didn't sound too worried.

"Humiliation!" I explained what happened, which she met with a long silence. "Chloe?"

"I'm here." She made a sniffing sound, and I wondered if she'd put me on mute to laugh. "Um, why was his music in your car?"

"It was on my phone. And it started playing when the Bluetooth synced."

"How is that possible?"

"I don't know. It happens sometimes if I'm trying to use Marco Polo or GPS. It's never happened when I'm just using the phone."

She was quiet for a moment. "Okay, but why was his music even on your phone?"

It was her reporter voice, the one where she was looking for answers. "Chloe, what do you want from me here?"

"You know what I want."

I sighed. "I listen to his music sometimes. His newer stuff. It doesn't suck."

"And why do you do that?"

"I told you, it doesn't suck."

"Well, your answer isn't convincing me, and it definitely won't convince him."

"I am literally begging you to help me keep my dignity intact. What do I do here?"

She tsked a couple of times, the sound she made sometimes when she was thinking hard. "Tell him it was research!"

"For what? A return to my stalking days?"

"*Is* that what's happening here?" Her tone was curious, not judgmental.

"No!"

"Tell him it was research to see if his music could help you figure out the right kind of place to find him."

"That's weak at best."

She snorted. "Maybe, but do you have anything better?"

"No, I do not."

"Byeeeeeeeeeee." She disconnected, and I tapped out my lame excuse to Miles.

Confession: caught me being a teacher's pet. Listening to your music to see if it can help me figure out the right property for you.

Cool, he answered. *Thanks for going the extra mile.*

I stopped into Miss Mary's kitchen on the way upstairs to drown my embarrassment in some banana pudding while she and Jerome did the last of the scut work. She joined me at her table when she was done and looked over the empty restaurant.

"Has it sunk in yet that you're leaving?" I asked.

"Yes and no. In some ways, I'm already gone, my mind living in that RV, imagining trips. And when it's not there, it's in my laptop while I'm working on my book. But in other ways…I don't know. I've been here forever, seems like. Hard to imagine a morning where I don't come in."

"I understand the second half. Hard to imagine you not here." I glanced around, sympathetic to why Miles had wanted it so badly. The layout was so good, and my mind began to overwrite Miss Mary's buttery yellow walls with the rich wood wainscot and burnt umber paint Miles had shown me from his "ideas" folder when we'd checked out other spaces.

Guilt chased the image out of my head. I didn't want to imagine anything different here until Miss Mary's last day.

I listened to Miss Mary talk about her book until Jerome was ready to go, then went upstairs and binged *The Bold Type* until I was too tired to stay awake. As I settled into bed, I reached for my phone but hesitated.

Lately, I'd been listening to one of Miles's songs before I went to sleep. It was called "June Nights," and the lyrics did more to settle my mind than even my most reliable mantras did. *Nothing is better than a summer evening/Fireflies and crickets putting on a show/It's hard to find the words to say what home is/But it's those plus you, that's all I know*.

I liked it because it was about the feeling of a place and not a person. The song felt like if you could wrap yourself in a perfect Sunday afternoon and carry it around with you like a comfort blanket.

But it would be overload to listen to Miles before sleep when I'd be seeing him the next day. Tomorrow needed to be all about distance.

Permanent distance. The lines were blurring for me, and it was time to hand him off to another agent completely. I owed him the courtesy of telling him to his face.

That was much, much harder to do when I came face to face with Miles the next day. It was such a cute face, I just kind of wanted to look at it some more when I parked beside him at the address he'd texted me. He was leaning against his Mustang and straightened as I climbed from the car.

"Hey," he said and reached out for a hug like he was Dylan or something. He did this with everyone. If he'd met them once, the next time he greeted them with a hug like they were his favorite cousin.

His hard chest met mine, and the zipper of his soft hoodie grazed my cheek. I had a quick image of pulling the zipper down with my teeth and sliding my hands inside the hoodie to slip my arms around his waist and match our hips up too.

Oh no. No, nope. Uh-uh.

I stepped back and pushed my hands into my pockets instead. "What are we here to see?"

"You ever been to the community center? Or seen Tambourine and Fan?"

"Of course," I said. "Home of the second line." A second line was a jazz parade of at least a dozen musicians on brass and drums, parading down the streets to celebrate all kinds of things. Weddings, graduations, Saints wins. There were multiple ones every weekend in the Quarter, some weekdays too, where the wedding party and invited guests walked along with the band, who didn't march so much as dance through the streets. Everyone from bystanders to family could fall in and dance down the street with them for as long as they liked. It was common to step into an antique store to browse and walk out to find a small parade going past, led by a bride in her wedding dress, holding her groom by one hand and a frilly parasol in the other.

"Central might argue with you, but yeah. Most of them start here," Miles agreed. "Jerome Smith revived the brass bands through Tambourine and Fan, and you're about to meet Jordan Goodman, who wants to do the same thing for jazz piano."

He led me around to the front of the modest cinder block building. Freshly painted script lettering on the front glass window read, "Tremé Music Center" in red letters outlined in gold.

"This is what keeps me busy when I'm not thinking about the Turnaround," Miles said, holding the door open for me.

I stepped into a lobby like a dentist's office, except instead of waiting room chairs, there were display stands full of music books. A middle-aged receptionist looked up from behind the counter. "Hey, Miles," she said, her smile a bright flash in her brown face.

"Hey, Miss Addie," he answered. "This is my friend Elle. Elle, Miss Addie runs this place."

"Can you tell that to Jordan? Because he seems to forget that."

"I'll set him straight," Miles said, grinning. "Come on back, Ellie."

It felt good to hear him call me Ellie again. I followed him past two practice rooms, the small ones with doors that cut some but not all of the sound of musicians practicing inside. Through the window of one, I could see a young guy around fourteen or fifteen, working on a piece of sheet music at a Yamaha keyboard.

As we approached a door at the end of the short hall, the sound of music grew louder, bursting into full cacophony as Miles pushed open the door. I followed him into a space the size of the music room at my old high school, and the sensory overload crashed over me.

The smell of Axe body spray, feet, and musty carpet. The sound of kids practicing different songs on different instruments at the same time. The sound of a trumpet-player hot dogging, completely unable to help himself. A trombonist making the weirdest swooping noises he could with his slide.

About a dozen kids—mostly brown, a few white—sat at different spots around the room, obviously waiting on their director to wrangle them, but not in any hurry while they waited.

The only other adult in the room was at the piano, standing over another young man who looked as if he was listening intently, his hands tracing over the keys as his eyes read the music.

"Got it?" The man said, straightening and offering knuckles. He was a dark-skinned guy in his early thirties at most, thin as a rail in jeans and a Jazz and Heritage Festival T-shirt with funky black glasses that were cooler than anything I'd ever owned.

The pianist nodded and gave him a fist bump.

"Miles," the man said, smiling when he saw us and starting over. "You brought company."

"Jordan, this is Elle Jones. She's helping me find a spot for the Turnaround. Elle Jones, meet Jordan Goodman. He's my partner at the Turnaround."

We shook hands and said our hellos, but I wasn't sure what I was doing here yet. "Am I going to start finding a new location for this place too?"

Miles smiled. "No. I'm trying to make a point, but I'm not going to tell you what it is yet."

"Uh…"

Jordan laughed. "That sounds extremely annoying," he said to me. "If I knew what it was, I'd tell you."

"I'm all for surprises, but I'm not sure what I'm supposed to do here," I admitted.

"Are you?" Miles asked.

"Am I what?"

"All for surprises? You seem like you wouldn't be."

"You're right. I'm not," I admitted. "I usually find them irritating."

"Try to lean into this one. I promise that by the time you go home for dinner, you'll know exactly what I'm up to."

"Okay," I said. I looked around the room. "What do I do in the meantime?"

"I thought I'd have Jordan explain what he does here," Miles said. "Jordan?"

Jordan nodded and swept his arm to encompass the whole room. "Behold the work of a madman."

"Or genius," Miles interjected.

"Madman," Miss Addie said. I turned to find her leaning against the doorframe. "And genius."

"You know Tremé has birthed some amazing musicians," Jordan began, and I nodded. Everyone from New Orleans knew that. "The Dirty Dozen Brass Band formed its roots over at the community center, but I've seen a need for the same kind of renaissance in piano jazz."

I wrinkled my forehead, trying to figure out what he meant by "piano jazz." I knew my music roots pretty well, but piano jazz covered a broad spectrum. "Can you be more specific?"

Miles's smile widened, and Jordan grinned. "Yeah. I can. Boogey," he called, and the young man at the piano straightened. "Miss Elle here would like to know what do I mean by piano jazz. You got it?"

Boogey smiled. "I got it."

"A one, a two, a one two three four," Jordan said, and Boogey's hands exploded across the keyboard, sending out a rush of notes that climbed and waterfalled, dancing with each other then separately, then on top of each other, his eyes closed the entire time. Wherever that was coming from, it wasn't his sheet music. In sections, I could hear the sound of New Orleans jazz with trombones, trumpets, clarinets, but then new chords would mix in and transform into something else, something alive and electric, improvising over a two-beat rhythm, finally concluding after a few minutes with a wild crescendo that ended on a spicy chord.

The kids in the room broke out clapping. They all looked like high schoolers too, and friendly shouts of "Get it, Boogey," and "You *did* that, Boogey!" flew around the room.

I clapped too, but it didn't feel like enough, so I stuck my pinkies in the corner of my mouth and gave the whistle my dad had taught me to do for Saints touchdowns.

Miles's jaw dropped slightly, and Jordan grinned. "Respect," he said. "Kids, talk amongst yourselves. I'm going to step out in the hall with our visitors. Boogey, you run point." Boogey nodded, and we followed Jordan into the hall.

"I wanted you to meet Jordan because he's the reason the Turnaround is going to be something special," Miles said. "He'll be managing it and helping scout local talent to perform there. It'll give a lot of these folks some of their first official paying gigs, though a lot of them do well busking down in the Quarter."

"Sounds like you're going to have a deep pool to draw from," I told Jordan.

"Indeed. I've been working here for six years, so I have a long list of excellent young musicians ready for a spotlight. I hear you're helping Miles find a property in the Bywater? Best place for it. I grew up there."

"No kidding." Now I knew why Miles had wanted me here. He wanted to show he had Bywater credentials and increase his chances to get Miss Mary's place, but it was going to take more than a guy he'd barely started working with to do that. "Do you eat at Miss Mary's?"

"We were too broke when I was coming up to eat out, but I get over there at least once a month now. Best chicken biscuits in town."

"You tell no lies," I agreed. "So how do you and Miles like working together so far?"

"We've been at this a while," he said. "What, five years? Almost as long as I've been working here. He doesn't like it when I say anything, but he's the reason all those kids in there have instruments."

Five years? Hmmm. So they didn't just start working together to talk me into leasing them the café.

Miles's ears flushed a dull red. "Enough, Jordan. This is about how this man has a brilliant eye for talent, and I wanted you to see that. We'd better get going." He took me by the elbow—gently but as naturally as if we did this all the time—and guided me toward the exit. "See you around, J. We'll get the property straightened out. Bye, Miss Addie."

"Bye, baby," she said.

He let go of my elbow when we reached the sidewalk, and I was glad, but

I also missed his touch as soon as it was gone. Gah. I needed to get this man a property and get him out of my professional space as soon as possible. That meant that as impressive as Jordan was, I still wasn't moving Miles into my downstairs property.

"So what'd you think?" he asked as we rounded the building toward our cars again.

"He sounds like a great choice to manage your club."

"Right? And he understands the Bywater as well as you do."

"Better," I acknowledged. "But that doesn't mean this is the right fit for replacing Miss Mary. You're wanting to change that corner from one type of vibe to a completely different one, and I'm not down."

"The vibe I have in mind is one hundred percent in keeping with Bywater. I've been doing a lot of research this week, really getting to know its history. Can I show you one more thing?"

I didn't have any more appointments for the day, but it was a bad idea to spend more time with Miles. When I was too long coming up with an excuse, he grinned. "I promise, this'll be worth it or I wouldn't be trying to eat up your time."

"What is it?"

"It's over in the Quarter. I'll drive you over and get you back to your car before dinner, I swear."

Miles by himself, I could have resisted. Probably. But another ride in that Mustang…

"Fine. I can give you an hour." I could technically give him the rest of the day if I wanted. But I couldn't give him more than an hour and still keep my head in the right place. Much longer than that and I found myself drifting into such an easy groove with him that I attuned to him, becoming aware of the subtlest shifts in him, from the weight of his gaze when it brushed over me to tiny changes in his breathing. It made me feel like Creepy Gabi, the obsessed high school freshman.

No, thanks. She and I were done.

I'd go pay some polite attention to whatever Miles wanted to show me, then I'd go home and work on my pitch about why he needed *anyone* else for his agent but me.

CHAPTER FOURTEEN

MILES DROVE me to Orleans Street and pulled into a six-car garage hidden behind a gorgeous cream stucco building that was vintage New Orleans. As we pulled in, I caught a glimpse of dark-green shutters and lacy ironwork on the second floor balcony running all the way across the front of the building.

"Where are we?" I asked. Two other cars occupied slots in the garage, a Range Rover and a very expensive BMW, the kind that cost more than I could earn in a year.

"Come in," he said. We stepped from the garage into an enclosed courtyard, a trademark of old French Quarter homes, then crossed the gorgeous garden space to the residence on the other side.

He opened the French door and waved me into a living room that had retained all the original charm of the building—crown molding, rounded corners, beautifully restored oak hardwood floors—with a contemporary vibe. Soft neutral paint and brass accents somehow tied together the house's historic roots with a current aesthetic.

"Do you like it?" he asked, watching me closely.

"I do." I wandered over to the twill sofa and studied the tiny touches in the room, from fresh magnolias in a vase to the tasteful accent tables. It screamed of high-end designer tastes while still making me want to curl up and relax.

"Thanks," he said.

"This is your place?"

He nodded.

It wasn't a surprise. It wasn't like I'd expected him to be letting me into someone else's house. "It's beautiful."

"Thanks. Would you like a tour?"

"I'd love one." There wasn't much I loved more than wandering through historic New Orleans properties.

Like most owners of old homes in the city, Miles knew a great deal about the history of his. The building itself was essentially a D-shape with the garage wing forming the spine. We started with the communal areas first as he explained the features to me that only a dedicated owner would know. The building itself was antebellum—pre-Civil War—and had been the city residence of a wealthy sugar baron. Miles hadn't focused on keeping antique furniture and décor the way some people did, but he'd very much respected the integrity of the architecture, showcasing original wood, glass, doors and fixtures wherever he could. But the real test was coming, and I was curious to see what would happen when we reached the former slave quarters. Would he acknowledge them? Ignore them? What had he done with them?

He led me through the formal dining room which wasn't that formal—comfortable upholstered chairs surrounded a long farm-chic table—and a kitchen that made me itchy to cook on its gleaming cooktop. It was big and spacious, and I wanted it.

"Do you do much cooking?" I asked.

He nodded. "For myself. Not so much for other people, but I know my way around a kitchen."

He'd never mentioned a girlfriend, and this seemed to confirm that he wasn't seeing anyone now. I'd broken down a few nights before and done some googling, bringing up years of his dating history. From ages eighteen to about twenty-two, he'd been the darling of TMZ as he dated a parade of Disney Channel starlets and two members of the same girl group. After that, the reports slowed down, but I wasn't sure if it was because the paparazzi had lost interest in him or if he'd slowed down dating. Every now and then, a story cropped up that showed him stretched out on a yacht next to a hot blonde or on a Miami beach chair next to a smoldering brunette, but if they stuck around, it wasn't making the tabloids.

I wondered how to work it into a casual conversation, something I could drop in like I didn't care about the answer. Something like, *This is a lot of house for just you*, maybe?

But the thought fled from me completely when he led me into the next wing. It was connected to the main body of the house now, but back then, it would have been detached from the main building to house the people enslaved by the sugar baron who'd built this place. Miles opened the first door on the right and flipped on a light, then stepped inside and made room for me to follow.

"These were the slave quarters," he said, his voice quiet.

I looked around, processing how he'd approached it. Some people turned these spaces into guest bedrooms or apartments to sublease. He'd turned them into a long gallery and converted it into a library. Books lined the shelves from floor to ceiling with artwork and sculptures dotting walls and pedestals.

"A library. I don't think I've seen one of these spaces used this way."

"Yeah." He scratched his head like he wasn't sure what to say. "I almost didn't buy this house because I hated the idea of owning a property that had ever been used to enslave people. But the former owner was a jazz musician. Rooster John?"

I nodded. He was a New Orleans legend.

"Anyway, John is the one who turned these old slave quarters into a library. He said he'd filled it with books and art that told their stories without anyone else's conditions on it. He said it was rebaptized and the ancestors approved."

I wandered over to the nearest sculpture, a bronze piece about eighteen inches high that showed a man playing a saxophone whose sound poured out like flowering vines. "This is awesome. You got to buy the whole collection?"

"Not exactly."

I glanced over at him, and even in the soft glow of library lamps, I could see the tips of his ears going dark red again. "He donated his collection to the library at Xavier University. I just thought it was a good idea, so I've been filling this place slowly with my own collection, trying to find local artists and writers to put in here. I mostly just buy what I like. You know, like what speaks to me?" He shrugged. "Most of it wasn't very expensive, but if it becomes valuable like John's collection, I'll put them on permanent loan somewhere and keep the replicas here."

I straightened and turned to face him fully. "You are something else, Miles Crowe."

"Yeah? Like…something good?" he asked, giving me the tiniest cheeky grin.

"Definitely something unexpected. Let's finish the tour."

He led me through the rest of the house, indicating where guest bedrooms were but not opening any of the doors. I wished he would have given me a peek at the main bedroom. I wondered how his style translated to his most personal space, but I had enough brain cells to rub together not to ask him to show it to me.

Finally, we circled back to the garage wing. The other half of it turned out to hold a recording studio on the first floor. I'd never been in a recording studio before, so I was surprised that it looked like every one I'd ever seen in a movie or TV show, complete with a fancy soundboard. "Do you still make a lot of music?" I asked. His most recent release on YouTube was two years old.

He shrugged. "Not so much lately. It's been more interesting to record other artists. Boogey from the center?" he asked, like I could forget him. I nodded. "He was here last month laying down some tracks. That kid is amazing. And he's sixteen. Another Jon Batiste, I think."

"Do you just not like writing music anymore?"

"Uh, I do. It's…complicated. Anyway, let's go upstairs. That's the last stop on our tour."

He obviously didn't want to talk about his own music, and that made me want to ask him about it more.

"This is my gym." He opened the door to a mini version of the big chain gym I went to. It had every machine I could ever need plus a ton of free weights, a treadmill, and… "Is that a Peloton?"

"Don't knock it," he said. "Those rides kick my butt."

"Yeah, I've noticed." And then I clamped my mouth shut. Oh, dang. I had not thought it through before saying those words out loud.

"Miss Jones, did you just hit on me?" Miles asked, and whatever shyness had lurked around him in the library and the recording studio was gone completely, replaced by a mischievous glint in his eye.

"No."

"I think you did."

"I think you misunderstood that."

"I think you just said I have a nice butt."

"I definitely didn't say that." I wanted a hole to appear that would allow me to drop into the studio below so I could then run out into the street and all the way to my place in the Bywater where I would ignore all calls and texts from him forever.

"I don't think there's any other way I could take that."

"I meant that I used my mom's once, and I know they can totally kick people's butts."

He crossed his arms and studied me, and I couldn't help but notice how well the free weights in this room had done their job on his biceps. I let my eyes travel over them on the way to meeting his gaze, which looked even more amused.

"Miss Jones, I'm going to have to call BS. I don't think that's what you meant at all."

"You're wrong, but even if you weren't, a gentleman would let it drop."

He gave an exaggerated look around the room. "I don't see any gentlemen here."

I had no idea what to do, but I wasn't about to flirt back. The only way through this was a bold-faced lie. I laid my hand on his forearm, fighting to not be distracted by how warm and strong it felt beneath my palm. Instead, I smiled up at him and said sweetly, "You're so not my thing."

He threw his head back and laughed and pulled me into a hug. "No one ever deserved that more," he said into my hair before giving me a fast squeeze and letting me go. "I'll quit teasing you. I lured you up here for a reason," he said, turning for the door. "Hang out for five minutes, and I'll be back. Is that okay?"

"Sure," I mumbled, too dazed by the hug to argue. He slipped out and shut the door behind him, and I stared after him while the aftershocks of his hug rolled over me. How did he go from slightly awkward to dead sexy in the space of ten minutes? From shy to the kind of cocky that made me want to kiss him stupid?

Every single one of my hormones was overheating. This was verging on disaster, and if I hadn't promised to wait, I'd already be heading for the sidewalk and escape.

I wandered around the gym for a few more minutes, wondering what Miles was doing. It was easy to imagine him in any of the spaces in his home because he'd done such a good job of making them reflect him.

Maybe I should grab one of these heavy weights and pump it like a bro-dude at the gym to clear my mind. I ran my finger along a thirty-pound dumbbell at the same moment the gym door opened, and Miles leaned against the doorframe.

"So?" he asked.

"So…what?" I felt like I was missing the first half of the question.

"Did you hear anything?"

Besides my overly loud heartbeats? "No," I said slowly. "Should I have?"

He grinned. "I just played live drums along with Metallica on blast downstairs in the studio."

"And you did that because…"

"Because I wanted to prove to you that you can live literally above the Turnaround and the sound will *never* bother you. Modern acoustic engineering is that good. I'll pay for all the upgrades. You'll never know we're there, I promise."

Ha. Like *that* was possible. I'd constantly be thinking about Miles, one floor below me, wondering what he might be doing. Performing? Nursing a drink at the bar? Flirting with the customers?

I opened my mouth to say no, but I couldn't.

I flashed to the mental picture I'd already had of how the Turnaround would look in that space. Of Jordan's face as he worked with the kids at the jazz center. Of Boogey's hands flying over the piano.

Instead, I sat heavily on the weight bench, knees pressed together in front of me, hands curled around the edges. I stared at the floor in front of me without really seeing it. Was I really considering this?

Miles straddled the other end of the bench, tapping at the padding with his knuckles, like he hadn't quite gotten the drumming out of his system. "What are you thinking?"

"I'm thinking maybe."

"*Yes.*"

"No, not yes. *Maybe.* Meet me tomorrow afternoon at Miss Mary's. You're going to talk us through every idea you have for the place. I need to know what I'd be asking my neighbors to deal with."

He reached out and wrapped his hand around my wrist, a loose hold that burned against my skin anyway. "Thank you."

"I'm not promising anything."

"Thank you for even considering it."

"You can thank me by letting me drive your Mustang back to my car."

His hold tightened slightly, and a slow smile tugged up the corner of his mouth. "You drive a hard bargain, Ellie."

I stood and pulled him to his feet. He ended up standing closer to me than I'd intended, forcing me to peer up at him. "I do. And don't you forget it."

"Couldn't if I tried." He reached for me, resting his hand at my waist, gathering the soft fabric of my shirt into his fist and pulling me even closer. I let him, helpless against the pull of his eyes drawing me in, refusing to let me look away. His free hand drifted up to brush my cheekbone. "Ellie." He said it so softly that my name was barely more than a breath.

I pulled away from him and headed for the door, desperately in need of an emergency exit.

He let me go.

CHAPTER FIFTEEN

"So this is it?" Miles asked.

"Yeah." I stared down at the papers that would make it official. "This is it. You are about to be the new tenant of Dauphine Street and my downstairs neighbor."

"Wild."

"Having second thoughts?" I was. But we hadn't talked about that final moment at his house, and he'd kept a friendly distance ever since, maybe so he didn't threaten the lease.

"Not even one," he said. "But I've dreamed about this for a long time, and I can't believe that signing on the dotted line makes it all start coming true even though I had to negotiate with terrorists."

I snort-laughed. Miles had made every concession I'd asked for and then some. He was even comping my neighbor's rent for two months to compensate him for the inconvenience of living over a construction zone. In fact, any time Miles had countered during negotiations, it had been to offer *more* than I'd asked for, which had driven Aaron straight up a wall.

"Yeah, well," I said. "Let it be known that I'm a battle-hardened businesswoman, et cetera."

Miss Mary had been adamant that we should lease to the Turnaround after Jordan stopped by for breakfast the morning after I met him. That was some dirty pool on Miles and Jordan's parts, but it had been highly effective. "I know his mama and them," she'd said. "Good people." Nothing I could have said after that would've convinced her we should lease to anyone else.

It had taken two weeks to work it all out, two weeks of regular meetings to look over their design concepts from tile to table placement to wall color. I had to admit, Miles and the design team he'd hired were pulling together exactly the kind of place where Chloe and I loved to hang out. It was sophisticated but warm, an interior that understood the history of New Orleans with mixed use of reclaimed wood, velvet, and leather, but that also looked toward the future with clean lines, modern tables and chairs, state-of-the-art technology, and sustainable materials anywhere and everywhere Miles could work it in.

I'd spent most of those negotiations wanting to keep my distance from Miles entirely, but I also needed to be sure I was keeping my promise to the Bywater and making sure Miles's vision fit the neighborhood. In fact, in one of those weird kismet moments, I'd ended up closing a deal on one of the properties up the street that Miles had rejected, and soon a new breakfast café would open, restoring balance to the Bywater.

It hadn't been easy to keep it strictly professional every time Miles and I spoke or met to go over plans. But I'd survived.

I glanced at his hands where they rested on the table now as we sat at the back of Miss Mary's. She and Jerome had already cleaned up and left for the day, but she'd assured me she had no problem with Miles and me meeting here to finalize the paperwork. His fingers were long and slender, easily stretching to cover two octaves. I'd watched him do it in his videos over and over again.

I kept a professional buffer between us every time we met, but I'd failed miserably in keeping myself divorced from his music. It was impossible. It was becoming the soundtrack to my life, and I knew I should worry, but I couldn't help it. There was something about the way his melodies drifted into the corner of my mind, the way his lyrics pulled out and defined feelings I hadn't put into words myself. About life. And home. And summertime. And dreams. And everything.

So far, Miles hadn't seemed to realize that I was dangerously close to being as obsessed with him now as I had been at fourteen, and weirdly, once he became my tenant, I could see him less. He could come and go in the restaurant, and we never had to cross paths unless I chose to. My entrance was totally separate from his. Even our parking was separate.

I just needed to get through this signing, and then I could claim all the space I needed away from him.

"I'm teasing," he said, concern in his voice, and I realized I'd been too quiet for too long. "You're super easy to work with, and I'm thankful for it."

"Can we do this?" Aaron asked. He'd been in the kitchen on a call, but he strode out now, looking impatient. "Let's get the paperwork and get on the road. I have dinner plans."

I wasn't sure exactly how much of Miles's business Aaron handled, but it didn't seem like much. Miles had done all the negotiating and made all the decisions on terms, but maybe Aaron wanted to be around for official things like signatures.

"Yeah, sure," I said. I extended a pen to Miles. "It's marked where you need to sign."

"I'll do it," Aaron said. "I'm the authorized signatory since this is running through Miles's S-corp."

"Right," I said, handing the pen to him instead.

He pulled up a chair and scrawled his signature on the designated lines. "We good?" he asked, tossing the pen on the table.

"We're good," I said. I picked up the pen and added my own signatures, trying to figure out why I felt deflated.

"All right, good to see you, Elle." He said it like he might say it to his mail carrier or grocery store cashier. Without sincerity, like he barely registered my existence. "I'm meeting Tami and her friends for drinks. You coming?" he asked Miles.

I had never heard of Tami or her friends before this, but I knew I hated them.

"No, thanks," Miles said. "I'm going to stay in, maybe spend some time in the studio."

Actually, Tami was probably a perfectly lovely person.

"Catch you later." Aaron walked out without a backward glance.

I cleared my throat and gathered up the papers, tapping their sides to get them into a neat pile. "That's it. We're no longer agent and client but landlord and tenant."

"Do I call you now when something is broken and that's it?" He sounded kind of sad.

"No calls until your check clears," I joked. "But yeah, that's about it."

He nodded and looked around the room, still fully Miss Mary's with her art and pictures on the wall. "Doesn't seem right not to have your input. You're like a guardian angel for this building or something. Can I still get your opinion now and then, or am I crossing the line?"

I should say no. I should say not to call me. To leave me out of it entirely. I was on the verge of getting all the distance I needed from him.

And I didn't want it.

Which…

"I'm crossing the line," he said, the tips of his ears turning red. "Sorry. I shouldn't have put you on the spot like that. I'm sure most of your clients don't do that to you. Chalk it up to celebrity entitlement."

"It's fine. You can call." Judging from his expression, I'd surprised us both by saying it.

"Yeah?" His voice was soft.

"Yeah." It was the fact that he didn't sound entitled at all, more nervous about taking over. I'd probably feel better knowing I had some say in the renovations happening beneath me anyway.

"Okay, thanks."

It wouldn't be a big deal. I could handle a phone call now and then asking questions about interiors, or maybe a text with a flooring choice.

And that was how it went at first. He'd text a picture of flooring samples, and I picked the warm, dark wood because it reminded me of the floor in the Ruby Slipper Café where my family did brunch on the first Sunday of every month. The following week, it was pictures of table and chair options. And somehow, before I knew how it had happened, within a month, he was picking me up to take me on appointments at the high-end antiques stores on Royal Street while he looked for bar and bathroom fixtures, or out to tile warehouses on Jefferson Highway so he could get my opinion on stuff.

One night, I came home around eight to an amused look from Chloe.

"What?" I asked as she folded her arms and grinned at me when I walked in.

"Where were you?" she asked.

"River Oaks." It was a newer brew pub and Miles had asked me to go with him to see if their chef was any good.

"With Miles?"

"Yeah."

She grinned. "You're dating."

I drew my head back like I'd smelled something bad. "We're not dating."

"He takes you places and buys you meals and you spend two to three days a week together. You're dating."

"You're high," I said. "He's getting my professional opinion on stuff."

"So you guys only talk about business, nothing else?"

"Yes." Except…no. Our conversations ranged all over the place. About his neighborhood growing up, his siblings, his family. About what it had been like in Hollywood. He'd asked me questions about college and work and growing up in the Bywater. But that was normal small talk.

"I don't believe you."

I couldn't argue because she was right about having non-business conversations. But it wasn't what she thought. "I think I'd know if I was dating someone."

"Yeah? What would be different with Miles that is not happening right now?"

"I'm pretty sure there would be more making out," I snapped.

"Ooh," she said, drawing her head back like I'd swiped at her. "Kitty has claws. You sound frustrated that there's no kissing."

"No, I'm frustrated by your questions. There's nothing going on. I don't want there to be anything going on. I'm giving him advice when he asks for it so that when his place opens, you and I are living over somewhere cool."

Chloe's expression softened. "Okay, I accept that you aren't dating. But are you sure that's how you want it?"

"Definitely."

She sighed. "He is fine. So fine." I agreed but knew better than to admit it aloud. "And it seems to me that what you guys are is friends, pre-benefits, but if you're happy, then okay."

"It's not about happy or not happy. It's about business."

Chloe's face was completely unimpressed. "You should be happy."

"I am. It's general happiness, not because of Miles."

"Good. Then it won't bother you when I show you this interesting item that ran in the paper today." She swiped on her phone a few times and handed it to me. It was an article entitled "Arts Benefit Draws Star-Studded Crowd." The picture showed Miles and a blonde I'd seen him with in a few paparazzi photos standing in front of one of those backdrops with the charity's logo all over it. The caption read "Singer Miles Crowe and model Anneke Jansen." He wore a black suit, and she was in a drapey silver mini-dress and sky-high heels. They made a striking couple.

I felt sick, and I hated it. The picture was a stark reminder that he lived a life totally different than mine, and I needed to remember that I didn't fit into it.

"They look good," I said, handing the phone back to her and trying to keep my face neutral.

"Uh huh." Chloe's tone dripped with doubt. "That's it? No further comment?"

"There's nothing to say. We're not dating. He's my tenant."

"All right, I believe you." But as she climbed to her feet and headed down the hallway to her bedroom, I heard her singing a snippet of Miles's song, "Sweet Sunshine," the one that served as my wakeup alarm.

Well, it was a good song.

Whatever. Miles would get the Turnaround open, and I would retreat completely, other than depositing his rent checks.

Until then, he'd get the same great service all my clients got.

It was just good business, after all.

CHAPTER SIXTEEN

Miss Mary looked out over the packed tables, each full of customers she'd known for years, and smiled.

"You okay?" I asked, watching her face.

It was a Saturday night, one of the few that the café had ever stayed open, and Miss Mary and a whole crew of her family had been prepping a giant goodbye gumbo for days. I'd come down several afternoons and helped Jerome with veggies, chopping up vats of onion, bell pepper, and celery—what we called the holy trinity in Cajun cooking—and slicing sausage and okra to get it all ready for Miss Mary to cook it up.

She'd spent all day on the gumbo yesterday, making the rich brown flour roux—had to be the color of an old brown penny, she'd told me for as long as I could remember—then she and Jerome had sauteed veggies and fried sausage and browned chicken, building the flavors of the gumbo layer by layer.

Gumbo was a thick stew served over rice, and it was everything you needed in one dish, so people didn't often bother with sides beyond oyster crackers on top for some texture. I'd once heard one of Miss Mary's grandkids complain about not liking okra, and Miss Mary had set her straight. "Okra is where gumbo gets its name, you hear? Our people brought okra from Africa centuries ago. Ki ngombo, it was called, and we used it to thicken our stews. How are you going to make a gumbo with no okra? Next you're going to tell me we don't need filé." She'd shaken her head. "Just cook it down all day and you'll never know the okra is in there."

I knew about filé from my own grandmother. It was a greenish brown powder made from ground sassafras and used as a thickener too. It didn't taste like anything by itself, but add it to the gumbo, and suddenly it was magic.

But both my grandmother and Miss Mary lived by the rule that gumbo was always better the second day, just like homemade marinara sauce. It had to do with letting all the flavors steep overnight, so yesterday had been Miss Mary's gumbo-making day, and today it was Miss Mary's gumbo-feeding day, opening up the café to people all day long to come in and get their last bowl of gumbo, all the proceeds going into the college fund she'd set up for her grandkids.

She'd also decided it was a good time to give the neighborhood a preview of what would replace her. Miles had refused to perform, saying he didn't want to overshadow her final day.

"You're crazy," she'd told him. "We'd get so many people here and word would get out about what's coming, and it'd give you a huge head start."

But Miles wouldn't hear of it. Watching the two of them try to wear each other down was like watching an unstoppable force meet an immovable object—basically, my grandad refusing to evacuate no matter the category of an incoming hurricane, Miles being my obstinate grandad and Miss Mary being the relentless hurricane.

Ultimately, I gave the final point to Miss Mary because she prevailed upon Miles to provide music, even if he wasn't doing it himself. And so against the back wall where Miles eventually wanted to put his stage, a trio of kids from the Tremé music center was getting ready to play. Boogey was on keyboard, there was another kid on an upright double bass, and a third on a scaled down set of drums, ready to play with brushes.

"I'm okay," Miss Mary confirmed. "It feels both harder and easier than I expected it to. I know in my bones it's time, but it's strange to think I'm not coming in tomorrow to prep for the Sunday brunch crowd."

I draped an arm around her shoulder. I couldn't imagine it either. "I'm going to miss you."

"Just make friends with Miles's new chef and bum food off him, same like you did with me. Miles will do fine," Miss Mary said, no concern in her voice. "When he showed me his concept for the new interiors, I knew there was nothing to worry about. He has his head on straight."

Miles walked out from the kitchen right then. He'd made himself comfortable with the staff entrance over the last week at Miss Mary's insistence, and he hurried toward us now with a smile.

"Miss Mary," he said, dropping a kiss on her cheek. "I stole a taste of gumbo, and now I have all kinds of guilt for taking over your place. I'm worried the neighborhood will run me out when you leave and take your gumbo with you."

She laughed and pulled him against her side in the half-squeeze she gave all her grandkids. "Stop it with that nonsense, you charmer. You know it's the chicken and biscuits that's going to get you in trouble."

Miles laughed and hugged her back. "You're right. I might be doomed before I even open."

"Don't you worry," she said, her eyes twinkling up at him. "I might have had the cook from the new café in here last week showing her how to make them, so Miss Mary's chicken and biscuits can live on and no one has to boycott your new place. Besides," she said, nodding in the direction of the trio, "I was listening to them warm up, and if that was anything to go by, your bigger problem is going to be finding enough seats for everyone who wants to get in."

"I hope so," he said with a soft sigh. "They're really good, huh?"

"They really are," she confirmed. "Why don't you go see if they're ready, and we'll kick this party up a notch?"

He slid from her arm only to step over and sweep me up into a hug. "Thank you for trusting me with this place," he murmured into my hair.

My arms came up in surprise, resting lightly against his back, then in spite of myself, tightening around him. "Of course. You were the right choice." We stayed like that for a second, long enough for me to register the faint scent of his shampoo and the warm leather smell of his jacket before he stepped back. Every place we'd touched felt suddenly too cool without his heat.

I thought I caught a smirk on Miss Mary's face, but when I turned to study her, she was already watching the trio as Miles strode over toward them. He moved with a different energy in this space, a crackle in his step, a sense of purpose very different from his usual laid-back amble everywhere we went.

He stepped up to the mic and cleared his throat. "Ladies and gentlemen, in a couple of months, this space will become the Turnaround, a dream I've had for as long as I can remember. But tonight is not about that. Tonight is about honoring the thousands of people Miss Mary has fed over the last forty years, the countless smiles, the hugs, the scoldings. I've only known her a month, and she's already fussed at me twice."

That drew a laugh from the crowd, louder from the ones who'd gotten their own scoldings too.

"Anyway, these young musicians are some of the finest talent in New Orleans, and Miss Mary deserved nothing less for her final night in the place she made home for all of us. Without further ado, I present the Tremé Trio."

They played a thirty-minute set, and as Chloe and I sat at our favorite table, eating Miss Mary's gumbo and listening to the jazz trio, every brilliantly executed note wrapped around me and carried me away into a future where the Turnaround existed fully and everyone leaned into the music like there was nothing else they wanted to do.

"Wow," Chloe said when their set ended to thunderous applause. "It's been a minute since I sat and listened to the real deal New Orleans sound."

"They're so good." I knew I sounded awed, but good music always did that to me. Made me reverent, in a way, while at the same time stirring up my blood like the notes were going to pull me right out of my body.

Boogey leaned into the mic. "We're going to take a break, but we'll be back later. Thank you for the love."

They stepped away from their instruments, Miles standing ready to clap them on their backs and offer words of encouragement.

"Heavens, you'd have thought these people never had a gumbo," Miss Mary said, zipping by with a platter full of steaming bowls.

"Need help?" I asked.

"Wouldn't mind it," she said without slowing down. Chloe and I jumped in, grabbing aprons from the supply closet and filling the never-ending stream of takeout orders coming in over the phone and online. I'd thought for sure Miss Mary would need to send home two gallons of it with every grandchild and still have some leftover, but after an hour, I began to wonder if we'd have enough.

Finally, close to nine, the crowd had thinned, and Boogey stepped up to the mic again.

"Since it looks like we down to mostly friends and family, I guess it needs to be said: ain't no party without some dancing, y'all."

He and the other two launched into a jazzy cover of "Whip/Nae Nae" which made Chloe burst out laughing, but Jerome and a couple of his cousins were already pushing tables aside to create space for dancing. Soon the floor filled with Miss Mary's family and Bywater friends, the longest standing ones who felt comfortable to stay without an invitation, and the whooping and cutting up began while I sat beside Chloe and watched it all, grinning.

"Whip/Nae Nae" became "The Humpty Dance," and after a half-dozen more dance songs, the crowd had thinned as people drifted home, full of gumbo and memories. Mr. Douglas took Miss Mary by the hand and called out, "Slow it down for us, Boogey!"

The opening strains of "Cruising Together" by Smokey Robinson began, and I flinched, a huge surge of feeling welling up in my chest. This was the song Miles had performed at his hometown concert on *Starstruck*, and I had no good memories of it. Worse, this tidal wave revealed a sudden and awful truth: my stupid, hopeless crush was back. Every ridiculous, outsized feeling thrummed through me at once. They'd been there all along, but this song made me see the truth as it called up all those old emotions.

I looked down at the packet of oyster crackers and began smooshing them, cracker by cracker, pressing them against the table until they were fine dust.

"That looks satisfying."

I glanced up to find Miles next to the table, watching me, an amused expression on his face.

"Making a self-contained mess?" I smooshed another cracker inside the wrapper. "Deeply satisfying."

"I hate to interrupt, but I don't want to miss a chance to ask you to dance."

I shot him a sharp look. He had to remember this song. "That's sweet, but this song isn't my favorite."

"I didn't figure it would be." He held out his hand. "I was hoping we could overwrite it with a better memory."

I didn't want to. I wanted to sneak out to my quiet apartment, but I wouldn't leave before Miss Mary did. Short of sitting and pouting, accepting Miles's invitation looked like the only option.

I placed my hand in his and stood, wishing I'd worn taller shoes when I realized I only came up to his chin in my flats. I wanted more height to feel like I was on equal footing. Or more distance, so I didn't feel the sharp pull in my belly when I caught a whiff of the soft spicy notes in his cologne. Or maybe that was just how Miles smelled. Maybe someone should bottle his pheromones and make themselves a billion dollars.

He led me toward the improvised dance floor, keeping my hand in his, and when we joined the three other couples dancing, he tugged gently, drawing me close to him to rest our clasped hands between us against his chest, his other arm sliding around my waist.

As simple as that, the rest of the world grew quiet, and we moved in time with my heartbeat. Maybe with his heartbeat too. But it was perfect rhythm, and I wanted to fight it, to step back and hold myself stiff. He might read too much into the way I relaxed into him, but I couldn't help it. The trio was only doing instrumental covers, but my brain supplied the lyrics. *Baby, let's cruise away from here.* Except…it was Miles's voice, singing quietly in my ear, his voice soft and husky like it was one of his acoustic performances when the arrangements were stripped down.

"Don't be confused, the way is clear," he sang softly, and my heart tripped. It had been a brilliant song choice. I'd always loved Smokey Robinson's impossibly smooth voice on the original, not realizing what a suggestive song it could be until I was much older. The arrangement the producers had given Miles for his *Starstruck* performance had been perfect for his boyish charm, emphasizing the idea of a road trip with some wholesome girl of his dreams.

But as he sang to me now, his voice tangled with the words in a way that was so sexy, I curled my fingers into his shirt to make up for my weak knees. This wasn't a sweet song about a road trip anymore. It was a seduction, and the soft rasp in his voice rubbed along my nerve endings, making my mouth go dry.

He pulled me more firmly against him, and I nestled my head beneath his chin so there was no danger of eye contact. I didn't want him to read the truth in them that I'd been trying to hide for weeks now. That I had tumbled, and I was verging on falling, not the way a kid does, but in the way a grown woman does for a man who is good and strong and smart and funny.

As he sang about inch-by-inch getting closer to every part of each other, he drew me even tighter, until even the music couldn't have snuck in between us.

I leaned my forehead against his chest. "What are you doing?" I breathed between the tones of the song's bridge.

"Private concert," he murmured into my hair. "It's the least I could do."

I drew back the tiniest bit to search his eyes now, trying to read him. Was this my friend and client Miles showing off for me? But what I saw in them looked so much like the wanting I felt for him that I couldn't look away.

The lyrics died on his lips, and we'd slipped into barely swaying, pressed against each other on the dance floor, everything else gone. "We signed on the dotted line, so that means I'm your tenant no matter what now, right?"

I gave a short, slow nod.

"Ellie." I saw my name on his lips more than heard it, watched the slow incline of his mouth toward mine, and I stretched up to meet it, still inside our bubble of only us and the music, but the notes for the last verse reached me just as Miles's lips brushed against mine. *If you want it, you got it forever…*

Heat flared between us and wrenched a gasp out of me. I stepped back, pressing a hand to my mouth like I'd been burned. And maybe I had.

"Ellie?" Miles moved as if he meant to draw me back toward him, but I pulled my hand from his and stepped back again.

"Thanks for the concert," I said, mustering a smile. I could barely hear myself over the music and my own heartbeat. "I should go see if there's any work left to do in the kitchen."

I turned, and it looked as if he would follow, but one of Miss Mary's daughters spun out of a cousin's arms and into Miles's, grinning. "Show me your moves," she said, and Miles swept her into a dance hold even as his eyes met mine in a question. I fluttered my fingers at him in a weak goodbye and almost ran for the kitchen.

There wasn't anything to do. Everything from the cooler to the cupboards had been cleaned out completely. At best, the twenty-gallon soup kettle held a couple of inches of leftover gumbo, but I pushed up my sleeves and began ladling it into gallon Ziploc bags for Miss Mary's family to take and freeze for another day.

Miles stepped in a few minutes later, the muffled sounds of "The Cupid Shuffle" leaking through the kitchen door as it closed behind him.

"Hey," he said softly.

"Hey!" I returned brightly like I hadn't almost gone somewhere dangerous with him on that dance floor minutes before.

"We good?"

"Of course." I dumped more gumbo into the bag I was holding.

"Because it sort of seemed like…"

I didn't want to know how he would finish the thought. "Yeah, I'm always itchy to be doing something. I don't want Miss Mary to have any mess to worry about tonight. Thought I'd come back and take care of it so she can go home, and the kitchen, at least, will be ready for you to take over Monday morning."

"Right." He leaned against the stainless steel counter behind him. "The perfect agent as usual, going above and beyond."

"It's the Crescent City Properties promise," I said, flashing him my professional smile.

"I'll be sure to give your boss a good report."

"Much appreciated." I scraped the ladle against the bottom of the kettle in pursuit of more gumbo.

"Will I see you again?"

I paused and turned to meet his eyes. "What do you mean?"

"This feels like it might be how you close all your deals before you move on to the next one."

"I'm not just your agent here; I'm your landlord." His shoulders relaxed until I added, "Of course we'll talk again. Old buildings always need some kind of fixing. You can call me any time."

He opened his mouth like he was about to argue, hesitated, then pushed away from the counter. "Fair enough. Thanks for helping me find this place. I'll see you around, Ellie."

The door had no sooner closed behind him than it opened to admit Miss Mary. "Hey, honey," she said. "What are you doing back here?"

"Scooping up the last of the gumbo so I can clean this kettle for you."

"Leave it. My grandkids will do it."

"I don't want any of you to have to do any more work tonight. You've earned the right to relax completely."

"*I* have," she said, "and you have too, but a little work won't kill those grandbabies. Leave it for them. Honestly." Her tone said clearly that she wasn't going to argue about it.

I hung the ladle on the lip of the kettle. "Yes, ma'am."

"Go on and wash your hands so I can give you something."

She hustled to the small office at the back of the kitchen, but I wasn't sure why since she'd cleaned it out as surely as she had the rest of the place. I washed my hands, and when she emerged, she handed me a white envelope. "Take this and follow the directions."

"What directions?"

She nodded her head at it. "Now I'm going to go enjoy one last dance with my kids. Mind leaving me and Harold to lock up one last time? I'll leave the keys on your doorstep."

"Of course not."

"Bye, baby. I'll call you when my book is done." And she slipped back out to the restaurant.

I looked down at the envelope. It had my name printed in her curly script, and beneath it, just four words: *Open in three months*.

What in the world?

CHAPTER SEVENTEEN

NOTHING COULD HAVE CONVINCED me to go downstairs for the next week, and I mean nothing. Not the most powerful gris-gris. Not money, love, or the possibility of saving the world from destruction. N.o.t.h.i.n.g.

I didn't want to deal with any weird Miles vibes. I didn't want to discuss our almost-kiss on the dance floor. And honestly, I didn't want to have to deal with all the demolition noise that started at eight o'clock sharp on Monday morning. They had to gut parts of the place to put in the soundproofing before I could have the blessed silence Miles had promised.

But in reality, avoiding downstairs—and Miles—became a non-issue by Tuesday evening when I returned home after work and found a fancy cream envelope tucked into my doorframe with my name on it, and an identical one tucked into my neighbor's doorframe across the hall.

I plucked mine out and let myself into my apartment as I studied it. It had been hand-delivered, no address on the outside.

I was pulling the card from the envelope when Chloe walked out of her room with a suitcase. "You're taking it, right?"

I blinked at her. "Taking what?"

"That." She nodded at the envelope. "It's from Miles. He's offering to put us up at a hotel or an Airbnb for the entire week or as long as it takes to get the soundproofing in."

"Wow." I was impressed. It wasn't something I had negotiated for in the lease.

"Yeah, well, you can thank me for it. I left a nasty note on his car yesterday complaining about the noise, and this is how he decided to solve it."

"Chloe!"

"I did *not* sign up to live over a construction zone, and I figured you'd like it better if I complained to him, even if *you* are my actual landlord."

"I can't decide if I prefer it that way or not."

"Trust me, you do," she said, pulling out the rolling handle of her suitcase with a sharp click. "It was a mean note. I don't like being woken up by sledgehammers. Not when I can't run down and get some of Miss Mary's coffee to ease me into the land of the living."

"I see," I said. "Why do I suspect that your note was less about the construction noise and more about missing Miss Mary?"

"It was definitely about the construction noise."

I raised an eyebrow at her.

"But missing Miss Mary made it sound cranky. Anyway, you have two choices. Fancy hotel," she said, holding her hands out like scales and letting one drop slightly with the weight of that option. "Or an awesome Airbnb. Which, by the way, is the right option." She let that hand drop almost all the way to her knees.

"I don't know. Getting spoiled at a four-star hotel sounds pretty great."

"Yeah, but you're still going to feel like a guest. If we go to the Airbnb, it's huge, it's in the Marigny, and we can cook our own food and stretch out instead of being in a cramped hotel room."

"That's true."

"Did I mention he threw in a gift card for a food delivery service that should cover us for two weeks no matter which way we decide?"

"It doesn't make up for losing Miss Mary." I opened the card and found the voucher she was talking about along with the hotel and Airbnb information. "But it *is* better than a poke in the eye with a sharp stick."

"So you'll do the Airbnb with me?"

"You mean instead of staying in a hotel with a bunch of tourists?" I rolled my eyes. "I don't know how I'll ever decide."

"You were always going to pick the Airbnb, weren't you? Why play with my feelings like that?"

I grinned at her. "A girl likes to feel wanted. I'll pack and meet you over there. How about you order dinner for us tonight and I'll order tomorrow?"

"You got it."

I checked the card to see if he'd included anything else. Like, *Almost kissing you was amazing.* He had added a note, but only to let me know that if I would give him permission, he would have some window guys come out to replace all our residential windows at his cost with triple-paned glass for even better sound protection.

He wasn't required to do that as part of his lease, but this was business, and it was too good of a deal to turn down just to be polite. He was a multi-platinum millionaire. It wasn't like upgraded windows were a sacrifice. I texted him to approve the plan, then packed enough clothes for the week and drove over to join Chloe and discover that Miles had hooked us up with a house that I couldn't afford on even triple my salary. It was gorgeous, and even if it didn't feel like home, it was fun to come back to at the end of every workday. I was almost sorry when I got a text on Friday afternoon from Miles.

Hey. Demo finished two days ahead of schedule. All clear for a quiet return if you want. Or enjoy the Airbnb for a few more days! Either way. It's paid through Tuesday night.

It was the first time I'd heard from him besides the envelope in my door. It was a friendly, polite message, exactly the kind I would expect to get from him.

But there was still a part of me that had waited every day to hear from him like I had for the past three weeks when he would check in daily about the property search.

"Stupid," I mumbled aloud. I'd set a boundary; I shouldn't be complaining when I actually got my space. I texted Chloe before leaving the office. *Miles says we can go home or stay at the rental until Tuesday. Going to head home.*

I missed my bed. I packed and drove home, and when I stepped back into my place, I noticed the windows right away. His installer had gone with an expensive upgrade and rebuilt the worn casements with new freshly painted built-ins.

Nice.

But it wasn't a surprise that Miles paid extraordinary attention to detail. From his plans for his club to the lyrics in his songs, his awareness of the small things other people didn't consider made him stand out. As a client. And a songwriter. And as a person.

Ugh. I didn't want to think about him right now. I'd avoided listening to his music all week, knowing that after our moment on the dance floor, his voice would have only served to pull me under, and I was already drifting too close to the deep end.

Still, in the early Friday evening quiet when the shops had closed but the restaurants and clubs hadn't begun bustling, I couldn't resist slipping downstairs to see what Miles had gotten done already.

Technically, I wasn't supposed to enter the leased premises without notifying him in advance, but I wasn't going downstairs in my official capacity; I was sneaking a peek as Gabi, the kid who'd grown up in Miss Mary's kitchen, curious to see what it had become.

I entered through the kitchen as I always did, and it looked almost the same. They'd pulled out one of the double ovens that had been temperamental for Miss Mary, and I knew Miles planned to replace it. Other than that, everything was exactly where I was used to seeing it, even if the pantry and cold storage were empty.

I hesitated at the door to the dining room, not sure I wanted to see it stripped bare. But it was probably the best way to help me process the fact that things were changing for good. I took a steadying breath and stepped through it, then almost yelped when I knocked right into Miles who'd been standing with his back to the door. He caught his balance with a step forward and a mild curse before turning to see me.

"I'm sorry!" I said at the same time he asked, "What are you doing here?"

"Sorry," I repeated. "I'm not technically supposed to come down here without twenty-four hours notice in writing."

"Did you do that with Miss Mary?"

"No."

"Then you don't need to do it now."

The invitation caused a small flutter in my chest. Nerves? Excitement?

Stupidity. That's what. "Thanks," I told him, "but I'll notify you from now on. I promise. I was just too curious to resist."

He swept his hand around the dimly lit hull of the café. "Not much to look at yet, but it's ready for them to do the sound-proofing on Monday, and by Tuesday you shouldn't hear a sound no matter what time they start construction."

I winced. "Yeah, Chloe said something about leaving you a note. It was nice of you to put us up for the week."

He smiled. "It's fine. She was right. No reason you should have to deal with the demolition noise." He glanced over the bare walls, the wooden floor faded around the darker spots where the permanent booths had sat. "Does it feel weird to be in here?"

My eyes followed the same path his took. "It does. But it's good for me. I'm not great at letting things go. This helps."

"For what it's worth, I found a place right around the corner. The Bywater Bakery?"

I nodded. Everybody in the Bywater knew it. Probably everyone in the city did.

"While I can verify that I know for myself no one makes a better chicken biscuit than Miss Mary, their coffee is just as good. Anyway, I set you and Chloe up with a permanent tab over there. Consider it a thank you for letting me lease this place."

My eyes widened. "You don't have to do that."

He shrugged. "I know. That's why I want to."

"Well…thank you. But you don't have to bribe me. You have an ironclad lease that keeps me from kicking you out of this place for at least five years. Unless you're planning to start laundering money through here or something?"

"I'm not," he said like he was taking my question seriously. "Not unless tourism dries up and people decide not to listen to music anymore. In which case I might have to turn to a life of crime. But I think we'll be okay."

"I'll do an addendum to your lease that requires you to give me thirty days' advance notice in writing if you decide to make this a crime front."

"Good plan."

I smiled at him, then crooked my head to the door behind us. "I'll get out of your hair. Sorry for barging in. I'll check with you first before I come down again." I turned toward the kitchen.

"Wait," he said, reaching out to grab my wrist in the same light hold he'd used on the dance floor. I stopped and turned back to him. "Last week, Miss Mary's gumbo party." He paused and it looked like he was drawing in a slow, steady breath. I tensed, knowing what was coming. "I didn't imagine that. Right?"

He sounded way more uncertain than I'd expect from a guy who had been photographed with major and minor celebrity girlfriends over the years, much less this month.

"It was nothing," I reassured him. "Anneke has nothing to worry about."

"Anneke?" his eyes crinkled in confusion, and it was so adorable it made my stomach dip. "Oh, did you see us on her Instagram?"

"What? No." The last thing I wanted him to think was that I was stalking him on social media. "Chloe mentioned something the paper ran in the People section, that's all. You were at a benefit together? Anyway, it's all good."

"Anneke is an old friend of mine. We're *not* dating. I get credit for more Hollywood hookups than I deserve."

"No judgment here," I said. Not judging him, anyway. But I'd judged that I was definitely not his type.

"I promise that of the two women I've had real relationships with in the last ten years, one of them has never been seen in a paparazzi photo and the other was identified as a friend I was grocery shopping with when one of the tabloids ran a picture of us coming out of the market in our sweats."

"Oh. That's...oh."

"Does that matter?" he asked softly.

Yes. No. Did it matter to him whether it mattered to me? I needed to say something fast before the silence said something I didn't mean it to. "No, it doesn't matter."

"Did you research me on Instagram?"

"No." I was thankful for the dim light so he couldn't see me turning red at telling such a bold-faced lie.

"I looked you up. I wondered what it had been like for you over the last twelve years."

This made my stomach churn harder. He'd been curious enough to look into me? It made me feel slightly naked, even though I knew exactly what he would have found. I'd kept any mention of *Starstruck* or that meme or video off my social media accounts. My personal accounts were private, and my public accounts mostly showed properties I'd found for my clients or pictures of places and food in New Orleans to show that I knew the city inside and out. Sometimes I put myself in the pictures to give clients a sense of connection to me. But I made it about the work.

"I didn't find much," he said, ducking his head like he was trying to see my face better. "Only proof that if you weren't already my property agent, I'd want to hire you."

"Lucky it worked out that way, then."

"I was hoping for more. Not that you owe it to me. But I was hoping to see more about what your non-work self is like."

This was veering too much into the personal territory where that dance had almost taken us. "Nothing to tell, really. Anyway, I need to"—*escape*—"head up and make some dinner. Thanks for the window upgrade. They look good." I made for the kitchen door.

"Ellie? Stop for a second?"

I did, turning to face him.

"For better or worse, you and I are going to be connected for a long time," he said. "It could just be as landlord and tenant, but I'd love it to be as friends. Could we go get dinner and talk? Possibly about nothing work-related?"

He might want to dig into our shared past to satisfy his curiosity, but I didn't. I'd created a healthy distance from all the trauma of the bullying and shame, and I'd never once benefitted from reliving those memories. Now more than ever, I wanted distance from them because it was too easy these days to remember how much I had adored Miles Crowe before I'd hated him.

"That's sweet, but I need to pass. Good luck with all the remodeling." I moved toward the kitchen again.

"Wow, not even a raincheck, just a straight up pass?" He sounded curious, not mad.

"Yeah. Landlord." I pointed to myself. "Tenant." I pointed to him.

"Got it." His jaw tightened. Then he sighed. "Will you at least promise me one thing?"

"What's that?"

"Please consider this your space as much as it was before. Come down here any time, wander through any time. I'm never going to be doing something I have to hide, and I'll feel better knowing I haven't displaced you. I'll put it in writing if it makes you feel better," he said with a quick grin. "And if you ever want to wander in for a cold beer with a friend, I'm here for that."

He wasn't going to feel better unless I promised to drop in, so I nodded. "Okay. Thanks. I'll wander in if the spirit moves me."

I went upstairs to make a quick chicken stir fry for dinner, considering the conversation as I dug ingredients from the fridge. I didn't want to start down the road that had opened up when Miles and I had danced at Miss Mary's party. I was already verging too dangerously close to the crush I'd had on him back then, and Miles might be attracted to me right now, but I was nothing like the women he'd dated in LA. I didn't have their level of glam. It would take airbrushing and a full-time makeup artist for me to reach their level of beauty. He'd get bored. Or a better offer.

There would be no such thing as a fling for me with Miles, and I didn't want to put myself back together again when he was done and on to the next woman. I didn't want to have to live above him or interact with him in a professional way if we dated and he moved on. There would be no moving on for me.

My mom always said, "Believe people when they show you who they are." And Miles had done that. He was a good guy. I could see that. But he was *not* the guy for me.

Still…

I hated the idea of Miss Mary's becoming a foreign space. What if Chloe and I could be as easy there as we'd always been with Miss Mary? What if we felt as free to pop our heads in to say hi to the kitchen staff and filch something to eat as we had the entire two years we'd lived here so far?

Miles made it sound like that's what he wanted for us. I tried to imagine how it would feel to drop by before they got busy each day, to say hey to Miles and wander through the kitchen on my way upstairs after work.

If we kept it at that—hellos and easy chat as I passed through—that could work, right? It would be good to have this place feel comfortable.

I ate my stir fry and pictured it. Friendly greetings with the Turnaround staff. I already knew Jordan. It would be fun to keep up with new talent he brought in.

Maybe…

Maybe this would be okay.

CHAPTER EIGHTEEN

Can I get your opinion?

It was a text from Miles. I hadn't stopped by downstairs in three days, not since our last conversation. But the soundproofing had gone in Monday while I was at work, and Tuesday morning, I hadn't even heard them start construction. I was curious about how it was coming along but stopping in at this point would be about seeing Miles. It wasn't like he had any other staff hired for me to get to know. I'd decided to wait until he started hiring and training before trying out his invitation to become a familiar face.

Now, though, I stared at his message. Was he sending it from downstairs? I'd barely gotten home from work. Had he seen me drive in?

My opinion on what? I texted back.

Decorating stuff. I'm lost. You always had good ideas when we were looking at properties.

I could do that. *Sure. What's the question?*

Want to run down and take a look?

So he *had* seen me drive in. Did I want to go down and look at fabric swatches or floor samples or whatever it was with Miles? I tried to think about what I would do for any other client.

I'd offer an opinion or refer them to someone who could help them if it was outside of my expertise.

But this was Miss Mary's space. I couldn't pass up a chance to give my two cents.

I made sure to dress down so it wouldn't look like I was trying to impress him. I wore running shorts and a tank and laced up my sneakers so I could hit the river trail when I was done downstairs.

I wasn't sure if I should go through the kitchen door like usual, so I walked around front and went in the main entrance. The club—the hull of it, anyway—was empty except for him. The crew probably got off at five every day.

He smiled when I walked in. "So I guess that's a yes, you'll give me your opinion?"

"Full-service leasing agent here," I answered.

"You're the best," he said, smiling slightly.

I liked that smile. It was his smile when he was thinking things he wasn't saying, and it always made me want to know what else was going on in his mind. He had so many layers, and I—

I was staring. I blinked. "You wanted me to look at something?" *Besides your lips?*

"I wanted to get your opinion on this wall over here. I'm thinking about bricking it over, giving it some Chicago blues club credibility."

"Or…?"

"Well, right now it's slated to be a plaster wall."

I raised my eyebrow. "Are you opening a Chicago blues club?"

"No."

"Does New Orleans need any kind of credibility when it comes to music?"

He cut his eyes toward me, and a small smile tugged at his lips. "No."

"Then it sounds to me like putting up a fake brick wall would be trying too hard."

His eyes slid back to the wall. "It sounds obvious when you put it that way."

"Yep." This one was definitely a no-brainer. "Exposed brick and fake brick facades are very different things."

"Fair enough."

"Great. I'm headed out for a run. See you around."

The next day he texted me at lunch. *Want to offer an opinion on light fixtures? Because that might be the decision that finally kills me.*

After work, I changed into my running clothes to give me an excuse not to stay and met him downstairs.

"Show me what you got." For the next twenty minutes, I looked at different fixtures on his phone.

Friday afternoon, shortly before I planned to leave work, it was, *There are more styles of chair legs in the world than I'm emotionally equipped to handle. Help?*

I laughed. *Feel their vibe.*

There are no vibes through the phone screen.

Of course there are, I answered.

He called. "I always thought I was a leg man, but these chairs are making me a liar."

I fought not to blush even though he couldn't see me. I had great legs, and I'd been parading them past him in my running shorts two days in a row. I hadn't meant to. I'd just been trying to give myself a reason to literally run out of the club every day.

"Ellie?"

"Here. Uh, okay, look, I'm heading home soon, and I'll pop in and take a look."

"Great." He sounded relieved, and I liked the flutter of warmth that created in my chest a little too much.

"Actually, why don't you text over the choices? Then you don't have to wait until I get home."

He paused for a second. "This works better if you stand in the space while you're looking at the options, don't you think?"

Miles Crowe wanted to see me, and he'd made up excuses three days in a row to get me downstairs. He wanted me in his space, and it didn't have anything to do with chair legs.

How did I feel about that?

I had been so good. Keeping it professional, keeping Miles at a distance. But my instincts said Miles would need only the tiniest sign from me to close that gap.

What if I did it? Would it be so bad to flirt with the cute guy downstairs? Would it be so bad to find out how his lips felt instead of wondering about it?

Maybe. But I didn't care anymore.

A smile curved my lips. "Sure, I'll check it out when I get home." And there was another warm flutter at using "home" to refer to a building we both occupied.

"See you then."

When I pulled in after work, I was glad I'd worn my favorite green top with a pencil skirt. I'd had a client lunch, and the outfit flattered my body while still being completely professional.

I walked around to the front and pushed through the front door of the club. "Show me what you're working with," I said.

Aaron snorted, and I realized that Miles wasn't alone. I didn't like the snort. It made my words sound vaguely dirty.

"Hey, Aaron."

"Hey, Elle."

That was a surprise. I didn't think he even knew my name. But he didn't look up from his phone, so that at least was normal.

"I don't know how I can like three such different chair designs, but I do. I'm serious. This is what breaks me." Miles placed his phone in my outstretched hand, his fingers brushing mine and sending tiny sparks through my palm.

I gave the screen a quick glance and handed it back. "You know what to do."

He stared down at the options. "The first one?"

"Bingo."

The brick was the only place he'd gone wrong. I could imagine everything else he'd shown me over the last few days in here, and I liked the way the pieces worked together in my mind.

"I feel better." He slid his phone into his pocket. "I'm hungry for dinner. Want to grab a bite?"

Aaron's presence changed the whole vibe, and for once, I probably owed him a thank you for snatching me back from a stupid mistake. I gestured down to my clothes. "I need to go change and get in a run but thanks for thinking of me."

"Next time then." Miles's tone was laid back, like the rejection hadn't stung at all.

"I'd better get going while I've got some light," I said, turning toward the door. "Good luck with the rest of the renovation."

"I'll walk you out." He held the door for me like a perfect gentleman.

"Thanks for coming down. And Ellie?" he said, as I stepped past him to the sidewalk. "Seriously, feel free to come in through the kitchen next time."

I gave him a polite, noncommittal smile and headed upstairs to change. When I came back down, Aaron was waiting for me at the back door.

"Hey, Elle," he said. "Wanted to chat for a minute."

A chat with a guy who'd never once tried to make conversation with me? This should be interesting. And probably annoying based on every previous second I'd spent in Aaron's company.

"Can I help you with something?" I asked.

"Miles needs to focus."

I blinked, not even knowing how to react to that. "Excuse me?"

"He doesn't need any distractions right now."

"You know *he* called *me*, right?" I knew it was in my best interests to placate Miles's business manager, but I didn't like his tone.

"His head's not in the game, and he needs to get it back there."

"Are you high? Because literally every single minute I've spent around him, all he talks about is the club."

"That's the problem," he said. "He had a slump and some burnout, but he's pouring all of his creative energy into this club, and he needs to channel it back into his music career."

"It sounds to me like Miles knows exactly what he wants. Go have this conversation with him if you don't believe me." A desire to get away from Aaron, to bob and weave through the light sidewalk traffic until I reached the freedom of the river trail, pricked at me.

"He *thinks* he knows what he wants. His music sales have plummeted in the last few years, and he couldn't book more than a small theater show if he tried. Which he doesn't. And you want to know why it's all gone to crap?"

I was hungrier than I should be for details of Miles's life that I couldn't glean from internet articles. But I wasn't sure it was Aaron's place to tell me. I shook my head. *No.* It didn't stop him from telling me anyway.

"When he listened to me and the label guys, he had money pouring in hand over fist. Arena tours, merch sales through the roof, and a new album every eighteen months to keep it all running smoothly. But he lost himself somewhere in the process. I think it was the breakup with Anneke."

"Anneke?" I asked in spite of myself. The model from the benefit, who according to Miles, was just a friend.

"Yeah. He's had a hard time getting over her. They were inseparable for a year, and then they started fighting. It hurt him more than he'll admit, but it was a turning point. After Anneke, his songwriting changed. It became... melancholy. He started digging into hard things, and it's not what listeners are hungry for. It's not his *brand*."

I thought about how Miles had explained that pivot. He'd described it as growing tired of being a corporate product, but he hadn't in any way connected it to a breakup. "I got the impression that Anneke wasn't one of the deeply meaningful relationships in his life."

Aaron shot me a sharp look. "Who told you that?"

"Miles. He didn't count it as one of his two 'real' relationships." I hated myself for gossiping about him, but I was too thirsty for the information to stop myself from fishing.

"He's pretty private. It makes sense that he wouldn't go into it when it was a relationship that didn't end on his terms. He's still down in the wreckage of it, and so he's like..." He waved in the direction of the club. "He's literally building something new because his mind is like that. He's trying to distract himself from all the pain, when what he should really do is pour it back into the music that made him a star."

I considered everything he was saying, the pages of results I'd found with pictures of him with Anneke. They'd been in each other's company for a solid year, photographed coming out of restaurants, walking the red carpet at award shows, sunning themselves on a yacht off the coast of Mexico.

Miles had made it sound like spending time with Anneke was a publicity stunt. Aaron was saying that was a front for some deep pain.

"They went to a benefit together last week."

Aaron rolled his eyes. "Anneke comes around as often as she needs to for Miles not to get over her. Trust me, he'd take her back in a second if he could."

I thought about the layers upon layers in Miles's lyrics. He was a man capable of great depth. It gave weight to Aaron's words.

"Here's the thing," Aaron continued. "This club might be a good idea for another investor, but for Miles, it's going to hijack him from who and what he's meant to be. And right now, not to be crass, he's definitely got his eye on you, and unless you're planning to become a rock star's side piece and leave New Orleans behind, when he does snap out of it and start his comeback, you'll be part of what's holding him back."

Two competing feelings warred inside me; disgust for Aaron referring to me—or anyone—as a "sidepiece" coupled with a sick thrill that Aaron had noticed Miles paying attention to me. It meant that the vibes were stronger than just the two of us on a tiny dance floor.

What was *wrong* with me? This deluded sign-seeking and surging hope had led to my televised meltdown twelve years ago.

"The Turnaround doesn't seem like a phase. He seems super invested. And I don't mean his money." I was proud of myself for keeping my voice even. "It's hard to imagine him leaving it behind."

"He'll get bored," Aaron said. "He always does. But when that happens, Jordan will be ready to take over, and it'll run fine. Jordan's a good guy, and Miles won't have to worry about it. He can stop in when he visits his parents, but he'll be able to get back to his own music."

He'll get bored. Seemed like Miles was like that with women too, no matter what easy explanations he gave. Or maybe he had been telling the truth as he saw it; maybe *he* had always felt the situations were casual while the women had wanted something more. It made Miles less of a jerk if he really thought his flings were easy-breezy on both sides. But the idea of leaning into this attraction we felt and having him drift off when he was bored...

"Don't worry about it," I said, bouncing on my toes, ready to be done with this whole conversation. "I'll stay out of his way."

And then I took off running, ready to leave Miles and all my confusing feelings about him behind.

CHAPTER NINETEEN

ALMOST LIKE CLOCKWORK, on Monday afternoon, a text came in from Miles.

Rethinking this flooring. You have time to take a look?

I texted back a short, *No, sorry.*

No problem, he answered. *Maybe tomorrow.*

Probably not, I texted. *Busy week.*

He answered with a thumbs up emoji.

He texted again Tuesday anyway, wondering if now I had time to look at flooring. I told him I had a client dinner.

Wednesday morning, he asked me to weigh in on the bar construction. I declined.

Thursday I didn't hear from him. It was both a relief and a letdown. But Friday afternoon he texted about getting my opinion on tabletops as I pulled in from work. Clearly, he'd been watching for my arrival, timing the text so I couldn't make an excuse of not having time to look.

I didn't answer, letting myself into my apartment. "Chloe?"

"Present," she called from her bedroom.

"Let's go out. You in?"

"Perfect timing," she said, walking out. "Because I have something to celebrate." Her eyes practically danced with excitement.

"Tell me."

"The Kitchen Saint got her first sponsor!"

"What? Yay!" I squealed. "Tell me who. I want to know all about it."

"I'll tell you at dinner which should be somewhere excellent that I've already reviewed so I don't have to work while I eat."

"Deal! Let me change, and we'll do this."

She glanced down at her watch. "It's not even five-thirty yet."

"Yeah, but we won't even get anywhere until six, and we can enjoy some drinks first."

"It's a date."

Relieved that I had an actual plausible excuse, I texted Miles. *Sorry, plans tonight. Go with your gut.*

Saturday I spent doing some cleaning and laundry, then catching up on paperwork. But Sunday…Sundays were for me. I lived for Sundays, and I needed this Sunday more than ever.

On Sundays, I slept late, greeted the day with some coffee and yoga whenever I woke up sometime mid-morning, and if I felt like it, I drove out to see my parents for dinner.

When I rolled out of bed close to ten, I pulled on my oldest, comfiest sundress, threw my hair up in a messy bun, and slid into my flipflops to trek over to Bywater Bakery for my coffee. I only allowed myself the smallest twinge as I reached for my door that I couldn't nip down to Miss Mary's. Maybe one day I wouldn't feel that missing in my routine, but today wasn't that day.

I opened the door to find Miles there, his hand raised and ready to knock, a surprised look on his face to match the tiny gasp I'd made.

"Whoa, hey," he said. He was in a worn Tulane T-shirt and jeans, both doing his hard planes and angles a lot of unfair favors.

"Hey." I resisted the urge to reach up and smooth my hair. I *wanted* him to see me like this. Mainly so I would remember that I wasn't an Instagram model or rising starlet and quit thinking there was some sort of chance here. "Is there something wrong downstairs?"

"No," he said, almost sharply, and I looked at him, startled. "Sorry, no." He said it softly that time. "Or yes, but it's not a landlord thing. Um, could we…" He ran his fingers through his hair and stared up at the ceiling for a moment before taking a deep breath and meeting my eyes. "Could we talk? Maybe get some coffee?"

"Sure." He looked so stressed that the word was out before I could second guess myself. "I was heading over to Bywater Bakery."

"I already went. And I have coffee and sticky buns downstairs if you're up for it."

"Miles…"

"I promise not to hold you hostage."

I sighed.

"Please?" His eyes were soft and hopeful.

He was making it impossible to say no. "All right. I'll come down for coffee."

I followed him down and through the kitchen, the first time I'd come in that way since sneaking in the week before. Nothing had changed back here, but the progress was obvious when we stepped into the club space. Almost all the new ceiling tiles were in. Scaffolding rested against two of the walls, and plastic tarps and piles of tools lay everywhere. It was organized chaos.

In the middle sat a card table and two chairs with two cups of coffee in Bywater Bakery sleeves and a paper bag, the top rolled down.

"If that's not for me, I'm leaving and probably burning this place down."

"Wow, you really don't do well until you get caffeine, huh?"

"This is about the sticky buns, dude."

"It's for you," he confirmed. He pulled out a chair for me then took the other.

I opened the coffee and doctored it with cream as an excuse not to meet his eyes. "So what did you want to talk about?"

"The thing is…I feel like a total idiot here, like I'm my sister having friend drama in high school, but I'll jump in." He hesitated then groaned and rubbed his hands over his face. "Have I done something wrong? Because you're avoiding me, and I'm not sure why."

What was I supposed to say? *Yes, I'm avoiding you so I don't catch feelings.* No. No way. "I've been busy. I have sales goals to meet, and that means hustling."

"So busy that you don't have time for me now that I've signed on the dotted line?"

I blinked at him, a rapid flutter of lashes while I tried to process what felt like a punch in the stomach. "I've given you more time and attention than I do most clients after they've bought or leased properties. But that's mainly because they don't ask for as much." It wasn't fair to criticize my professionalism when I'd gone above and beyond for him.

He took a swallow of his coffee and set the cup back down, wrapping both hands around it and keeping his eyes on the lid like it held deep secrets. Then it was his turn to sigh. "Sorry," he said, flicking his gaze up to me. "You're right. Low blow."

I nodded and said nothing else. I didn't understand the currents swirling around us.

He rubbed his hands down his thighs. "I'm going to be completely honest with you." He flicked another glance toward me, like he was checking if that was okay. I didn't say anything because I wasn't sure I could promise the same thing in return. He bit the corner of his lip, then forged ahead. "I moved to LA for the show, and I've lived there ever since. I didn't keep any of my high school friendships, so when I come back to visit, it's to see my family. My cousins. I don't have a lot of other friends here. I mean, there's Jordan. But we work together, we don't hang out together. And even though that's you and me too, somehow…I don't know. Somehow, I guess it started feeling different? Maybe it's the shared history thing, and the fact that you forgave me when I didn't deserve it. But I've started thinking of you as a friend, only now you're ghosting on me, and I'm wondering why."

He didn't look at me once the whole time he said it, just played with his coffee cup. Maybe that was what did me in. I couldn't leave him sitting there looking awkward and stressed out. I wanted to reach out and still his hands, hold them and promise that he had me, no matter what. But I couldn't do that, so I did the only other thing I could think of to reassure him and threw Aaron under the bus.

"You didn't do anything wrong. It was Aaron."

His forehead wrinkled, and he finally met my eyes, his full of confusion. "Aaron?"

"Yeah. He told me I shouldn't encourage you with this club because it was costing you more than you could afford. Said you needed to get it out of your system and get back to your career."

"Aaron." He repeated it in a way that made me glad I wasn't Aaron.

"He made it sound like you're having a quarter-life crisis."

He took a big swig of his coffee, his face tight. "Aaron thinks that anything I do that isn't exactly what the record label wants me to do is a quarter-life crisis." He looked at me again as he set the cup down. "Aaron is very good about certain things. He's taken over the roles of people I lost when I left the label. He's my manager and publicist, sometimes my stylist, and every now and then, on a bad day, he's my punching bag. Metaphorically speaking," he added, like I thought he might be beating up his cousin.

"But he's not great at other things. He came on board at the beginning of my career and got used to all the perks right away. He liked taking late meetings at expensive restaurants, and he's never adjusted back to the everyone else's nine-to-five ethic. He's not even that involved in the business details anymore. He's excellent when it comes to promo and image, but the nuts and bolts? The business stuff? He understands it. But it bores him. So I handle most of it with my dad's help."

"Then why not fire him from that and let him do the parts he likes?"

"Did I mention he's my cousin?"

I shrugged. "Not sure what that has to do with keeping him for one job and not the other."

"Because the promo and image stuff, that's a flat salary if you hire someone. But the business stuff…"

"He gets a commission." I was beginning to understand their dynamic now.

"Bingo. And I don't mind," he hurried to add as if to head off any of my objections. Which to be fair, I had. Loads of them. "It's an easy way to take care of him without either of us feeling like it's charity. But when he tells you that I shouldn't be distracted, it's because he misses the LA scene, the power players, and the lifestyle. I don't. He doesn't get that. He thinks it's a phase I'll get over. I won't."

"How can you be sure?"

He raised an eyebrow at me. "Is loving the Bywater a phase for you? Or doing commercial real estate?"

"Of course not."

"How can you be sure?"

"I—" But I shut my mouth. How did I know? "I have roots here. Helping this city become the best it can be is my passion. It's not the kind of thing you grow out of."

"Neither is music. My style and taste may change, but the need to be around it?" He shook his head. "That never changes. And don't forget, my roots are here too. Why else would I have felt called back to it?"

"Point taken." It was true; I could sense in him the same love and connection I felt for the city, and I had no reason to doubt him except Aaron's words.

"Ignore Aaron." He leaned forward, his eyes now searching mine. "If it weren't for him telling you to stay away, would you still be coming by to offer opinions?"

The honest answer was that Aaron had done me a favor, and even though every day felt incomplete when I didn't see Miles, I needed that distance. When I didn't answer immediately, Miles leaned closer. "Ellie?"

I couldn't tell him any of that, but I also didn't want to tell him why I needed to keep my distance. "That was the only reason," I lied.

His face relaxed, the faint lines around his eyes smoothing. "Cool. You definitely get the Bywater, and I feel like you get me." My heart gave a traitorous lurch as he continued. "It's been so useful having you double check me on stuff. Or put me in check when I need it." He shook his head. "Faux exposed brick? What was I thinking?"

"You panicked. It's fine. You made the right choice."

"Thanks to you."

I saluted him. Cool. Casual. I could totally do this.

"So you'll come around more? I want you to love this place. I want you to help me make it a place that becomes an organic part of the Bywater DNA."

He was appealing to my strongest instincts. What choice did I have? "Of course," I said. "Can't have a carpetbagger ruining things." I threw an empty creamer pod at him to let him know I was kidding.

"Carpetbagger? Seven generations of Crowe ancestors just rolled over in their Louis Cemetery graves."

"Nah," I retorted. "That was them doing a happy dance that I won't let you screw this up."

"And I'm glad to have my friend back." He smiled at me over his coffee.

Right. Friend. As long as I stayed inside that boundary, I wouldn't screw this up either.

CHAPTER TWENTY

The next few weeks fell into a predictable pattern. Miles had extracted a promise from me that I'd come in through the kitchen door in the future, so a few times a week, I'd pop down after work when he wanted to ask my opinion or to show me some renovation progress.

The first time, he'd tried to turn it into dinner afterward, but I'd put him off by saying I had more work to do.

The next time, I'd straight up lied and told him I had a date to get ready for. I wasn't proud of the fact that it was a test to see how he reacted. All he'd done was give me an easy smile and tell me to have a good time.

Which sucked.

But it was exactly how I needed him to react to keep my boundary lines bright and shiny.

The next day, Miles ran up and knocked on my door when I got home.

"How was the date?" he asked when I answered. Hope thrummed in my chest. He *did* care.

"Fine," I answered.

"Good," he said, and the hope died. "Want to come see the paint?"

After that, he didn't ask if I wanted to do anything after coming down to the club. He'd show me whatever had been done that day, we'd chat, and I'd head upstairs.

There were things I liked about this. I loved seeing the progress every day.

It hurt less to watch the old traces of Miss Mary's place disappear when I felt like I'd had a hand in the changes. The walls became a shade of umber, warm and dark. The redone floors shone with a deep walnut stain, all the character still there but more elegant. And yet, the space was retaining a comfortable feel, the kind of place people could come and relax while they listened to live music. Booths with leather bench seats went in against the walls. Soon the tables and chairs would arrive to fill in the floor space.

My favorite part was watching the progress as the stage was built. More than anything else, that marked the conversion from café to club. When it had been a café, from the entrance, the kitchen door was on the left side of the back wall and the hallway to the restrooms ran up the right. The contractor had built a hallway in front of the kitchen that extended halfway down each side wall. The stage went in against that. Now, as a club, standing in the same spot, it looked as if the stage backed up to the main wall, when really, now a hidden passage ran behind it so servers could come and go from the kitchen and customers could come and go to the restrooms without distracting anyone.

The stage had started as sturdy plywood and struts. It wasn't high, maybe two feet, but it would need to hold the weight of a baby grand and up to six musicians with portable risers for even larger groups. Gradually, the floorboards had gone in, then the footlights, each new addition making Miss Mary's a more distant memory.

With every bit of progress, I could imagine the musicians more clearly, plucking an upright bass, using brushes on the drums, doing riffs on the piano. It made my fingers itch. I'd quit piano lessons after junior high, and I only played every once in a while when I went over to visit my parents. I was rusty, but the skills were there.

"How do you feel about this?" Chloe asked me one morning when I stopped in to check on the progress before work.

"Guilty."

"Guilty? Not the answer I expected."

"Maybe disloyal is the right word. I loved Miss Mary's so much, but honestly, every time I come down here, I get more excited about the renovations."

"I get that," she said, slowly. "But if her Facebook is anything to go by, I don't think she's missing the café at all."

I laughed. "True. Did you see her post from yesterday?" She and Mr. Douglas were on the road in their RV and they'd stopped at an RV park near the Great Smoky Mountains for a couple of nights. Apparently, she'd decided to cook breakfast for all the other travelers staying in the campground, and her post had shown her beaming in front of a portable griddle surrounded by at least a dozen other people, all holding plates of pancakes and giving a thumbs up.

"Leave it to Miss Mary." Chloe shook her head. "Of course she would turn an RV park full of strangers into family. Anyway, I don't think she misses being on her old café schedule at all."

"I know. But I still feel guilty about how much I love this new place."

"Feelings aren't logical, so I won't try to talk you out of them. But if you don't feel guilty about loving our apartment more than you love your parents' house, there's no reason to feel guilty about loving the changes here."

"Hey, ladies," Miles said behind us as he stepped out from the new kitchen hallway. "Good to see you this morning."

"We'll get out of your hair," I said. "Just wanted to see how the stage was coming."

"Almost done. The floodlights go up today." He slid an arm around each of us, resting them on our shoulders. I stiffened slightly, surprised by the touch, but Chloe snaked her arm around his waist like they were the oldest of friends. It was the first time I could ever remember being jealous of her.

He gave a happy sigh as he studied the stage. "Definitely stop by after work so you can get the full effect."

"Sounds good," Chloe said. "And now I'm off to work. I have to cover a zoning hearing this afternoon, and I need to read up on some statutes. Try not to be jealous."

"So jealous," Miles said as she slipped away. "Have fun."

Now it was only the two of us, me still standing like a wooden post next to him. I wanted to relax into him and slide my arm around his waist like Chloe had. It was the kind of thing I should be able to do as friends. Instead, I made an excuse to step away.

"Is this hickory?" I asked, walking toward the stage like I wanted to investigate it.

"Yeah. Same as the floor." He sounded almost confused by the question, which made sense since I'd helped him pick the hardwood.

"Right. Good call. Well, I should get going."

"See you after work?"

"Sure." I tossed it over my shoulder as I headed for the kitchen exit.

"Ellie?" Miles called when I was halfway through the door. I paused and glanced back at him. "Good to see you this morning too."

I nodded, trying to figure out why his words had made me blush as I exited the kitchen and walked out to my car. People said that all the time. Clients. Tenants. But somehow, coming from Miles, it had felt intimate.

Instead of driving into work, I headed out on Franklin to the I-10. I wanted to drive Pontchartrain Bridge. My parents had moved to Mandeville a few years ago, the city at the other end of the bridge, but that wasn't why I wanted to drive it. The lake was massive and driving the twenty-three miles across it felt like driving over the ocean. I needed the wide-open space to clear my head.

For almost a month now, I'd avoided playing Miles's music. I'd stayed away from his social media, and when thoughts of him drifted into my mind multiple times a day, I shoved them out. I'd kept my visits after work short and focused on the club.

But those had been my downfall.

I looked out over the water stretching as far as the eye could see on either side of the causeway, my wheels humming quietly over the concrete.

I craved seeing him every afternoon the way I craved my coffee in the mornings. Worse, even. I felt like an addict who thought she had it under control, promising myself the tiniest hit, promising myself it would be the last one, then going back the next day. I told myself it wasn't a real problem because I always made myself leave within twenty minutes. But the truth was, I couldn't get through a weekday without popping in to see him, and Miles was always there, the work crew gone, like he was waiting for me.

He'd told me once that it was the only time he could be in the space while it was quiet to think about future plans or even his to-do list for the next day. But a part of me believed he was hanging out, waiting for me, no matter how much I tried to talk myself out of it.

"Is this a crush?" I asked out loud. The waves didn't answer. Neither did the road.

"Siri, what is the difference between love and a crush?" Because what I felt for Miles had the same intensity it had when I was fourteen. But wasn't twenty-six too old for a crush?

"A crush is about perfection. Love is about imperfections," Siri explained in her mellow voice. "Would you like more information?"

"Yes, please."

"Here is an entry from Ask the Love Genius. A crush is based on attraction and does not require a relationship. Love is deep affection for another person based on knowing them. Attraction is often part of this affection. Would you like more information?"

"No, thank you, Siri."

I ran the answer through my mind. *A deep affection based on knowing them.*

In high school, I'd made up a whole version of Miles, of what I thought he would be like. I imagined interactions between us, what he would say, how he would look at me. I watched every interview I could find with him. I'd been so sure that once we met, he'd see how perfect we were for each other and our love story *together* could begin.

But I hadn't known him. Not even a little.

I couldn't have imagined my current reality, where we saw each other almost daily, for twenty carefully rationed minutes. I couldn't have imagined that we would talk that whole time, joking about light fixtures and arguing about flooring.

I could have easily imagined the many times I stood quietly in the doorway watching him for a few seconds before announcing that I'd arrived. Sometimes he was on his phone, sometimes working at the card table in an open notebook. "Ideas," he'd said once when I asked him what he was writing. But no matter what he was doing, when I made a small noise to announce my arrival, he always turned toward me, a slow smile growing on his face when he saw me. Maybe that smile meant nothing.

But it didn't feel like nothing.

Sometimes, I caught him watching me as I studied whatever new change he'd made that day. Other times, I could swear he was staring at me, but when I glanced his way, he was doing something else. Looking at his phone or elsewhere.

Did I know Miles now?

I knew how he liked his coffee. That he laughed at stupid puns. I knew he was kind to the jobsite workers but firm with the contractor. I knew he obsessed over details and spared no cost when he found what he wanted for the club. I knew he loved the Saints and spent several hours a week mentoring the kids at Jordan's music center. I knew he spent his free time looking at pet rescue sites because for the first time in forever, he felt rooted enough in one place to adopt a dog. He called his obsessive scrolling "window shopping," and he showed me dog TikToks almost every time I came downstairs.

I knew that when he was thinking hard, his fingers tapped out chords on the nearest surface. I knew because I did the same thing. Usually, it was because I had an earworm and I was trying to figure out the notes. Lately, I'd had snatches of original melodies floating through my head. But when I watched his fingers moving across a tabletop, I knew where his head was.

Yeah, I knew him.

Love is a deep affection based on knowing them.

I felt a deep affection for him based on knowing him. And attraction was part of that affection.

A very strong attraction.

An attraction that made me slide my hands into my pockets and subtly shift away from him every time he was near. I didn't want him to feel the heat coming off me or hear my heartbeats because they sounded so loud in my ears when he got too close. I didn't want him to sense the way my lungs throbbed or how I could feel each individual hair on my head because the energy coming off him was so strong that it charged all my molecules.

So according to Siri…

"Dammit, Siri."

"I'm sorry, I didn't catch that."

I sighed and leaned against the head rest, watching more of the gray sky and brown water roll past. Then I rolled down the window and shouted the truth to the wind where it could be snatched up and carried away with no one else to hear it.

"I think I'm in love with Miles Crowe!"

The wind didn't answer. Neither did Siri.

But neither of them had to say anything. The pit in my stomach said it all.

CHAPTER TWENTY-ONE

THE PIANO IS HERE! Come down!

It was Miles's usual afternoon text, and like every other day when he invited me down to inspect a change, I absolutely wanted to see it. But I'd been reeling since my epiphany on the bridge this morning, and if I ran down the stairs right now, Miles would see the truth on my face. How much I wanted him. I didn't trust myself not to blurt it out.

For the first time in weeks, I texted back an excuse. *Can't today. Dinner plans.*

The typing bubbles appeared and disappeared a few times on his end before a sad face emoji appeared.

Driving the causeway had made me an hour late for work, and that had put a ton of pressure on my schedule. Maybe that was why I'd done it; I'd wanted to force myself to be so busy that I couldn't think.

I succeeded spectacularly and came home exhausted from running between appointments, barely making each. It hadn't even worked that well. Miles was still the only thing on my mind, and I only knew of one way to deal with this that didn't end up with me very, very drunk.

For the first time in almost two years, I pulled out my Moleskine notebook from my closet shelf. I'd been keeping song lyrics in it since middle school, but I'd written so few lyrics since I'd deleted my YouTube channel that I still had enough pages for fifty more songs. I hadn't written in it since college.

I grabbed a pen, turned to a fresh page, and went to work. This was the only place in the world I ever told the whole truth, and I needed to get the words out somewhere because I was never, ever going to say them to Miles.

An hour later, I had half-formed verses and incomplete ideas, and nothing even close to good unless, "I love you, Miles Crowe, but I don't want you to know" was a masterpiece in embryo.

Ha.

My stomach growled, and I put the notebook away, giving up for the moment. Fifteen minutes later, dressed in shorts and a gauzy tank top as a nod to the heat, I left down the back stairs, skirting the restaurant completely. Only I ran into Miles one block up, staring into the window of a record shop.

"Ellie," he said, surprised. "Hey. On your way to your dinner plans?"

"Hey," I said, trying to figure out how to make my face look normal when every muscle in it suddenly felt like it was made of goo. Was I smiling? Was it a friendly, professional smile? HOW DID SMILES WORK?

"You okay there?" he asked, his eyebrows furrowing in concern.

"Yeah, fine." He nodded, then it fell quiet. "So, uh, I guess I better get to those plans."

His eyes narrowed. "Yeah. Plans. What were they again?"

"Dinner?"

"Right. Where?"

Why was he testing me? And why couldn't I think of a fast response? The truth was that I was going to Frady's Grocery which was a counter joint, not the kind of place where people went when they had "plans." "Up the street."

"I'm always looking for good new places to eat. What is it? Maybe I'll check it out tomorrow." But his tone held a slight challenge, like he knew I didn't have an answer.

"It's Frady's," I confessed.

"So…you don't have actual dinner plans."

"I *plan* to stuff my face very full of poboys," I said. "And it's a very good plan."

"But by yourself. Not with anyone else. Like me. Who you knew was right downstairs, probably starving around dinner time."

"It's not like I invited Chloe either. I need to decompress, that's all," I mumbled. It was embarrassing to be caught ditching someone, and it made me cranky to be called on it.

"You can say that, you know." He said it quietly. It was the first time in a long time that he wasn't giving me the "good vibes only" smile that he wore no matter what.

"Sorry. I needed…" I trailed off, not sure how to finish the thought. *I needed to get away from you* sounded rude, even if he'd figured out that was the truth of it.

"Am I driving you crazy? Too much in your space?"

YES.

He looked slightly anxious, so instead I said, "No. Sometimes I like to be by myself, but I'm with people all day, and Chloe's there when I get home, and…"

He winced. "And you have my needy butt dragging you downstairs every night. I'm sorry. You probably regret leasing to me more with every passing day."

I did. In many ways, he was exactly right for the Bywater. He was just all wrong for me.

But I hated seeing him look as vulnerable as I felt, so I smiled and shook my head. "You're a great tenant. And I changed my mind about my plans. If you don't mind a sandwich for dinner, I'd love some company."

"Are you saying that to make me feel better?"

I smiled wider, a real smile this time. "I was when I said it, but as soon as the words came out of my mouth, I realized they were true. So, sandwich?"

"Sandwich," he agreed, and we headed up the sidewalk toward Frady's.

"How are you feeling about the Turnaround?" I asked.

"I'm not sure I've talked to you about anything besides the club in… weeks? And my brain needs a break from it. *You* probably need a break from it. Let's talk about something else."

"Like what?"

"You pick."

"Okay. Music."

He shot me a questioning look. "What about it?"

"Anything," I said. "How's the music center doing? Listen to anything good lately? Who are you dying to book at the club? Working on anything yourself? What's your favorite radio station?"

He laughed. "Let's see, Jordan and the kids are great. I like Esperanza Spalding's new album. I'd love to get Kamasi Washington at the club. And I like W-YLD."

"Huh." There was a conspicuously missing answer.

"Huh what?"

"You didn't talk about your own music."

He shrugged and paused in front of a contemporary art gallery to study the sculpture in the window, a piece made from reclaimed cypress. It was abstract, but it made me think of how I felt inside on my most tired days.

"How hungry are you?" He glanced over at me. "Would you mind if we popped in here for a second? Or like ten minutes?"

"I've got time. Kreyol's always has interesting pieces. I wouldn't mind looking around."

"Cool, let's do it."

Air conditioning met us as we stepped in, and Keisha, the owner, looked up and smiled. She was my mom's age and looked exactly like you'd expect an art gallery owner to look, her hair bound up in a colorful orange and red scarf, long gold earrings dangling from her ears, a sleeveless dress made from Ankara fabric skimming her large body. Keisha was always big smiles and even bigger splashes of color.

"Hey, baby," she said. "Haven't seen you in a minute."

"I know. Since Miss Mary's goodbye?"

"Yeah, that's about right. Been even longer since you were in here. It's good to see you."

"Miss Keisha, this is Miles. He took over Miss Mary's place."

She cocked her head at him. "Jazz club? Is that what I'm hearing?"

"Yes, ma'am."

"Good. We got some weekend music places around here, but it'll be good to have some for every night. Welcome. Y'all go on and look around. Got some new pieces."

"I'd love some advice on pieces I could put in the club," Miles said. "I want to feature local artists."

Keisha's smile grew even bigger. "You came to the right place. Wander, see what you like, and we'll start talking. If I don't have what you want, I know where to find it."

Her place was small, and it took all of ten minutes to look at everything, even pausing here and there for Miles to comment when pieces caught his eye.

"What do you think?" she asked as we circled back to the front of the gallery. "Anyone or anything jump out at you?"

"My two favorite paintings were by the same guy. Elijah Remy?"

Miss Keisha smiled. "Yeah. He's good. He's from right here in the Bywater. He's mostly a muralist, but he works in acrylics sometimes, and I always snap those up. Tell you what, you come back when you got some time on your hands, and we'll look at more of his work together. I can even tell you where to find some of his murals if you want to see them in the wild."

"That sounds great," he said. "Thank you."

We waved goodbye and walked the last two blocks to Frady's, discussing the pieces we'd seen. It *had* been a long time since we'd talked about anything but the club, I realized.

"Maybe I don't want paintings for the club," Miles concluded. "Maybe I need murals, something that speaks to the soul of music." I smothered a smile, but Miles caught it. "What's so funny?"

"You. But not funny, exactly."

"Then what?"

"I don't know." I tried to think about what had made me smile as I pushed open the door. "The way you're so into the art and the club. It's…cute." It was the safest word I could think of to describe the feeling of listening to Miles do a monologue on stuff he cared about deeply.

"Cute? I think…I'm offended?"

"Fair," I said. "I'd probably be offended if someone said my passion for my work was cute."

"Then pick a different word," he said, a half-smile on his face. "I don't want to be cute."

I could think of two words: dead sexy. His passion for his work was dead sexy. But I wasn't about to say that out loud. "How about admirable?"

"Stuffy. Like I graduated from being a dumb puppy to an antique sofa."

"Let's go with 'relatable.' I find the way you think about things relatable."

"Relatable," he mused. "I dig it."

We ordered our sandwiches and wandered back down Dauphine but on the other side. I knew the Bywater like the back of my hand, but in the same way you sometimes forget you have a freckle or birthmark until someone else points it out, it was a slightly different experience seeing it through Miles's eyes. It wasn't like he was commenting on everything he saw, but even the places he'd pause or let his eyes linger brought them to my attention in ways I didn't notice on my own.

He stopped in front of a pink house with magenta trim with a hand-painted sign in the front window showing a palm and offering other psychic services including séances.

"There's places like this all over Venice Beach," he said. "Do you think they're more accurate here?"

"Palm readers? Why would they be more accurate here?"

He shrugged. "I don't know. Just seems like they would be. New Orleans has that…"

"Vibe?" I finished for him.

"Yeah. Some cities are like that. Prague. Vienna. Kyoto. Edinburgh. Cairo."

"You're just naming old cities."

"It's not that," he insisted. "Paris doesn't feel this way. Rome either. Or Dubai. But New Orleans does."

"That may be true—*is* true," I corrected myself when he looked like he was about to argue again, "but this place can't read your palm any better than I could."

I started to move on, but he stayed where he was. "Let's try it," he said.

"Try what?"

"A palm reading. Or a tarot reading or whatever."

I laughed until I saw his face. "Wait, you're serious?"

"Serious about trying it. Why not? Could be fun."

"You can find a dozen psychics in Jackson Square every day."

"But we're here."

I flicked another glance at the window. It wasn't like I had anywhere else to be. "I'll go with you, but I'm not getting one." I had better ways to spend the fifty dollars advertised for palm and tarot readings.

A small handwritten sign above the doorknob read, "Just come in," and we stepped into the dim interior of the living room. The walls were painted a nice shade of murder red, and a white woman in chinos and a pink polo smiled at us from her seat at a small oak table where she was working a crossword. She wore her hair in a ponytail and had a bedazzled water bottle next to her. She looked like a suburban mom named Heather who spent her days running her kids to too many activities. It was not who I'd expected.

"Hey," she said. "What can I do for you?"

I let Miles take the question while I checked out the interior on reflex, appraising it like I did any commercial property. Nothing besides the intense walls met my expectations for a seedy psychic shop. There were no pillows piled on the floor, no gauzy fabrics or bead curtains hanging anywhere. Besides the table and four chairs in the center of the room, a simple oak cabinet sat in one corner with a collection of houseplants atop it, and a few larger potted plants nestled in each corner. Shelves lined the walls displaying candles, books, and incense for sale. Tidy low-grade carpeting covered the floor, and the dim light came from low wattage bulbs in the utilitarian light fixture overhead.

"We're here for a reading," Miles told her.

She glanced at her watch. "What kind? My sister isn't here. She's the psychic."

"Um, what kind do you do?" Miles asked.

"I do tarot. I'm waiting for a seven o'clock appointment, but I have a half hour. I can squeeze y'all in"

Miles looked at me, and I shrugged. This was his idea. I was tagging along to humor him.

He looked back at her. "Well, I'm Miles and this is Elle." He stopped and shook his head. "I guess you knew that."

"I knew your name but only because I know your music," she said. "Welcome, by the way. I'm Heather."

Heather? HA. Who was the psychic now?

"Right. Heather. Hello. So I don't know what kind of reading I need, really. You tell me."

She ran an eye over both of us, her expression thoughtful. "I told you, my sister's the psychic. I don't have any talent with divination. I do intuitive readings. I'd say you need a three-card reading. If that sounds good, come sit down."

Miles took the seat across from her, and I hung back awkwardly, not sure how the rules worked if I wasn't getting a reading.

"Come on," Heather said. "I don't bite."

"Is that okay even if I'm not getting a reading?"

One of Heather's eyebrows went up. "Sit down," she said, her voice firm but kind. I sat. She looked from Miles to me and back again. "Y'all have a distinct energy. You're definitely getting a reading together."

She went to the cabinet, and Miles shot me a grin. I smiled back, glad that things had been easy between us this evening.

Heather resumed her seat and set a wooden box carved with vines on the table. She opened it and removed a deck of large cards and set them down in front of her. They looked old and well-used. "This is the Rider-Waite-Smith deck. Let's begin."

"Just like that?" I asked, confused. "Don't you need to ask us some questions?"

"Like what?" she asked as she shuffled.

"I don't know. About our childhoods, or maybe about our jobs and hobbies?"

She shot me a knowing look. "Why? So I can do some basic conning where I make educated guesses on the information you give me to convince you I'm the real deal?"

"Busted," Miles said, trying not to laugh.

"No," I said. Her eyebrow went up again. "Yes," I admitted.

She fanned the cards. "That's not how tarot readings work. I don't make any guesses. I interpret in a general sense what the cards reveal. It's not going to give you the winning lottery numbers or the name of your future husband. Let's begin."

Her fingers skimmed the cards, touching a couple before she drew one and turned it over. It showed a cloaked man on a horse with a wreath around his head. "This card is your past. It's the Six of Wands reversed. This means public recognition, but in a negative way. The kind that may have happened long ago but that still affects you now."

Miles's eyebrow shot up, but I fought the urge to scoff. She'd obviously recognized both of us and knew about the viral moment.

She skimmed the cards again and chose another. "This card is for the present. Five of Cups." She studied it, looked between us, then back to the card. A man in black stood on a riverbank, staring down at five chalices around his feet, two standing, three tipped over. "Interesting. I'd intended to do a pair reading, but your energy seems to be driving the cards tonight, Elle. This card reminds you that you need to leave the past in the past. Mourn it but look toward the future."

"Like our walk down to the river the other day," Miles said. "We did that."

I wasn't impressed, but I didn't say anything. That was another easy guess, the kind of thing that could be true based on how either of us wanted to look at it.

When she turned the third card, she gave it a long look as a smile played around her lips. "Well, well, well."

"What?" Miles asked. I leaned forward to see it better in spite of myself.

"Are you two together?" she asked.

"No," I said while Miles shifted uncomfortably in his chair next to me.

"But do you want to be?" she asked, and heat flooded my cheeks. I didn't want her to say whatever she was about to say. "Because it looks like you'll get a couples reading after all. This is the Two of Cups. It symbolizes the beginning of a new relationship, one that is balanced. It will be strong with equal energy on both parts. It reflects attraction and a great deal of potential for a committed, monogamous relationship. It's the card lovers are happy to see."

I looked down at the card. It had far more going on than the other two. A man and woman stared into each other's eyes, each holding a large trophy-looking cup. A caduceus topped with a lion's head hung over the goblets. The Two of Cups, she'd called it. I didn't dare look at Miles. Was he trying not to laugh? Feeling stressed that she'd pretty much announced I was madly in love with him?

I wasn't even sure what to do. Get up and walk out? Find a joke to make? Deny it?

I went with option three. "Nice try, but you probably should have asked those getting-to-know-us questions. If you had, you'd know you're way off base."

Instead of looking offended, she simply collected the cards, efficiently tapping them into a neat deck. "I didn't 'try' anything. I interpreted what the cards said. Believe them or don't."

"Thanks for the reading," Miles said, reaching for his wallet. "And ignore my friend here. I think she's still hangry and her stomach hasn't told her brain yet that they're both fine." He tossed a hundred-dollar bill on the table. Seriously, was he made of them? I glared at him and headed for the door.

"What did I do now?" he asked when we hit the sidewalk.

"Did you seriously tell her that she should ignore me because I'm at the mercy of my emotions?"

"No, of course not..." But he paused, his forehead scrunched like he was recalling the conversation. "Oh. Yeah. I did. I'm sorry. Hang on." He opened the door and poked his head back in. "Also, for the record, Ellie is not super emotional, and she definitely meant the very logical thing she said." He paused again like he was listening, mumbled, "What?" and stuck his head further in the door for a few seconds, then said "Bye" and shut the door again.

"What was that?" I asked.

"What? Nothing. She was clarifying something." He started down the sidewalk.

I had to do a two-step to catch up. "Clarifying what?"

"Doesn't matter. You don't believe her anyway, right?"

"Right." I wanted to press him on whatever Heather had added, but the whole reason I'd left was because I didn't want to talk about what she'd told us in the first place, so why was I pushing now? If anything, I should be changing the subject. "So those were good sandwiches, yeah?"

He looked at me like he couldn't figure out why I was lurching from one topic to the other like a drunk tourist. "Yeah, good sandwiches. Thanks for telling me about them."

"Yeah, sure." It fell quiet, and I wracked my brain for something else to talk about as we walked but it was blank, and Miles's mind seemed to be somewhere else completely.

When we stopped in front of the Turnaround, he stared at the front door in mild surprise. He blinked. "Want to come see the new addition?"

"Raincheck? I think I'm going to go up and unwind," I said. "See you tomorrow, maybe?"

"Definitely."

I kept walking around the corner of the building to take my back stairs.

"Ellie," he called when I was halfway there.

I turned around to find him smiling at me, his gaze fully present again.

"You got it bad," he sang softly. I recognized the melody immediately. It was an Usher song he'd covered on *Starstruck*. "You got it, you got it bad," he continued, smiling slightly.

I froze like I'd just been pantsed onstage at a half-time show. "It's not funny," I ground out. Then I whirled and sprinted for my stairs.

"Elle, wait!"

"Go away, Miles!" Then I rounded the building and took the stairs two at a time, racing into my apartment and slamming the door.

But it wasn't hard enough to keep the humiliation from following me inside.

CHAPTER TWENTY-TWO

CHLOE DIDN'T COME when I slammed the door, so I knew she wasn't home. I threw myself on my bed and stared up at the ceiling. Why had he made us go to that stupid tarot reader? And why did she have to guess right—and out loud —while he was sitting *right there*?

Worst of all, how could Miles tease me like that? The snatch of melody ran itself through my mind over and over again. I hated it. I was prone to earworms, and the only way to get them out of my head was to play them all the way through, but I didn't want this one running through my mind. Every time the words played on their loop—*You've got it bad*—a new wave of heat stung my cheeks. It was like an old episode of *Grey's Anatomy*—Chloe and I had binge-watched it last summer—when this girl came in for a surgery because literally every emotion made her blush and she hated it.

I hated this. A new wave of embarrassment tortured me with each repeat of the melody.

"Gah!" I shouted at the ceiling.

I shoved in my earbuds and grabbed my phone, determined to play the whole song and get it out of my head. I listened to it on repeat for an hour, and the whole time, I saw Miles in my mind's eye, singing it to me with a grin.

I hated feeling so exposed. Hated it. It wasn't fair that my emotions were sitting out there, all naked and shivering.

I ripped out the earbuds and went down to the club, letting myself in through the kitchen. I wasn't even sure why I was down there other than wanting to take back some control. Maybe if I saw the "new addition" on my own terms instead of seeing it on Miles's terms, it would make me feel like we were more even.

I saw it the second I stepped into the club space. The baby grand, sitting on the stage, glinting even in the dim light of the security bulbs. Miles had shown me the lightboard the other day, so I went to the back corner and found the switch labeled "Stage spot 1." It sprang to life, illuminating the piano.

It was impossibly beautiful, a Yamaha in classic black, waiting for someone to play it.

I couldn't resist.

I sat down at the keys and played a couple of chords, the rich sound vibrating through my chest. It sounded even better than it looked, like God himself had designed it and placed it on this otherwise empty stage, a single perfect object shining in the beam of light.

It was such a reverent moment that my fingers picked out an old hymn almost on their own, and it came to me with ease. It reminded me of a song we used to sing in choir, "How Can I Keep From Singing," and I played that next, stumbling a few times but remembering it far better than I would have expected.

Before long, I'd moved onto a Lady Gaga song I'd loved in high school, then, inevitably, I picked out the Usher song. After about ten minutes, I had the melody down. I sang it from start to finish. The last two verses in particular tugged at things inside me the way the first chords on the piano had. Words about your whole life getting off track because you missed your friend. Words about staying stuck in your house because nothing is fun without them, or thinking about them even when you're out with other people.

I let my hands fall into my lap and stared at the keys. Yeah, I had it bad.

It was too quiet with the piano falling silent, so I played again, this time a snatch of melody that had been running through my head for weeks, teasing out the notes and weaving in some harmony.

It felt like…something? Like an actual song was coming together. I'd written a lot of music in eighth and ninth grade. Not good music, but it made me happy. I'd used to post it on YouTube, but after everything had happened with Miles back then, I'd gotten so much hate in the comments that I'd deleted my channel. I hadn't written much since. A couple of songs in college, but that was about it.

Right now, though…the familiar itch I used to get when words needed to come out flared up, and I pulled out my phone, recording sections as they came to me. I lost track of time as I worked out the melody and added lyrics, the words coming together. When I set my phone to record the whole thing, I realized over an hour had passed.

I pressed record and played it through, pouring out all my confusion and longing over the last two months since Miles had reappeared in my life.

You're the one that I want
The one I'm always thinking of
All I see, all I breathe
You're the vein of every need and dream
Let me love you like I can
Hold your dreams inside my hands
Let me lift you up
Let me steal your every touch
I'll wait until you see
That it should be you and me

I kept the pedal down, my eyes closed, the fading note cradling me.

A soft clap started, and my eyes flew open, peering past the bright edges of the spotlight. "Who's there?" I asked.

Miles stepped forward, still a shadow in the darkness beyond the stage. "I didn't know you sang. Or played."

"I used to." I pulled the lid down over the keys.

"Don't stop," he said. "You're good."

"Sorry, I'll head upstairs. I thought you were gone for the night." This felt even more naked than the tarot reading, and I was so tired of the feeling.

"No, don't. I got a free concert, and that's not fair, especially if it wasn't something you're ready to put out there."

"It wasn't." My words were barely audible. He didn't even ask me who it was about. He didn't need to.

"We got new security cameras. It was a condition for insuring that beast." He nodded at the piano. "You set off the motion sensor, and when I saw you on the screen"—he held up his phone—"I couldn't believe I didn't know you were an artist too, so I came to see for myself."

"I'm not. An artist," I clarified. "I just…I don't know. I saw it, and I haven't played in a few weeks, and I wanted to figure some stuff out, and that's where it decided to come out, I guess."

"Look, I was going to come over to your place tonight anyway to see if we could talk. Again. Or mostly I could talk. I wanted to say some stuff, and…" He sighed and shoved his fingers through his hair. "You showed me yours. How about if I show you mine?"

I shook my head a tiny bit. "What are you talking about?"

"Been working on something. What if you be the audience and I put something out there?"

"Sure." I started to slide from the bench.

"Stay," he said. He hopped up on the stage and sat next to me, lifting the lid and running his fingers lightly over the keys. "It sounds good, huh?"

"Yeah. So good it kind of…"

"Kind of what?" he prompted me softly.

"Kind of makes my chest hurt." I cringed at how stupid that sounded.

He nodded like that made perfect sense. "I feel that. I like it so much it doesn't want to stay inside my body."

It was that exactly. I tumbled even further toward loving him in a way that I couldn't come back from. I should get up and leave for self-protection, the only tool I'd had over the last month to keep me safe. But I didn't. I stayed where I was. It felt too good to sit next to him. He smelled like soap, and the short sleeve of his soft blue shirt brushed my arm, sending tiny sparks down my spine.

He rested his fingers on the keys and made a small throat-clearing sound before playing.

"We were so young when our paths first crossed
I was too immature and the moment was lost
Now we're grown and together again
With a chance to make it what it should have been."

. . .

I went totally still. This song was about me. There was no way it wasn't. He did a chord change, and my heart rate accelerated because it meant he was leading to the chorus, and the chorus of a song always told the truth. It was always the bottom line.

"We can write our own brand-new beginning
Scenes still waiting for us to write the ending
Let me show you how this story could unfold now
I can be your hero, baby, let me show you how"

I tumbled all the way down. I could not fall any farther, and I did not care.

He let the last note die out. "That's all I have so far."

I kept my eyes on the keys, afraid of what they would show if I met his.

"Did you like it?" he asked.

"Was that about me?" I asked. It was barely more than a whisper, hope almost squeezing my throat tight.

He turned his head, and I could feel his eyes on me. "Ellie." I turned my head too but couldn't lift my eyes above his chest. "Elle, I don't…" He sighed and seemed to gather himself. "I know I hurt you back then, but I've changed, and I've been trying to show you how much almost since we met."

"Why?" I asked, finally meeting his eyes. "Why does that matter? Do you need me to think you're a good guy? I do."

"No. It's because the words in my song, they're true. I fell for you when you laughed at me for getting powdered sugar on my shirt. And I've been trying to figure out how to show you that I'm not the sixteen-year-old jerk who shot his mouth off about you on TV. I didn't know you. But I do now, and I…" He trailed off and searched my eyes.

"You what?"

He swallowed hard, and I was mesmerized by his Adam's apple moving up and down. "The song you were singing before. Is there any chance it's about me?"

I met his eyes again. "What do you think?"

His eyes darkened. "I think I'm going to kiss you right now, Ellie Jones, so if that's not what you want, say so."

I didn't say a word.

He slid a hand around my neck and pulled me toward him, brushing his lips against mine. His were warm and soft, and I loved the way his callused guitar fingers felt against my skin. I kissed him back and whispered, "Is that all you got?"

His laugh was a soft puff of breath against my cheek that I barely had a second to register before he was kissing me again. This time it was hungry, his mouth pressing against mine, his free hand moving to my back to hold me closer. A streak of heat like nothing I'd ever experienced shot through me, and I shifted, trying to find a better angle to explore him.

He gave a small growl of frustration and leaned away. I gave a wordless protest, but he was only shifting to straddle the piano bench before he drew me back for a deeper kiss, a slow exploration that turned me boneless.

I wanted the same kind of access to him, so I twisted and resettled myself on the bench, but I didn't kiss him again. Instead, I traced the outline of his lips with my thumb and searched his eyes. "Say the part from the chorus again. I want to feel you say it."

"I can be your hero, baby, let me show you how."

I stole the last word with a kiss, and he sucked in a sharp breath. I wondered if I'd gone too far until he reached behind my knees and drew my legs over his, pulling me even closer.

"Ellie," he murmured, when he pulled away minutes—hours? years?—later. "I swear to you if you keep ditching me after work, my entire next album is going to be songs about broken hearts."

I pressed another kiss to his lips and smiled. "I won't. I promise."

"I don't want you to run away from me." He rested his forehead against mine. "If you were doing it because you thought I didn't feel the same, don't. Because I do." He trailed kisses down my neck. "Will you sing for me again?"

"Tomorrow," I murmured, barely paying attention.

"Why not now?"

I pulled away and blinked at him, trying to clear the fog of lust hijacking my mind. "Because I'm doing this right now. And because I need to figure out the chords on the song I want to play for you."

"Fine. But I want you to play for me every day. I love your voice. I can't believe I had no idea you could sing."

"One condition," I said, pressing another kiss against his jaw.

"Anything."

"You sing a song for me every day too."

He pulled back to give me a cocky grin. "You don't get enough of me in your car?"

I pinched his side, hard. He yelped and pulled me into a hug, burrowing his face in my hair. "Want to know the truth?" he asked.

"No, lie to me, please."

He pulled back to smile at me and smooth my hair from my face. "I'd listen to you sing that every day if I could. Would you come record it for me?"

I shook my head before he was even done asking. "That's not my thing."

He pressed a kiss against my forehead. "All right. I won't push. But just for the record, Ellie Jones, you are very much my thing."

That deserved some more making out. A lot more making out. Beard-burn-and-swollen-lips making out.

We finally separated for oxygen, and he blinked at me sleepily. But the bedroom eyes kind of sleepy that made me want to taste him again.

"Sing for me again?" I asked instead.

He smiled and maneuvered us so we were both facing the keyboard. "Whatever you want, Ellie."

I rested my head on his shoulder and slid my hand down his thigh. "I was thinking Marvin Gaye."

He groaned. "Girl, you are killing me." And he started playing, but avoided any Marvin Gaye, instead choosing "Lovesong" by The Cure, which I only recognized because my mom used to play it all the time when I was a kid.

The music and his voice wrapped around us, each the warmest blanket, and when that ended, he played Otis Redding and Aerosmith and some Beach Boys. It all wove a spell, and I didn't even realize how late it was until a yawn caught me off guard.

He gave a soft laugh and let the last notes of the Harry Styles song he was singing taper off. "You need to go to bed," he said, turning to drop another kiss on my hair. When he dipped down to also steal one from my lips, I ducked and pressed my finger against his mouth. "If you start that after singing me 'Watermelon Sugar', I'll never make it upstairs."

He smiled, and I slid off the bench. "Come down for breakfast with me in the morning," he said.

"Okay." It felt good not to make up excuses about why I couldn't see him.

"And every morning."

That made me smile. "Let's start with tomorrow."

"I can do that. But fair warning, I'm going to string together as many tomorrows as you'll let me."

It was a good thing I'd already told him I was going upstairs by myself or we might have thoroughly scandalized Chloe.

CHAPTER TWENTY-THREE

I CAME DOWN for breakfast the next morning like I'd promised, unsure of how this was all going to go. Sometimes it was easy to believe a thing at night only to have it look totally different in the morning. Maybe Miles would regret it. Maybe today would be like every other one, with me being stiff and awkward.

But when I walked into the club, Miles looked up from a conversation he was having with Jordan and crossed over to pull me into his arms for an unhurried kiss and a long hug.

"Oh, it's like that," Jordan said, grinning at us.

"It's like that." Miles slung his arm around my shoulder and walked me back to Jordan. "You've met my girl, Ellie."

His girl. My inner fourteen-year-old squealed. Then my inner grownup did too.

"I have. Good to see you again," Jordan said, holding his hand out for a shake. "What do you think of the progress in here so far?"

"It's amazing," I said.

We fell into a conversation about the changes to come. Turned out Jordan spent most mornings with Miles at the Turnaround before heading over to the music center. Today's big plan was interviewing chefs.

"I realize I know a whole lot more about the property development side than the business development side, but isn't it kind of late in the game to be hiring a chef?" I asked.

"We had one," Jordan explained. "We were keeping it under wraps. He didn't want to advertise he was leaving his current place until he was sure it would work out. But he let them know last week so they'd have time to replace him, and instead, they made him a counteroffer that he couldn't refuse."

I winced. "That's hard."

Miles sighed. "Yeah. It wasn't great. We love the concepts he had for the menu, but I don't think we're going to get a top-level chef who wants to come in here and execute someone else's vision. We need to let them bring their own ideas to the table."

"So there you go," Jordan said. "You *do* know the food matters as much as the music."

It sounded like a point from an ongoing argument. That made me smile. New Orleans might be the only city in the world where the music wasn't an afterthought.

"Of course I know that," Miles said. "I don't know why you always act like I don't. And I want a homegrown chef too. Don't need to import talent from LA when there's so much here. So we went back to our stack of resumes, and we're trying again."

"Did you get a lot of applicants?" I asked. I wished I'd confessed my feelings to Miles sooner because I could have been around to hear these conversations and had Dylan apply for the job. He'd only been at Redbird for six months, but he was always eager to push to the next level.

"So many applicants," Miles said.

"Yeah, not hard to find someone who can cook around here," Jordan said. "More an issue with finding someone who has skills plus vision plus the ability to manage a staff."

I wasn't sure Dylan had that last skill yet. He had bottomless ambition and mad skills in the kitchen, but a short-temper and perfectionist tendencies. I didn't know how he'd do running a whole team. "That makes sense," I said, and left it at that.

"Guess what I found out about Ellie?" Miles asked Jordan.

"She's a secret agent? She won the lottery? She works for the health department? I don't know, man. That's an annoyingly wide-open question," Jordan said.

"Wow." I smiled up at Miles. "He does *not* care about your fame or money, does he?"

"Nope," Miles said, cheerfully. "Just cares about music. Which is what I wanted to tell you." My stomach gave a slight lurch. "Ellie here can *sing*."

"Oh, really?" Jordan's eyes lit up. "What kind of music do you do?"

"None," I said with a tight smile. "I mess around on the piano sometimes, but that's it." I slipped from under Miles's arm and headed for the exit. "I need to get ready for work, boys. Catch y'all later."

I barely made it into the hall before Miles came after me.

"Whoa, what was that?"

"What was what?" I headed for the stairs without slowing down.

"I said something wrong again, obviously. Should I not have told him you can sing?"

I stopped at the foot of the stairs. "I don't."

"That's not what I heard last night."

"You weren't supposed to hear last night. I thought I was alone." I dropped a kiss on his cheek. "It's not a big deal, but I need to get to work, so I'm going to go grab my stuff."

"You run," he said.

I stopped halfway up the stairs. "Excuse me?"

He leaned against the wall and crossed his arms, watching me. "If you don't like how something feels, you leave."

"So? Am I supposed to hang out when I'm uncomfortable?"

"Did I make you uncomfortable?"

"Yes."

"Okay. This, by the way," he said pointing from himself to me, "is not running. It's talking. I like doing things this way. Are you up for it?"

"Sure, but there's nothing to talk about. I told you it's no big deal."

He straightened and slowly climbed a few stairs until he was two steps below me and eye-level. "Good. Then can we talk about this? How about if I ride with you to work while we talk it out, and I'll take a Lyft back?"

"Can it wait?" I asked.

"Depends. Is this going to bother you today?" I hesitated, and he smiled. "Let's handle it, and then you don't have to carry around this thing all day that actually *does* bother you."

I searched his face. "You don't seem nearly dysfunctional enough."

He snorted. "For what? A guy?"

"A rock star."

"Retired. A retired rock star. But when you meet my family, you'll understand. I'm not allowed not to be grounded."

Warmth spread through my chest at the idea of meeting them, followed immediately by dread. "Wait, are they going to hate me?"

"Why would they hate you?" He sounded genuinely confused.

"Because of the meme?"

That made him laugh out loud. "You should have seen how mad my mom got after I said that on *Live with Laura*. She'll probably try to cut me out of the will and adopt you instead." Then a look of worry crossed his face. "Is your family going to hate me?"

"Uh…"

He rubbed his eyes. "Crap. I should have thought about that."

"I don't have any magic words for you, but I wish I did. It might take them a while."

"Kiss it better?" he asked.

"Will it help?"

"Might cure me."

"Then I guess I'd better." And I did, which is why Chloe found us making out in the stairwell five minutes later.

"I haven't had enough coffee for this," she said from the top of the stairs.

I dropped my head against Miles's chest where he leaned against the wall. Because I'd pushed him there. "So I have some news," I mumbled.

"Uh huh. Let me use my incredible reporter skills to figure this one out. Based on the clues, y'all figured out what everyone who has ever spent three minutes around the two of you together has known for months?"

"You're a genius, Chloe," Miles said, nudging my chin up for a quick kiss. "But I knew it months ago too."

"I admit, it was hard with so few context clues."

I could hear her eyeroll even though I wasn't looking at her.

Miles gave me a light swat on the butt. "Go get your stuff, and I'll meet you at your car."

Chloe gagged and skimmed past us down the stairs. "For real, not before my coffee."

"Love you too, Clo," I shouted after her.

A few minutes later, Miles was buckling himself into my passenger seat. "So tell me why you don't want people to know you can sing. And Ellie?" He made sure he had my attention before he continued. "Not just sing. You're as good as anyone I've ever worked with."

I stared at the steering wheel for a moment, then put the car in reverse and backed out while I considered his words.

"I know I am." I pulled into the street and signaled for my turn at the corner. I *did* know that. I'd started coming into my voice around eighth grade when it had deepened enough to put me squarely in mezzo-soprano range.

"I'm glad you know. You're so good," he said. "Your voice reminds me of…"

"Sara Bareilles," we said at the same time.

He turned his head to grin at me. "Guess it's not the first time you've heard that."

I shook my head. "You should hear me cover 'Brave.'"

"I'd like to."

"I'll do it for you some time." It felt easy now that he'd already heard me.

"But only for me and no one else?"

"No. I don't sing in public anymore."

"Why the hell not?" His voice was totally baffled, not sharp.

Miles knew everything about the *Starstruck* fallout but this. It was the last piece, and I didn't want to give it to him. Only this time, it was because I didn't want to hurt him by bringing it up.

But he was right. I tended to walk away from anything uncomfortable, and I wanted to work on that. I took a deep breath. "I don't know how to explain this to you without making you feel bad."

"It's okay. You can tell me."

I turned onto St. Claude and tried to think of a nice way to say it, but there was no saving the situation. He was going to feel bad no matter what. "I used to have a YouTube channel," I finally explained. "I'd do covers. Every now and then, I'd try an original. And I got an okay number of views. Around 20,000 on each video. But after I went viral, the trolls came out."

He cursed, then sighed.

"Yeah. I'll spare you the comments, but it was constant. It wouldn't stop. People would post the crying GIF or the meme in the comments over and over. It got to the point where I hated even opening YouTube, so I quit posting videos. Then I deleted my channel completely."

"I'm so sorry," he said. "I had no idea that I'd cost you so much."

"You didn't. I sing now for friends and family. Like at Christmas and stuff.

But I worry about having another viral moment and someone doing some digging and finding my connection to Gabi the Meltdown Girl, and it makes me tired. So I don't sing anywhere else. I don't want to. I'm good with it." I meant it. Even the thought of singing for anyone else besides the people closest to me made me feel panicky.

"That doesn't seem right," he said. "I only heard you sing part of one song, and I couldn't get enough of your voice. I woke up wanting to hear it again. Immediately. Other people should hear it."

I shook my head. "You're thinking like a rock star. I'm seriously fine if no one but the people closest to me know I can sing."

"I…can't imagine that," he confessed.

"I know. Your voice is a commodity, and there's nothing wrong with that. But mine's only for me."

"And me sometimes?" he asked.

"And you sometimes," I said, smiling. "If you're good."

"What about today on the stairs? Was I good?"

"Pretty good." I smiled wider.

"Good enough that you'll sing with me? Do our own carpool karaoke?" He was already reaching for my phone. "What's your passcode? I'll find us something good."

"You can't have my passcode," I told him.

"Why not? You already made out with me. Are you saying your passcode is too intimate? You can have mine," he said, rattling it off.

"We're at passcodes already?" I wasn't sure how I felt about that.

"I am. I can wait for you to catch up, but basically we're at stage four of modern love."

"Fascinating," I said, every single molecule fluttering that he'd used the word "love." "What are the first three?"

"I ask you out. Which I did a million times. You say yes. We have a good time. We kiss. We do that a bunch. Then I call you my girlfriend. Then we trade passcodes."

"I disagree with stage three. It needs editing."

"Calling you my girlfriend?"

"Yeah. You can't just go around saying that." I worked hard to keep my tone neutral so he wouldn't know how hard I was fighting not to smile.

"You don't want to be my girlfriend?"

"I'm saying that requires a discussion," I informed him. "I'm not into unilateral decision-making."

He dropped his head against the seat and groaned. "Anneke is going to love you."

"Excuse me?" Hers was not the name I wanted to hear at the moment.

"Vocabulary nerds. Both of you. Hang on." He pulled out his phone and tapped out a text, reading the words as he typed. "My…girlfriend…just…accused…me…of…unilateral… decision-making."

"I'm not your girlfriend," I told him. Even though he'd just called me that to Anneke. Even though it had felt so good to hear him say it.

"Okay, but what if you are my girlfriend in my mind?"

"Then you're delusional."

"What do I have to do to change your mind?"

"Probably ask."

"Ellie?"

"Yes?"

"Are you always going to be this difficult?" He sounded like he was trying not to laugh.

"Yes."

"Good to know. Ellie?"

"Yes?"

"Will you be my girlfriend?"

"2769." It spelled CROW.

"What?"

"That's my passcode."

He busted out laughing, and the sound of it made my cheeks stretch into a bigger smile than I'd even thought I could make.

"I want to kiss you stupid right now, but since you're still driving, I'm settling for karaoke."

"Okay, but the real reason I didn't want you to have my phone is because I don't want you to see how many times I've played all your songs. It's embarrassing." But I was still smiling. I didn't care if he knew anymore. He was my *boyfriend.*

He set my phone down. "That deserves a serenade. What can I sing for you?"

"Can't Hide," I said. I didn't have to think twice about it.

He slid his hand into mine where it rested on the console between us and pressed a kiss to the back. "Don't need the filter, just looking for real," he sang softly, and I let the sound of his voice, stripped down but still warm and gorgeous, curl around me in the car. When he got to the chorus, I joined him, blending my voice with his.

His eyes widened but he kept singing, and I could feel his eyes on me the whole time as our voices wove together.

"You smile and I fall, can't hide how I feel," we sang as I pulled into the parking space.

I cut the engine and turned to face him in the quiet, even though it still felt like the notes were lingering between us. His eyes searched mine, and I met them, okay with sitting here and being seen completely.

"I knew it," he finally said.

"Knew what?"

"That you were something special. And I just keep finding more layers."

I had no defenses left against this man. None. And I didn't care.

His phone vibrated, and he looked down at it. Smiling, he handed it to me. It showed a text from Anneke.

You're in trouble for waking me up. Also, GIRLFRIEND? Unilateral?! I looooove her.

I knew he was showing me so I could understand that he and Anneke were only friends, but it still gave me a jealous pang that he was texting her about this stuff. Friendships between men and women often turned to more, didn't they?

I wouldn't know. I had lots of friends, but not a lot of people who I let get close to me. I didn't have a guy friend on the level of Chloe, and maybe I would feel differently about it if I did. But I couldn't forget Aaron's voice saying, "He's had a hard time getting over her."

Still, being weirdly possessive veered toward irrational crush territory, and not this-is-a-grown-up-relationship behavior, so I smiled at Miles and didn't comment.

"I'll wait with you for your Lyft," I said instead. "What should we do while we wait?" His eyes glinted, and I laughed. "Besides that. I meant what we should talk about."

"Let's talk about how you're going to drop by the Turnaround after work so we can mess around."

"Miles!"

"On the piano," he said, giving me a scandalized look. "What did you think I meant?"

I punched him in the arm.

"Fine. Let's talk about the chef search, and how it's hard in different ways than I expected."

I thought about suggesting Dylan again, but he seemed pretty intent on proving himself at Redbird, so I didn't. Instead, I listened to Miles as he listed the top three candidates he had in mind.

"Anyway," he concluded after he'd described all three of them, "I'd love to go with Le Anh, but I almost worry that she's too ambitious. Like her version of modern classics might skew too far from the basics. I get nervous when people start throwing around the word 'deconstructed.' Makes me think I'm going to get a pile of ingredients on my plate."

"Have your two top candidates come in and cook for you. A main and sides plus a dessert, see what they can do."

"Is that insulting? To put them in there and make them play *Top Chef*?"

"I didn't mean it like that," I said. "Have them come in on different nights, bring in people who know what they're talking about to try the food with you, then make a decision from there. If they each want the job, they won't mind doing it. Pay them well and it'll make it worth their time no matter what."

"You're brilliant," he said. "Now will you help me find people who can try the food with me?"

"You're from here. You know people."

"Right, but this is a ploy to get to know more of your circle."

I rolled my eyes. "You've already met my entire inner circle. Pick two weeknights, not back-to-back, and I might be able to get Dylan to come. Chloe knows food. You'll definitely want her opinion. And if Miss Mary is in town, I'll see if she and Mr. Douglas want to come down. Jerome might even be willing to stop in as well."

"You're the best."

"I know. Your Lyft is here," I said as it pulled up in front of the building. "I'll drop by the club after work."

He leaned forward and kissed me, soft and sweet, like it was the easiest thing in the world. I still felt a tiny bit shy about it, unsure yet if I was supposed to get in his space that way without an invitation.

"Just so you know," Miles said climbing out of the car but leaning in to talk to me, "I'm going to steal every free minute you'll give me, so you're going to have to speak up loudly when you need me to back off."

I climbed from the car and met his gaze over the roof. "See you after work, Miles. Today, tomorrow, and the day after too."

He slid his hands into his pockets and turned toward the Lyft with a little dance step, half-turning to grin at me. "Best answer."

As I walked into work, I admitted that the answer felt good to me too.

CHAPTER TWENTY-FOUR

THE NEXT COUPLE of weeks passed in a blur. On the work side, Miles was preoccupied with staffing and finding a restaurant manager. Jordan focused on booking entertainment. They were both constantly in a state of panic over what to do about a head chef. They'd scheduled demos with their top choices, but they each already had a favorite going in, and since the debate was in full swing this morning, there would be getting no work done here.

"Guys, want me to invite my brother to the tasting?" I asked. "He'll know exactly what you need."

"He won't mind?" Miles asked. "I got the feeling he didn't like me."

"He likes you fine," I told him. "He's protective, that's all." Miles and I hadn't brought each other home to our families yet. On my side, it would provoke the kinds of loaded and uncomfortable questions even I didn't know the answer to. I wouldn't put it past my dad to straight up ask him what his intentions toward me were.

Which is why I hadn't mentioned exactly who the new tenant was. They knew it was a jazz club. I just hadn't told them it was Miles, and I'd dodged having to explain it when they'd been out of town for Miss Mary's goodbye party.

My parents had left me to manage the building for over a year, focusing their time on multi-family residential units in and around Mandeville, a New Orleans suburb on the far side of Lake Ponchartrain. New Orleans wasn't exactly a fast-paced city; people took their time here in a way they didn't in most other big cities I'd visited, but my parents liked the even more low-key suburban pace.

I wasn't trying to hide Miles from them, exactly. But they were going to be super protective on my behalf, having lived through the *Starstruck* fallout.

"I'm going to run into the office to work." I gave Miles a quick kiss. "I'll talk to Dylan and see what he thinks."

On the personal side, the days had taken on a rhythm over the last two weeks, me starting mine downstairs until the regular renovation bustle took over and I headed out to work. I came home at the end of each workday to Miles waiting for me, pulling me in for a hug and a long kiss the second I walked in. Then he'd either coax me into singing something for him, or sometimes we'd go back to his place and hang out in his studio where he'd play something he was working on.

We ate dinner together most days too, sometimes cooking for each other, more often going out so he could "research" different chefs he and Jordan were considering. And before, after, and in between, there was so much making out.

Miles was becoming more familiar to me in a physical way as we learned each other, what made him growl low in his throat or close his arms around me so tight that it made it hard for me to breathe. Those moments also lit a fire low in my belly that raced out to every nerve ending.

If this was love, then I'd only ever felt twitterpated before. The rest of the room faded when our eyes locked, and when he sang to me, his voice alone made me boneless. He invented reasons to touch me, begged me for stories from all the years he hadn't known me, sang the Usher lyrics to me softly every time he walked me to the door, but with a small change. *I got it bad,* he would sing. And I would smile and give him one last kiss before he left or I went home.

But that was the thing: the only time he ever mentioned his feelings was in his music, and even then, other than the Usher lyrics, it was never a song specifically to me. He showed me every day that he wanted to be with me. But he didn't say, "I love you." Was the music enough?

I didn't say it either. Having my feelings splashed across tens of millions of screens when we were kids made it impossible for me to say the words first now. I needed it to be him.

We'd been officially together for all of two weeks. There was time. I didn't need to worry about this. It would happen when it needed to. Besides, every day when I walked into the club after work, if Miles was at the piano, he'd stop whatever he was doing and play "She Don't Know She's Beautiful." It was clearly for me, and I decided to hear them all that way, as if each song contained the words he meant to say to me.

"You excited?" I asked Chloe when she walked into our living room two days later. Tonight was the first chef showcase.

"Low-key excited," she said. "I do this a lot, so…"

"But how many times do you get to influence which chef a restaurant will hire?"

"I'm one of a bunch of votes tonight, Ellie. It's not like they know I'm the Kitchen Saint. I'm sure Dylan's opinion will count more."

Miss Mary and Mr. Douglas were still off "gallivanting," as she liked to hashtag her pictures, but Jerome had agreed to come. With Dylan, Chloe, Jordan and his wife, plus Aaron—unfortunately—there was a good-sized crew with trained New Orleans tastebuds.

"If only they did know," I said. "Then your opinion would be the only one that mattered."

"I would hate that," she said, leading the way out of the apartment. "I value my anonymity like you value…"

"My what?"

"I'm trying to think of something you love as much as I love keeping my identity a secret." I followed her down the stairs, and at the bottom, she announced, "Miles."

"Miles what?"

"I love keeping my identity secret as much as you love Miles."

"I don't—"

But she held up her hand to cut off my half-hearted denial. "Don't even try it. I won't believe you. Now let's get our grub on."

We went in through the main entrance to give the auditioning chef her space. Everyone but Dylan was there. Tanya, the no-nonsense middle-aged restaurant manager they'd hired, had set up two tables for dining.

"This looks so good," I said to Miles when he came to hug me. "I can't believe how good it all looks together." Tanya had used the linens and settings they'd be using for real when they opened for business.

"It does, doesn't it?" He ran his eyes over everything. "I think this is going to work."

"You better hope so," Aaron said, passing us to get to his seat.

I shot Miles a questioning look, but he just shook his head. "I think we're starting with apps," he said.

"That means appetizers *and* aperitifs," Jordan added. "Let's get this started."

I was about to text Dylan when he walked in. "Hey," he said. Normally, he walked in with a touch of swagger, but tonight his shoulders were stiff.

"Everything okay?" I asked.

"Yeah, fine. Just some friction at work."

I could almost *see* Chloe's story antennae go up. "Trouble at Redbird?" she asked.

"It's nothing," he mumbled. "Did someone mention drinks?"

"Coming up," I told him, leading him over to our table. Tanya had arranged the tables for two separate dinner groupings, but they were close enough that we could talk back and forth easily. "Before we start, I wanted to tell you—"

But before I could give him a heads up that Miles and I were dating now, Miles slid an arm around me and held his hand out to Dylan for a shake. "Good to see you, man."

Dylan's eyebrow went up, and he returned Miles's handshake. "So you're with my sister now?"

Miles looked down at me. "You didn't tell him?"

"I was about to."

"You don't tell me a lot of stuff," Dylan said, his face losing some of its animation again.

I had no idea what he was talking about. I loved my brother, but we weren't close. It wasn't like I knew what was going on in his dating life in any given week. "Did I do something wrong?" I asked, trying to figure out his weird mood.

"Nothing. It's fine. Forget it. Which one is my seat?"

Miles pulled out my chair and waved Dylan into the one across from me. Miles sat next to me with Chloe across from him.

"Hey, Clo," Dylan said, sounding a tiny bit less grumpy.

We settled into small talk until Tanya emerged from the kitchen to announce that dinner service would begin. "Tonight, we're eating from Chef Le's take on refined classics. We begin with a shrimp starter."

The servers brought us small plates, each with a gorgeous piece of Gulf shrimp in Cajun pesto resting on a triangle of toast.

"Points for the plating," Chloe said. Dylan nodded.

It proved to taste good too. So did every other dish she sent out. After the two dessert tastings—a coffee crème brulee and a torta ricotta—Tanya brought Chef Le Anh out to the floor. We gave her a sincere round of applause, and she returned to the kitchen to pack up.

"Hey, Jordan," his wife said, loud enough for us to hear her. "How about if you and Miles hop on stage and give us a preview of the entertainment?"

Jordan shook his head, but everyone else hooted and clapped, and Miles waved him toward the stage. Jordan shook his head again, but this time he was grinning as he rose and went to the piano. "How about some classic jazz?" he called out to more hoots. "Let's do a little 'So What' from Miles Davis."

He was flawless, his fingers lightning quick on the keys. We clapped when he ended, and he smiled out at us. "We'll bring in people to cover the standards, but we're also going to showcase singer-songwriters who have an interesting point of view. Sometimes that may verge toward Americana, other times toward soul and R&B roots, but from blues to bebop, the Turnaround will have it."

"How's the booking going?" I asked Miles as Jordan headed back to his seat.

His big smile tightened a tiny bit at the question. "Tougher than expected. We've got great regional acts coming in, but we've had a hard time getting calls back from some of the other acts I wanted."

"Use your name," Aaron said from the next table. "I keep telling you that, bro. All you have to do is use your name."

Miles rolled his eyes at him. "Eat your torta."

"What was that about?" I asked him.

"Nothing. Old argument."

"Get up there," Jordan told Miles. "It's your turn."

Miles leaned toward me instead, his eyes glinting. "These are all friendly faces. How about you get up there and sing? Do a cover if you don't want to do your own stuff."

My cheeks burned even at the thought. "No. Not even covers."

He lowered his voice, his expression turning serious. "It kills me that everyone else doesn't get to see how good you are."

"Dylan and Chloe know. That's half the room. And it's enough."

Miles looked like he wanted to say something else, but he closed his mouth and shook his head instead. "Okay. But I wish you'd change your mind."

"I know." He stressed me out more each time he brought it up. "But they'll be happy to listen to you. Go," I said, as Jordan called for him to go up again. "Do one of your new ones."

"Which one?"

"Any of them. I love them all." It was true. He'd played me three new songs over the last two weeks, and I'd loved each of them for different reasons.

Miles went to the piano and sat for a few seconds, like he was deciding what to play. As soon as he plucked out the first notes, I recognized it. He'd chosen his new up tempo one, a song about dancing like no one is watching. If the industry was a fair place, this would be everyone's new summer jam, and it was fun to watch everyone's head move and fingers tap, even cranky Dylan's.

And once again, when Miles sang about love, I pretended the words were for me. For now, it was enough.

The second chef showcase went well too. Jordan brought in Boogey to play while we ate so we could get more of the full Turnaround experience, and while the second chef was good, the group voted six to two in favor of the first chef, Le Anh.

As if hiring her made the prospect of opening real, suddenly everything went into high gear. Keisha from the gallery had connected Miles with the muralist she'd mentioned, Elijah Remy, who came in and transformed the walls into something magical. He designed it with moments of color in a dark grounding, meant to be seen by the low lights of the jazz club. That also required another visit from the electrician to install strategically placed lighting floods to bring the art to life. Miles called Jordan over the next morning, stood us in the center of the club, and switched on the lights. We all caught our breath.

"It looks amazing," I told him.

"Yeah," Jordan agreed, moving closer to study one of the murals. "Like this place has been here forever and was always meant to be here."

"Won't be if you don't get the bookings up."

We all turned to Aaron, who had offered this cheerful prediction.

"The bookings are fine," Miles said, his voice mild. "We're booked the first three months solid."

"But sales aren't," Aaron said. "We haven't even sold out the first week completely. We still have half the tickets left for opening night."

My stomach clenched. That didn't sound good. Opening night was only three weeks away.

"You know how to fix this," Aaron added.

But Miles shook his head. "Drop it."

"No, I won't drop it. Because you've dragged yourself back here to do this, and it's not working. My job is to make sure you're making the right business choices, and this is a bad one."

Jordan caught my eye. "Hey, Ellie, want to go look at the…kitchen with me?"

"Yep." I jumped at the chance, already turning to follow him, but Miles said, "Don't leave, guys. You can hear this."

He faced Aaron, his arms crossed, his jaw tight. "I don't know how many times I have to tell you this. I won't put my name on the club. I don't want my name in the PR. It's not the draw you think it is, and I want the Turnaround to succeed because of the talent we bring in and the food we serve. So I'm going to say it one more time. Drop. It."

Aaron made a disgusted noise and grabbed his keys from the table. "Whatever, bro. I'm going to the gym."

He walked out, and Miles blew out a frustrated breath. "Sorry, y'all. I just need him to hear me, and so far he hasn't."

"No problem," Jordan said. I didn't know what to add to that.

"I'm going to go check on some paperwork. Catch you after work?" Miles asked me. I nodded and he gave me a quick kiss before he headed into the office.

When he was gone, I turned to Jordan. "How bad are ticket sales?"

"Not good," he admitted. "It'll pick up as we get closer, but I'd hoped we'd be sold out right now. We haven't even gotten RSVPs from some of our VIP invites. The mayor, a couple of the social club presidents. Stuff like that."

"Would it help if Miles used his name? If they knew he was backing it?"

He gave a slow nod. "Yes, but I understand why he won't. He thinks his reputation as an artist is so different from what we're spotlighting here that it'll only confuse people about our brand. If they come here expecting one thing and get another, then we risk bad Yelp reviews. Stuff like that."

"What can I do to help?"

He gave me a small twist of his lips, like he wasn't sure whether to smile or frown. "Tell your friends."

"I will," I said. "I don't have a huge social network, but I can start putting out the word in my professional ones."

"Everything helps," he said. "Then tell your friends to tell their friends."

"You got it."

I went to work, but I worried about it the rest of the day. The worry didn't ease over the next two weeks either. Everything was on schedule with the club. Tanya had the wait staff hired, Chef Le Anh had put together a killer menu, and we all got to sample her dishes every day for dinner as she trained her line cooks.

Intense energy crackled through the staff and crew, but every few days, I quietly checked in with Jordan on ticket sales, and the news didn't get better. New sales were coming in at a trickle, and it lent all the pre-opening energy an edge of desperation, like we were collectively holding our breath and leaning forward, hard, as if we could psychically tip the balance toward more ticket sales.

Miles and I spent most of our time at the club. I came home from work, changed, and met him downstairs to eat whatever Anh was working on, then we'd each work on our separate stuff at a table in the center of the floor. Emails, vendor orders, other paperwork. But when the kitchen staff cleared out and it was only us left, sometimes I'd sit at the piano or Miles would pull out his guitar, and we'd take turns playing. He was always working out new music, rarely working on the same song two nights in a row.

I'd finished "Let Me Love You" and lately had been noodling around on a new one. I had a melody but it hadn't found words yet. That was fine. I liked just being on the piano. I was getting better at it by the day, my muscle memory coming back.

Tonight, when Anh popped her head into the dining room to tell us she was leaving, Miles thanked her and went to get his guitar. Instead of joining him on the stage, I waited for him, my hands in my pockets to keep them from fidgeting while I worked out what I wanted to say.

"Hey," he said, giving me a curious half-smile when he walked back out to find me standing instead of already claiming the piano bench. "What are you doing?"

"I want to talk?" I hadn't meant for it to come out like a question, but that had been happening more and more lately. Maybe it was because I was still never exactly certain where I stood with him, but I hated it every time my voice went up at the end of a statement, like I couldn't speak a straightforward sentence.

"Sure, babe. What's up?"

"It's about the opening." His smile faded, a wariness creeping in instead. "It's in a week and Jordan says you still haven't sold all the tickets."

He shrugged. "It'll be fine. We'll give comp tickets to the artists for their friends and family and they'll fill the place." He settled onto his stool and strummed an E chord.

"It's not enough to fill it. You need influencers, people who love music, who are going to come and tell their friends, then those friends will listen and come too. If you're filling it with friends and family, then they're only going to come when it's their person up there." I took the guitar from his hands, gently lifting the strap off his neck, and set it on its stand. He turned on the stool to watch me. "I know marketing isn't my specialty, but Aaron is right. You need to trade on your name."

He was shaking his head before I could even finish the sentence. "Nobody is coming to see a washed-up talent show winner. This might be a slow start, but we've got the fundamentals right. Great ambiance, good food, and cool artists coming in."

"Yeah, but you booked all locals. *Lesser-known* locals."

"Because that's our aesthetic." He jammed his hand through his hair. "I don't know why I keep having to explain that to everyone."

I tried not to bristle at the trace of condescension in the words. He was on edge with the opening so close. "You don't. But you should listen when people are telling you to reconsider. If you want to do the best possible thing for the Turnaround, you need to start using your name, and quick."

His jaw worked back and forth, like he had to grind his words down before he could spit them out. "It won't work like you think it will."

"Why not?"

"I told you, I'm not that much of a draw."

"You're more of a draw than you think. Putting your name out there, offering the artists as 'Presented by Miles Crowe,' is going to generate some interest even if it's only people who are curious but skeptical about what a lineup curated by you would look like."

"I don't know." His shoulders slumped slightly.

I hated seeing him like this. "Think about it, Miles. I know you want to save the spotlight for new faces, but right now, no one is going to see them. If you want to give them the best possible shot at exposure, *use your name*. Even if you back away from it later, at least it gets the faucet running, you know?"

"I'll think about it." He dug his keys from his front pocket. "I'm not up for hanging out tonight. It's not you," he said, hurrying to reassure me even though I hadn't said anything. "But I need to think."

"That's all I'm asking." I didn't like the vibe between us. I didn't feel like he was mad at me, but for over a month now, I'd felt like parts of him were off limits to me, times he was away somewhere in his head, or times when he was singing and I'd convince myself that his lyrics were about me, but then he'd blink like he'd just realized I was standing there.

"I'll see you tomorrow." He dropped a kiss on my forehead—a kiss he might as well have been giving a favorite auntie—and headed out. "Oh," he said, stopping at the door. "Do you mind locking up?"

I shook my head. "I'll take care of it."

"Thanks," he murmured as he walked out, and once again, I was left with the distinct feeling he'd already forgotten he was leaving me behind.

CHAPTER TWENTY-FIVE

"You were right."

I jumped as I walked out of my apartment to the stairs. Miles was sitting halfway down them, his back against the wall. I hadn't heard from him at all yesterday, even when I'd texted, and now he was hanging out and smiling up at me.

I leaned against the wall and stared down at him. "What are you doing?"

"Waiting here for you."

"Duh. Why?"

"Because you said duh."

"When?"

"Just now."

I blinked at him. "You're sitting on my stairs because I said 'duh' just now?"

He patted the stair two steps above him in invitation. "Join me and I'll catch you up?"

I stayed put and eyed him.

"Please?" he added.

None of this made any sense, but I sat on the step he indicated because he'd at least asked nicely. "You didn't answer my text last night."

"I'm sorry. That's why I came in person today. I was so busy, but I wanted to explain everything to you in person, and I kept meaning to text you that I was going to explain everything in person, and suddenly it was ten o'clock, and I had a feeling I was already going to be in trouble, so I decided to come today to explain and also beg your forgiveness."

I'd never heard him speak such a long, uninterrupted sentence before. He was losing breath toward the end there. "I'm listening."

"I did too. Listen, I mean. That's what I want to tell you." He leaned forward to grip my knees, and even though I was still annoyed with him, my belly did the same flip it always did when he touched me. "I thought about it, and you were right. So I dragged Aaron out of bed yesterday morning and put him on the case. We were working our contacts all day yesterday. And get this, Channel Five is coming to do a profile on us next Tuesday for the evening news."

"Wow." It was a sincere wow. "That's great."

"And look at this." He handed me his phone. "I put it on Instagram and everything. And I called Anneke, and she's coming."

"That's good." I tried to keep my tone neutral, but I didn't like that he was so excited about that. I didn't fool him.

"Seriously, don't worry about her. She's friends with a couple of guys on the Saints who will show up because that's what athletes do: hang out with swimsuit models. She's doing me a big solid because once the word is out that those guys are coming, the tickets will sell out, the news story will keep the buzz going, and we can sell out the next few weeks of shows too."

His clear enthusiasm made me smile. His energy was back. I put my hands on his and gave them a light squeeze. "That all sounds great."

"You were right." He flipped his hands over to grab mine and tugged me until I tumbled into his lap. "It doesn't matter if the buzz is people trying to be where the party is. If it sells tickets, it'll get our artists the attention they deserve." He buried his face in my neck and took a long, deep breath of me. "I should have been listening to you from the start. And I'm sorry again I didn't call you yesterday. I do this sometimes, get hyper focused and shut everything out. Fair warning: it gets bad when I'm putting together an album. I can disappear into my head for a while."

I brushed my fingers through his hair. "You feel better about everything?"

"Yeah."

I could feel it in the lines of his body, his thighs beneath mine, his chest against my side, his arms around me. Every bit of him was more relaxed than I'd seen him in weeks. "You don't have to apologize for being hyper focused.

But you're probably going to have to apologize every time you don't return a text."

"Fair," he murmured, but his tone was distracted as his mouth nuzzled toward mine, looking for a kiss I was happy to give him.

We didn't break apart for a few minutes until there was a groan from the top of the stairs where Chloe glared down at us.

"Seriously, you guys? Again?"

"Here, there, and everywhere," Miles said cheerfully. Chloe reached into her purse and hurled a small packet of Kleenex at him. It bounced off his shoulder. He just grinned.

She skimmed down the stairs and stepped over us, disappearing through the rear exit, no doubt in a hurry to get her bakery coffee before she tried to deal with the rest of the day.

"Forgive me?" Miles asked.

"Forgiven," I promised, and kissed him until not only he believed it, but until he had no room left for any other thoughts.

By the time Channel Five came on Tuesday to do their "Weekend Preview" segment, the tickets had already sold out from Miles and Anneke's Instagram posts, but the station wanted to profile the Turnaround. The reporter, a woman named Kyla, was intrigued by the guest list.

"That's quite a who's who," she said to Jordan as he rattled off the confirmed VIPs.

I watched the interview from a booth off to the side. At first, I hadn't wanted to come. I swear, for about a week straight after going viral, I'd gotten as much coverage on the local news as a hurricane until the national press lost interest in me. The local news had too, within another week. Too bad the meme hadn't died as quickly.

But Miles had wheedled. "Come on, it'll be fun. You can see me doing my rock star thing. I want to show off for you."

"You don't have to show off for me," I'd told him. That had ended with him hoisting me onto my kitchen counter and kissing me stupid until we heard Chloe fumbling with the front door. But I'd agreed to come watch him do the Channel Five interview.

"What made you decide to come back to New Orleans?" Kyla asked Miles. Aaron settled in across from me and watched his cousin give a smooth answer about wanting to give back to his hometown.

"I don't know how the camera doesn't make him totally nervous," I whispered to Aaron.

He shrugged. "The label gave him a lot of media training."

It didn't make him any less interesting to watch. Maybe I wouldn't have torpedoed my whole life if I'd had the same kind of training during my viral moment.

Kyla asked a few more questions, then thanked Miles. "We'll take some establishing shots of the murals and speak with your chef, then I'll find you if I have any follow up questions."

Aaron slid out of the booth. "Let me show you to the kitchen," he said.

Miles took Aaron's place. "How'd I do?"

"You know you were great."

"Yeah." He grinned at me. "I just want to periodically remind you I'm awesome so you'll remember that you're happy you're dating me."

It was a funny way to phrase it. "Have I ever made you think I wasn't?"

"Sometimes I feel like I talked you into this, and I don't want you to regret it."

I stretched my hand across the table to take his. "No regrets. I promise."

We talked through more of the details for the opening, going over the lineup again and again. It was my job to listen, mostly. Miles had it covered but liked to talk it out to make sure his own head was clear.

He was reviewing the cocktail list when Kyla stepped out from the kitchen with the camera crew behind her. Her eyes lit up as they landed on us in the booth. "Miles, there you are."

"Hey, Kyla. Did Chef Le treat you right back there?"

"She sure did. But Aaron was filling me in more on your background. Do you mind answering a few more questions?"

"Not at all," he said, sliding toward the end of the bench.

"Oh, you're fine where you are," she assured him. The lighting guy and the cameraman were already maneuvering into place for a shot of the booth. A shiver of alarm skittered down my spine, but they were in place within seconds, and Kyla was already turning to face the camera. The guy pointed at her to talk, and she drew back her shoulders and spoke in her newswoman voice. Why was she keeping me in the shot? I tried to scrunch my shoulders and slouch.

"Miles Crowe started playing and singing in French Quarter clubs when he was a young man, and now he's come full circle, opening his own New

Orleans club to give other young artists the same opportunities. But that's not the only way he's keeping in touch with his past."

Miles wore his usual, pleasant public expression, his listening face, but the dread swelling in my stomach told me exactly where this was about to go.

"Miles rose to fame on *Starstruck*, but many of you may remember that he captured the national spotlight before he even won thanks to a moment with another familiar New Orleans face."

I was going to be sick. This wasn't happening. This couldn't be happening.

"During his hometown performance in the semifinals, Gabrielle Jones rose to fame after the producers spotted her in the audience and zeroed in on her reaction to Miles Crowe's performance. Her emotional response to watching her hometown hero turned her into one of the earliest viral moments of the emerging YouTube era. After Miles Crowe won the show, his appearance on *Live with Laura* led to one of the most famous memes on the internet."

I had no doubt that when this aired, she'd be voicing over a clip of me at my snottiest and most red-faced in the old footage followed by flashing the Meme That Would Not Die.

"Gabrielle and Miles have since reunited, and by the looks of things, she's very much his thing now."

It was a hammer to my gut. I shot a panicked look at Miles. Why wasn't he saying anything? But he wasn't even looking at me, just watching Kyla with his same pleasant smile.

She turned to face us. "So how does it feel to be sitting here with your teenage crush?" Her voice was so friendly, but I had no words. They had drained out of me along with the blood that was now pooling in my stomach. Definitely none of it was staying in my brain, oxygenating, helping me figure out what to do.

Miles spoke up. "Ellie and I never met back then, so it's been great getting to know her now."

Getting to know her. Like we didn't spend every spare moment together. Like he wasn't the first person I saw when I got up in the morning and the last person I saw before one of us went home for the night. Like we hadn't talked music for hours, sung together, traded lyrics and more kisses than I could count.

Why wasn't he cutting off this line of questioning?

"Ellie has been essential to getting the Turnaround open," he added. "She found us this property and connected us with so many skilled contractors and local businesses. She's a major asset."

A major asset.

All I felt like was a major ass.

Kyla turned back to the camera. "Let me do this outro." She walked over so the lit neon sign spelling out the club's name on the stage wall were over her shoulder. She'd made it clear this was going to be a short segment, and apparently she'd decided she had everything she needed. "Miles Crowe and his partner Jordan Goodman took the club name from a jazz term, but it's a metaphor too. A place for artists to come and reinvent themselves. Hopefully a place that will give birth to the next New Orleans great. It's sold out for the weekend with a slate of stars to welcome it to The Big Easy, but you can check their schedule for future dates."

It only registered at the very edge of my consciousness. The loud roar of blood in my ears drowned almost everything out.

"Ellie," Miles said, and I realized it probably wasn't the first time he'd tried to get my attention.

I lurched from the booth without looking at him, grabbed my purse, and walked straight out the back exit to my car. Miles tapped on the window as I was buckling in.

"Ellie, talk to me." His voice sounded like it was underwater through the noise-dampening features in the car.

I pushed the ignition instead, and the car purred to life.

"Ellie, come on." He was louder now, more insistent, so I lowered the window halfway.

"How could you do that, Miles?"

"Do what?"

"Drag all of that up for her? Let her sit there and talk about it? She's going to run that tomorrow, and everyone in my office, every client I work with right now, and probably every client for the foreseeable future, is going to know that's me in that meme. It took me almost six years to live that joke down, and now people are going to throw that at me everywhere I go. 'Don't have a meltdown, Ellie.' 'Thanks for showing me this property, but it's so not my thing,' wink-wink. They'll think they're being funny, but every time it happens, they'll be forcing me to live for a few seconds as the worst version of myself."

"I know it sucked, but it won't be as bad as you think. It'll be annoying for a few days, but people will forget again. Play it off, roll your eyes, say, 'So glad I grew up,' and people will let it go."

"Let it go," I repeated, my voice flat.

"Yeah. You kind of have to."

"What about the fact that everyone is going to think that I'm working with you because I was madly in love with you back then? They're not going to take me seriously as a professional."

"Miles?" called one of the lighting guys from the back door.

He took a step back from the car, casting a glance toward the building. "Ellie, I—"

"Go, Miles. You've got a lot to do."

"I do, but I want—"

"Don't worry about it. Take care of business. I understand." I understood that Miles still didn't get how hard those years had been for me, how I'd had to reshape my dreams and find new ones that I could chase without dragging the baggage of my single stupid moment with me. I understood that he had no idea how painful it had been for him to smile through Kyla's ambush and treat me like a polite acquaintance for the sake of publicity.

"It doesn't seem like you're okay," he said, not making a move to leave.

I banged my fists against the steering wheel. "Of course I'm not okay. My boyfriend just used the worst thing that ever happened to me as a PR move to promote his club. Nothing about that is fine. Move, Miles."

He took a step back almost on reflex, opening his mouth to argue or defend himself, but I reversed and pulled away, not looking back.

CHAPTER TWENTY-SIX

I WALKED INTO MY PARENTS' place thirty minutes later, a graceful Georgian home in Mandeville. "Knock, knock," I called to announce myself. My mom had to be home because her Cadillac was in the driveway.

"Honey, what are you doing here?" she asked, walking out of the kitchen.

"Nice to see you too, Mom."

"You know that's not what I meant." She pulled me into a hug. "I just can barely get you to come out on a Sunday, much less the middle of the week."

And without meaning to, without even the faintest warning that I would do it, I burst into tears.

"Oh, baby," she said, gathering me close, and even though she was two inches shorter than me, I was a little kid again, wrapped up in the warmth of her hug. "Do I need to call Daddy?"

"No, it's okay," I sniffled, staying where I was.

"Come on and sit down." She led me to the sofa and gathered me right back into a hug. "Tell me what's wrong."

I couldn't at first. She and my dad were going to hate that I was dating Miles. They'd hated every mention of his name after his *Live with Laura* appearance, my dad threatening more than once to beat his scrawny behind because clearly Miles had gotten no home training.

Finally, my sniffling subsided enough for me to sit up and rub my eyes like an overwrought preschooler. "Sorry."

"Don't be sorry. Just tell me what's the matter."

I drew a deep, shuddering breath, then a less dramatic one. How should I bring up Miles? If she would have hated the idea before, now she'd be ready to kill him.

I flashed back to his calm smile, heard him call me a "major asset," someone he didn't even want to publicly admit to dating. Maybe I was okay with some light murder. But I didn't want her to think I was stupid. And I'd been so very, very stupid.

"There's going to be something on Channel Five news," I said. "Maybe tomorrow."

"Okay," she said, taking my chin in her hand. "What's that got to do with anything?"

"I did something so idiotic," I forced myself to say. Or whisper, anyway.

"Did you get tangled up in something at work? Do I need to call a lawyer?"

"Mom."

"Well?"

"Honestly, can you imagine me doing something illegal?"

"Of course not. But I'm trying to think of why you would worry about making the news."

"Remember how I told you that I got a tenant for my building?" She nodded. I shifted uncomfortably on the sofa. "It's Miles Crowe."

Her eyes narrowed into slits. "Is that so."

It was a flat statement.

I shifted, wishing I could take it back. But there was nowhere else I wanted to be right now while my heart unraveled like it had when I was fourteen. I forged ahead. "He used Crescent City Properties to find a space for a jazz club he wanted to open. He was supposed to be Brenda's client, but he asked to work with me."

Her gaze sharpened. "Did he recognize you?"

"No. He said he wanted to work with me because he could tell at our first meeting that I wasn't a fan of the sites she'd chosen. I tried to get myself fired with the first few properties I showed him, but…I don't know. The more I worked with him, the more I realized that he understands New Orleans, and he's the opposite of slick corporate."

"So you moved him in with you?" Her tone was complete disbelief. "That boy nearly destroyed you twelve years ago."

"Mom, no. Come on. I wouldn't have offered him Mary's spot, but she mentioned retiring in front of him and he couldn't get it out of his mind. I still wasn't sold on having him in the space. You know how protective I am of the Bywater."

She nodded. We all were. I'd learned it from her and my dad.

"Anyway, he brought me over to this music center in Tremé to meet his business partner. Between the two of them, I believed in their vision for Miss Mary's place. If I'd leased it to another restaurant, I would have always felt like it was falling short, that I should have found something better. It felt right to go in a different direction."

She'd listened with tightly pursed lips. "All of that sounds like good reasoning until you get to the part that it's Miles Crowe."

"From a business standpoint, I stand by that choice. They're going to be great in that space."

"Then how is it you ended up on the news?"

"You are not going to love what comes next."

"Spit it out, Gabrielle Marie." But she gave my arm a gentle squeeze.

"We started dating."

"Oh, Gabi," she sighed. She only remembered to call me Ellie half the time. "At what point did you decide he was a decent human being? What could have possibly changed your mind?"

I stifled an impulse to defend him. The whole reason I'd run to her crying was because he'd proven that he didn't want to be publicly associated with me now any more than he had then.

My phone went off. A text from Miles. *Call me? We have gotten things so twisted.* I turned it off and dropped my phone into my purse.

"Dylan stopped in when we were having lunch at Miss Mary's once," I said. "He told Miles who I was, and his reaction was different than I expected. He apologized, and he'd had no idea how much that whole mess followed me. He figured it had burned itself out after a couple of weeks when the next viral thing came along. And it had some pretty tough repercussions for him too."

My mom snorted. "Like what? Million-dollar recording deals?"

"Yeah, like that. Because he got pigeon-holed as a teen idol, and his label wouldn't let him move beyond it. He wanted to explore different sounds, reinvent himself, and they wouldn't let him. He left and went indie, but without their giant machine behind him, he didn't find the same kind of success."

She smoothed my hair back. "Why am I only hearing about it now, and how did it lead to you crying on my couch?"

"We've been dating for almost two months. And I'm crazy about him. I've had hints that he's not as into me as I'm into him. And maybe that's subconsciously why I haven't brought him around before. I didn't want you to think this was me reliving my freshman crush and not see it for something real."

"But *is* it real?"

I slowly shook my head, my eyes welling again. I hated the burning feeling of the tears. She tucked a tissue into my hand without a word. "I should have known. Maybe I did. He's never said he loves me. He sings me love songs, but he never says the words to me. I hoped it would be a matter of time. But then, this afternoon, Channel Five came to do an interview, and…" The tears spilled over, and I swiped at them with the tissue.

"Oh, honey. It's okay. You can tell me when you're ready." She pulled me back into her arms and held me while I cried some more. This time it was a slow, steady trickle of tears that somehow tasted saltier and sadder than the first ones. I wasn't sure how long I stayed there, cuddled against her shoulder, before those ran out too.

I straightened and pushed my hair off my cheek where the tears had stuck it. I reached for a fresh tissue and twisted it around my fingers, winding it up, straightening it out against my leg, winding it up again. I watched Miles in my mind's eye as he spoke to Kyla, replaying his words on a loop.

"He told Kyla that it had been fun getting to know me and that I've been a major asset in helping them open the club." The words left a pit in my stomach. Nothing about the nights we'd spent with the two of us at the piano, or daydreaming about the future of the club, or the countless kisses, from sweet to the scorching. "He still wants to keep his distance publicly. I may be his thing in private, but even he says that most of his public relationships are for publicity. I don't fit his image."

She pulled me down into her lap and stroked my hair like she used to when I'd gotten sick as a kid. "He's not worth it, honey." That was all she said about it. She pet my hair until I fell asleep and woke me with a gentle shake when my dad got home.

"I told him," she said. "You don't have to re-explain."

He pulled me into a big hug, sat next to me, and turned on Animal Planet. It was a dog training show, and he sat with me in silence, his arm around my shoulders, while my mom made dinner.

She popped out at one point to say, "Dylan called. Said Chloe called him, worried about you. Better let her know you're okay."

I didn't want to turn on my phone. I didn't know what I wanted more: to find a dozen texts from Miles waiting for me, or none at all. "Can you tell Dylan to let her know I'm fine and I'll call her tomorrow?" With Chloe and Dylan both knowing how to get hold of me, I could just email Donna to handle any clients who called the office and keep my cell phone off and buried.

My mom nodded and disappeared into the kitchen again.

An hour later, we had smothered chicken, and I was reminded again of who Dylan had gotten his talent from. It tasted like everything I needed: familiarity, comfort, love, all stirred right into the sauce.

"Can I stay here for a few days?" I asked. "I'll run home and get some clothes tomorrow, but I need some space."

"You never even have to ask," my dad said.

This was exactly why I hadn't wanted to date Miles, even when I'd wanted him so desperately, I thought I would die from the wanting: there would be no escape. I'd always be watching for his car in his spot, trying to figure out when my apartment was wholly mine and when he was invading the space beneath me.

So stupid.

But I didn't want to cry anymore about it tonight. Instead, after dinner, I changed into an extra pair of my mom's pajamas and sat down at the piano. The one good thing that had come out of my time with Miles was the practice I'd put in.

"That was lovely," my mom said, when I finished the last notes of "Moonlight Sonata," a piece I hadn't played since high school. "It does my heart good to hear you playing again." A yawn escaped her, and she clapped her hand over her mouth. "Sorry, honey. That's not a comment on your performance. Want to sing me to sleep?"

I smiled. It had been a joke between us since I'd first learned to accompany myself. She loved for me to sing her a song before we all went up to bed. "Of course, Mama. What do you want?"

"Do 'Brave' by Sara Bareilles."

She'd always loved bragging to her friends about her Baby Bareilles, even though most of them had no idea who Sara Bareilles was. As the lyrics came back to me, I found myself singing them with conviction instead of humoring her. *Say what you want to say, and let the words fall out.* I'd be singing it to myself as I fell asleep tonight.

She padded over to the piano bench to drop a kiss on my forehead. She'd sent my dad up to bed an hour earlier when he'd dozed off in front of the TV. "Stay as long as you need to. And as far as I'm concerned, Channel Five doesn't exist in this house anymore."

I meant to sneak over to my place early before I knew Miles would be at the club. I needed clothes and my laptop. But when I woke up Wednesday morning, my eyes were sore and puffy-feeling, and sinus pressure I only got from pollen or crying pushed against my cheekbones. I didn't feel like crying anymore, but I didn't want to go to work either.

I shuffled downstairs and found my purse, fishing out my phone. I let it wake up while I foraged in the kitchen. It was too early even for my mom, who would usually brew some coffee—always Community coffee, always doctored with two creams and a sugar. I dug through the fridge for something to reheat while my phone vibrated like crazy, announcing two million messages that had come in while it was off.

I gave up looking for something to reheat and pulled grits from the pantry. My phone kept buzzing. I set a small saucepan of water to boil and finally checked it. Thirteen missed calls. Thirty-seven texts, all from Chloe or Miles. Hers started around six and ended around the time Dylan had called my mom. The final one read, *Glad you're okay. Call me if you need anything.*

I didn't want to read the texts from Miles. There had to be at least twenty-five. The last one he'd sent, the one that showed up in my texts list, read, *Seriously. That was totally unfair. Call me please? I just want to...*

The rest disappeared, too long to fit in the preview window. I didn't open it. I would talk to Miles eventually. But I needed to work out some stuff first.

I texted Donna instead to tell her I wasn't feeling well and wouldn't be in the office. I rescheduled two client meetings, turned off my phone, and curled up to watch more Animal Planet and eat plain buttered grits.

About a half hour later, my mom came down, dropped a kiss on my head, and went to put the coffee on. My dad came down a few minutes later, hair wet from a shower, and I ate a second breakfast with them, this time with eggs and bacon.

"It's nice to have you at the breakfast table," my mom said as she gathered up our dirty plates. "It's been too long. Last Christmas, at least. You and Dylan are too independent. I miss fussing over you."

"Thanks, Mom."

"You going to be okay if we go into the office, sugar?" My dad's forehead furrowed like he wasn't sure he was going to believe me if I said yes.

"I'll be fine, I promise. I want to decompress and maybe play the piano for a while."

Eventually, they decided to take my word for it and left together for work. The house fell completely quiet as soon as the door shut behind them.

I went over to the piano and tried the melody I'd been messing with for a week, but it felt more wrong than ever. Before, I could sometimes sense the edges of what it was about, but today, I drew a blank.

Instead, I picked out a different melody with my right hand, something bluesy, the traditional C-F-G chord progression feeling like the right fit for my mood this morning. Today was a day to write about love gone wrong. I hopped off the bench and lifted the lid, digging through it until I found the sheet music for an old Allen Toussaint song, spending a couple of hours learning it until it came to me more fluidly. Then I pushed it aside and went back to the melody I'd been picking out earlier.

By lunch I had two verses, and after a quick cold-cut sandwich, I sat down and finished the rest of it. I played it for myself several times, and I was ready to do a quick recording on my iPhone when I realized that reaching for it would only mean seeing more texts from Miles. I set it back down without turning it on. If I forgot the chords and lyrics, that could be his fault too.

Instead, I curled up on the sofa and watched more Animal Planet. When my mom got home around four, she walked into the den and sighed. "Honey, I was really hoping to find you watching Real Housewives of anywhere."

I wrinkled my nose. "Why?"

"Because if you'd moved on from sad animals to being judgy it would mean you're feeling better."

I scrunched down further into my cushion and drew my knees to my chest. "I don't feel better. And I wrote a blues song," I mumbled into my knees.

"What was that?"

I sighed and lifted my face up. "I wrote a blues song."

My mom winced.

I knew writing it was a bad sign. The last time I'd written a blues song was when Miles had dissed me on *Live with Laura*.

"What can I do to help?" she asked. "Do you want to go shopping? Get some ice cream?"

I uncurled from my protective ball and climbed to my feet, still in my pajamas that I hadn't bothered to change. I stretched and caught a whiff of my own slightly musty smell. I needed a shower. But I didn't want a shower. "I'm going to take a nap."

I stumbled upstairs to bed, feeling the weight of her worry the whole way up.

I ended up sleeping all the way through until morning, an uneasy fitful sleep, and I woke up feeling as if I'd been on the edge of waking up the whole time.

When I opened my bedroom door, my overnight bag was sitting in front of it. I wondered if my mom had gone to get me some clothes, or if Chloe had dropped them by. I hauled it into my room and threw it on the bed, digging inside it to find clean underwear, yoga pants, and my favorite T-shirt. Chloe, then.

I still wasn't in the mood to go into the office, and I'd have to reschedule another client today, but I definitely didn't want to be in my stinky pajamas anymore. I grabbed the clothes and headed for the shower, rinsing off two days of moping.

Progress, basically. If you measured progress with super pathetic benchmarks.

When I walked into the kitchen with wet hair, my mom smiled at me. "You look better. How are you feeling?"

Like I wanted to write another blues song. But I didn't want to worry her, so I said, "Fine."

"Very convincing."

I poured myself a cup of coffee and took a sip. I didn't like plain chicory coffee, but I needed the caffeine more than I needed to take the time to put cream and sugar in it.

"Chloe's worried. She wants you to call her."

"I will."

"Soon?"

I didn't answer. I'd used up all my grit on showering and getting dressed.

My mom had been on her laptop, probably checking the headlines, but she shut it and rested her hands on top. I could feel her looking for the words to say next, but when she stayed quiet, I leaned back against the sink and studied her over the rim of my mug.

"What, Mom? I know you want to say something."

"I called Miss Mary last night."

I raised my eyebrows. "That's good. How's she doing?"

"Fine. Having a grand time. But I didn't call her to catch up. You said she'd met Miles, and I wanted to get her take on him."

"You could have asked Dylan or Chloe."

"I wanted a mother's perspective. She knows what it was like last time. And right now, all signs point to you spiraling again."

"I'm not spiraling, Mom." It was an irritating assessment. "I just need a minute to process this."

"That's what I thought when you were fourteen, but it took three years. And this past forty-eight hours has been heartbreakingly familiar."

I digested that with another swallow of coffee. Those three years had been hard on her too. She'd never lost patience with me then, so I'd find some for her now. I owed her that. "Okay. What did she say?"

"She said she left a letter for you, and you should read it. Do you know what she's talking about?"

I'd forgotten about the letter Miss Mary had given me at the goodbye party until she mentioned it. "I do."

"She said to tell you to read it right away."

"It's at my apartment."

"Then go and get it."

"No way. The grand opening is tomorrow. The Turnaround will be busier than a kicked-over anthill."

"Then they won't notice one more person coming and going. Miss Mary seems to think you need to read this now. I'll drive over and pick it up if you tell me where you put it."

I could tell from the stubborn set of her chin that she wouldn't be letting up on this. "No, it's okay. I need to get more clothes for the weekend anyway. I'll get it."

"I'm coming home at lunch to check on you. I want a report on that letter."

I rolled my eyes. "Gabrielle Marie Jones."

"Fine," I said. "I promise. I'll get it. I'll read it. I'll write you a book report."

"You are lucky you are sad and broken right now because you are not too big for me to paddle your butt."

"Sorry," I mumbled. But I meant it.

That seemed to satisfy her. "I'm going to the office. See you in a little while."

I tried to procrastinate leaving for another hour, but there wasn't enough for me to do. I gave up and grabbed my purse, pulling out my phone and turning it on again as I walked out to my car. It went off with at least a dozen more alerts. Down by almost two-thirds from yesterday.

"You don't have much endurance, do you, Miles?"

But there was no answer. I glanced at the phone, the visible message another variation of *Let's-talk-about-this-please-call-me*.

I drove back to the city, drawing up a game plan to avoid Miles. It involved parking a block away, pulling on a hoodie I'd swiped from my dad's closet, and slinking in through the back door. I could hear the clatter from the kitchen as I skimmed up the back stairs, but no one poked their head out as I made it up to the second floor. Chloe's parking space was empty, so I had the apartment to myself. I wasn't in the mood to talk about this anymore. Or maybe ever again.

I'd tucked the letter into the drawer of my nightstand, so I grabbed it and my song notebook and headed back out, not drawing a deep breath until I'd made it safely to my car. I reached the causeway in record time, Miss Mary's letter staring at me from the passenger seat the whole way.

What could she possibly have needed to tell me that required three months of time and distance before she was ready for me to hear it? What had she seen coming?

The question had me pushing my car faster toward my parents' house, and when I pulled into the driveway, I didn't even bother getting out of the car before I slid my thumb under the seal and pulled the letter out.

Seeing the elegant cursive I knew so well from her "Daily Special" chalkboard made me homesick for Miss Mary.

July 15

Hey, honey.

If you listened to directions, it's been three months since I closed my café and left to enjoy time off with Douglas. I promise you, I know already that these have been some of the best three months of my life, and I haven't even lived them yet. Don't believe me? Check my Facebook and see if I'm lying. I bet you I'm having more fun than a decent woman should.

Anyway, if my Facebook proves I'm telling the truth and I know a little bit about what may be coming, it's not because I fool with the Sight. I don't have it. What I do have is an abundance of common sense and a pretty good read on human nature.

You are going to fall in love with that boy again, Ellie. It's written all over your face, and I know as I write this that you don't see it coming yet, but I know as sure as you're reading this that it's already happened.

Here's what you may not know: that boy is already half gone on you, and unless I miss my guess—and I won't—he'll be as crazy for you as you are for him.

This is going to go one of two ways. Either you'll let yourself feel it, and by the time you read the advice I'm about to give you, it will be a moot point. I hope that's what happened.

But I'm afraid the second possibility is more likely, which is that you're going to get in your own head too much, and then you'll get in your own way. In some ways, your tendency to overanalyze has made you successful at work. But in your personal life...it holds you back.

Don't let it. If you're reading this and the two of you have not gotten together, or even worse, got together and fell apart, I want you to listen to me: Miles is the goods.

Go back and read that again.

Read it one more time.

He is a good man. Steady and true, like my Harold. He's more guarded than people realize, but I've seen glimpses beyond his impeccable manners and charm, unguarded moments when he watches you, or when I can tell he's drifted on a daydream as he rearranges my café into the club of his dreams.

Don't get in your own way on this one, Ellie-girl. You deserve to be happy, but you get in your own way because of how this very same man burned you when he was a boy. But I believe he has done as the apostle said and put away his childish things. The lesson you took from back then was to only put your trust in things you can quantify and measure. But that's not how love works.

And this is love. Or it will be if you let it.

Let it, Ellie. I love you like one of my grandkids, and I'm telling you, even though I love you to death, I know you already messed this up. Go fix it.

Love,

Mary

. . .

It was her signature that got to me. Something about her signing it that way, just Mary, not Miss Mary, told me that she was inviting me into adulthood in a way she never had before. Even when I'd lived above her on my own and became her landlord, I always knew she saw me as my skinned-knee childhood self no matter how much polish I acquired.

I read the letter again, stopping to reread some of the lines. One in particular. "He'll be as crazy for you as you are for him."

That wasn't how it had felt when I'd been sitting there in the crosshairs of Kyla's ambush. I'd felt like a PR opportunity, not a girlfriend.

But Miss Mary had been right about everything else in the letter. And for so many things in my life. And she was as protective of me as my own parents were. So why would she push me toward Miles, knowing…

Miles is the goods.

I reread the line a half dozen more times before I cut the engine and headed into the house, thinking. Miss Mary hadn't been here for the last two months that we'd been dating, two months where Miles sang pretty words around me, never *to* me. Two months where he'd never said the word Miss Mary threw around so easily: love.

He'd never spoken love.

Still, only an idiot would brush off Miss Mary's advice about anything.

I curled up on the couch and opened my text messages. I'd at least read what Miles had to say over the last two days. Then I could tell her in good conscience that I'd given him a chance.

CHAPTER TWENTY-SEVEN

THE FIRST SEVERAL texts were variations of *Ellie, I'm worried. Where are you? Please call me.* As the timestamps got later, it changed to versions of *Can you just talk to me? I can fix this.*

The messages stopped around midnight and picked up again yesterday morning. Around 1:00, he changed direction. *I didn't use you as a PR stunt. That was all Aaron feeding the reporter that info. I would never have brought it up. But when it came up, all my old media instincts took over. Sanitize. Minimize. Tell half-truths. Throw them off the scent. Please talk to me.*

There were only a couple more messages after that. The first said, *I would never do that to you. It hurts that you think I would.* And the final one said, *I fired Aaron. Should have done it a while ago. But it won't change that stuff like this will keep happening. As long as you're with me, your past will come up. And it's not fair. I want nothing but good things for you, but I can't protect you from that. I'm sorry, Ellie. Thanks for trying.*

I stared at the letter on the coffee table in front of me, then back to the phone, skimming his messages again.

Miles is the goods.

Miss Mary was right. The surety sat behind my breastbone like a light in a distant window, small but steady.

Miles Crowe was the goods.

It didn't make what had happened with Kyla okay. But he had done what he'd been trained to do. And I had been naïve not to realize that as long as he and I were together, to some extent, that old part of my past was going to come up.

Could I live with that?

Was he worth it?

Miles is the goods.

I got up and went to the piano and played "Brave," singing it softly to myself, replaying his texts in my mind.

As long as you're with me, your past will come up.

Was I brave enough for that?

I can't protect you from that.

Did I need him to?

I let the notes die beneath my fingers and rubbed my palms against my thighs. They were clammy. People would know it was me again, in that meme. It might take on new life, not that it had ever died.

I hated the idea.

I stared down at the piano keys and thought about the weeks I'd spent watching Miles play in the Turnaround, sharing his music with me, the stuff he wouldn't play for anyone else, the incomplete lyrics, the snatches of melody. The way he let me see everything in process before it was perfect and ready for everyone else. How he shared his worries and fears about the club. And his hopes and dreams for it.

Maybe he hadn't said "I love you" in the exact way I wanted to hear it, but he'd opened every other part of himself to me. I'd repaid him with doubt, forcing him to explain and defend past relationships. Forcing him to prove his worthiness to lease Miss Mary's place. I hadn't even told my parents about him, so why should he bring me home to his?

I hadn't given Miles any reason to stay, but he had.

He had a dozen reasons to leave, but he hadn't.

Miles Crowe is the goods.

Suddenly, I couldn't fumble my phone into my hands fast enough. I owed him an apology. We'd figure this out in a few days when he got past the grand opening, but I couldn't leave him thinking I wanted to walk away.

I'd learn how to deal with new notoriety. We'd figure this out.

He answered on the third ring. "Ellie. Hey."

His voice was subdued, and my heart gave a hard twist. I had done this to him. "Miles, hey. How's everything going over there?"

He sighed. "It's chaos, but it was like this before all my tours too, and it will work out. I'm choosing to believe it'll work out before opening tomorrow."

I could hear the stress in his voice, so I tried to wedge as much positivity as I could in mine. "It's going to be great."

"I hope so." But he sounded subdued. "Hey, look, I'm really sorry about the interview. I called and asked her not to run that part, but she did anyway."

I digested that. "I didn't see it. My mom decided Channel Five doesn't exist in her house anymore."

"Right."

We both fell silent, and I didn't know how to segue into the next thing I needed to say. There was no smooth transition. I cleared my throat and jumped in. "I'm sorry I freaked out about it. I shouldn't have accused you of setting me up."

"I would never do that to you."

I could hear the hurt.

"I should never have said that. I was thinking after the opening, we can talk this all out. I know it's crazy right now, but I didn't want to add to your stress thinking that we were breaking up or something."

"We aren't?" He sounded confused.

"Of course not. It was a fight. We'll figure it out."

A long pause. "Will we?" he asked softly. "I'm not so sure. The reality of my life is not going to change for a long time. I can't do anything about it."

"I know. But I'll figure out how to live with it."

An even longer silence.

"Miles?"

He cleared his throat. "I don't know, Ellie. One thing you learn after being in this industry long enough is that if you have even two people you can count on to ride out the crazy with you, you've got a hundred percent more support than most people. And if you count on the wrong people, you get burned.

"Sometimes it's because they're self-interested people. Like Aaron. He wasn't always like this, but I finally had to accept that he's changed. I can't count on him anymore. Sometimes it's because life in the spotlight is too much for people, and it's not fair to expect them to deal with it. Like you. So I thought I had three people, but I guess I just have Anneke. And one is still more than most people have, so maybe I'm still lucky after all."

I hated hearing the words. Every single one burned. I hated not being counted as one of his people. I hated the exhaustion in his voice. "Miles, I know this was a bad moment for me to have a breakdown or whatever, but I've had some sleep and some advice and now I have clarity. Let's talk about this on Monday, when you're through opening weekend."

He gave a soft sigh. "Sometimes I feel like I've lived fifty years instead of twenty-eight. But the upside is that it helps you figure people out sooner than later. You are all the good things, Ellie. But I'll never be good *for* you. Take care of yourself, okay?"

"Miles—"

"I can't," he said. "I need to go. See you around some time."

The call went the kind of quiet that meant he was gone.

I called him back immediately, but he sent me to voicemail. "No, no, no," I murmured, dialing again. "I need you to pick up. Come on, Miles." But I got voicemail again.

I got up and paced, trying a few more times. Nothing.

I stared down at my phone. He wasn't going to pick up. What should I do? Drive over there?

But no. I couldn't force him to deal with personal drama when the opening was barely twenty-four hours away. He'd been winding tighter and tighter each day for the last week, and the last thing he needed was me showing up and dragging him into a deep talk.

Worse, I realized as I tried to make sense of the acidic feeling in my stomach, I wasn't sure that even once he got through this weekend, he would want to talk. I might be able to get him to believe that I was truly sorry for accusing him of trying to use me for PR. But for a minute, maybe even a day, I had believed it. And he knew it.

Even if he could forgive me for that, his experiences had taught him that I wouldn't fit in his life. That I couldn't and be happy. And he wanted me to be happy. I knew it in every fiber. He would keep me at a distance to make sure I would be.

But that's not what I wanted. Why could I only see that clearly now that he had given up?

I wanted Miles. I wanted nights at the piano. I wanted hours spent debating light fixtures and cocktail options. I wanted walks on the Crescent Park trail, and I wanted mornings at a table in front of Elizabeth's Café, eating.

I wanted all of him, and his fame and its baggage…that was a feature, not a bug. It had shaped him. It had enabled him to use his wealth and experience to create new opportunities for other people. He was writing the second act of his life, scripting all of it the way he wanted it, and now he had written me out.

It would take so much more than a conversation to convince him to change his mind, and I had no idea how to do it.

I sat back down at the piano again, mindlessly picking out a tune. *You make me new.* The words floated through my head. I played the snatch of melody again with the words. *You make me new, I'm whole with you.*

It was the melody I'd been noodling on the Turnaround piano with Miles, the one whose words wouldn't come to me, but now I could feel them almost tripping over themselves to get out, and I knew.

I knew how to get through to Miles.

CHAPTER TWENTY-EIGHT

I TUGGED at the neckline of the black strapless sheath Chloe had loaned me. "Are you sure this is okay?"

We were standing behind our building, the very muffled thump of bass leaking from the back door. As soon as we got the text from Jordan, I would slip in through the backstage entrance instead of through the kitchen, the way I always came and went.

"You look amazing," Chloe said. "I'm not worried about that. But Ellie, are you sure you want to do this?" She curled her hands around my upper arms and held me in place, staring into my eyes.

I drew a shaky breath. "I'm sure."

Her hands slid down to take mine. "Your palms are clammy, and I can see your pulse jumping in your throat. This looks like more than stage fright. Don't do this to yourself. You can find another way."

I shook my head. It had to be this. It had to be this because Miles would understand exactly what it was costing me to do what I was about to do, and he needed to see the lengths I was willing to go to.

She pulled me into a hug. "You've got this. You're going to be brilliant."

"You don't know that," I said. "You haven't heard me sing. Not really."

She gave me a small, secretive smile. "I might have snuck down a few times to listen to you and Miles. You're amazing."

I nodded, too preoccupied with what would happen next to feel any pleasure at the compliment.

My phone vibrated in my cleavage, and I pulled it out. It was from Jordan. *You're up next.*

Chloe slipped the phone from my suddenly numb fingers. "Go time?"

"Go time." It was almost a croak.

She looked as if she wanted to object again, but instead she pressed her lips tight and nodded, slipping her hand through mine and leading me through the back door. We took the hall past the dressing rooms, weaving in and out of performers either waiting or decompressing from their performances, then hooked a sharp right. The music grew louder as we neared the stage and the brass ensemble playing. Chloe stopped, and I did too, but she let go of my hand and gave me a gentle push in the middle of my back. The stage was ahead about ten feet, but it might as well have been a mile.

"If you're going to do this, do it now," she said. "Because if you don't take the next step, you'll regret it."

"I thought you wanted me to find some other way to get through to him," I whispered.

"I do, but I know you. *You* need to do this. Go, Ellie."

I took a deep breath, and she gave me another gentle push. I was wearing the red heels I'd worn for my first appointment with Miles, and I unstuck my feet, the first step shaky on the stilettos, but I forced one foot in front of the other until I crossed the threshold to the stage, and I turned to look at Chloe. She shooed me further in, and I stepped into the darkness of the stage left wings.

The ensemble ended in a crescendo, with the trumpet trilling high and pure, cymbals crashing, the raucous applause of the audience rising above it all.

This was the worst possible act for me to follow, but there wasn't going to be a good place to slot me in for what I was about to do. Jordan was doing me an enormous favor, and soon I heard his voice blaring out of the speakers as the first members of the brass ensemble ran off the stage, all grinning, the high of their performance written on their faces.

"Let's give it up one more time for the Horn Dawgs," he called into the mic, and the audience was more than happy to comply. "All right, we have a change of pace for you," he said as it began to die down. "We pride ourselves here at the Turnaround on searching out undiscovered talent, and our next performer is the very definition of undiscovered."

I could imagine the confusion on Miles's face. The next act was supposed to be a well-known blues duo from Biloxi.

"This young lady hasn't performed in public in over a decade, and if the rumors are to be believed, her voice is one of the best-kept secrets in contemporary music. Please put your hands together for Miss Elle!"

I forced myself to step onstage as the audience applauded, feeling good after an hour of cocktails and the Horn Dawgs. I waved as I walked past the music stands they'd left behind, crossing to the piano. I tried to smile too, but the curve of my lips felt hard and plastic, and I kept having to force myself to blink.

I sat at the piano and put my hands on the keys, but they shook, and my stomach churned hard. Jordan came over to adjust the mic for me, switching it off as he positioned it, quietly asking, "You good?" next to my ear.

No. I wasn't good. I was terrified. I hadn't sung for an audience since high school, and I was a nobody. But when I'd called Jordan and explained what I wanted to do, he'd agreed. "Miles is miserable. If this'll help, let's do it. He says you can sing, and he would know." When I'd sent over the recording I'd made on my iPhone so he could figure out where to slot me, he'd texted back, *Dang. He wasn't lying.*

I clung to those words now, settling my hands in my lap so I could squeeze them tight to steady them. "I'm good."

He nodded, switched the mic back on, and withdrew.

I took a deep breath, my hands still tightly clasped, trying to will them apart. Restless sounds rose from the front tables, and even though I wasn't ready, I'd run out of time. It was now or never.

I put my hands back on the keys. They shook again, but I played the first chord, determined to get through this, to show Miles how much I wanted us to work.

But I couldn't calm the nerves, and I stumbled twice in the intro measures. This was a disaster, and the rustling of the audience grew louder, but there was no way I could make the words come out. I lifted my hands from the keys, squeezed them tight in my lap again, forced myself to take two deep breaths, and started over.

I stumbled in the same spot.

Tears pricked the backs of my eyes, and I didn't know what to do, so I kept playing, passing the point where the lyrics began, hoping I could settle in before I tried to add my vocals. Because right now, my throat was closing like I'd just developed a deadly allergy to the mic in front of me. And the notes didn't get better. The more I fumbled, the more I fumbled. I was ready to stand up and run when a warm hand touched my bare shoulder and Jordan was back, leaning down to whisper again.

"I can play if it would help. I listened to it a few times yesterday. Could you sing if I do that?"

I nodded. "I think so."

"Go to the main mic," he said. "I'll cue the sound guy to turn it on." He slid onto the bench and I slid off, walking over to the lead mic on legs that were as shaky as when they'd walked me to the stage. But at least here, I could hold the mic and the stand and keep my hands still.

As soon as I took my mark, the melody I'd been messing with for weeks poured from Jordan's fingers as flawlessly as if he'd been the one practicing it the whole time, and this time, after the intro, I came in with the lyrics.

Been hard to get over it but I was trying
If I said it didn't matter I'd be lying
But there's a point I have to let it go
And now I just need you to know…

My nerves began to settle as I let the words sink in, trying to fill them with the same emotion that had poured from me when I wrote them. The audience had gone quiet again, at least. And maybe, maybe if I could sing this right, wrap each note with the love and longing that I'd been feeling for Miles for months, maybe he could see me standing here, terrified, but doing this. Doing this despite the shaking. Doing this despite the fear. And he would see that I could do this. *We* could do this.

You make me new, I'm whole with you
You're all I ever want or need
We're the love story I want to read

. . .

I eased into the second verse, my voice coming a little stronger, the emotion quieting my nerves.

I don't want us to be a "what might have been"
Let's turn the page and begin again
This chapter doesn't have to be our ending
We can write our own brand new beginning

It took me back to the feeling of driving down the causeway, the wind blowing into my car and clearing from my mind everything that wasn't the truth of my feelings. That I loved Miles. And that was everything.

As the verse built to the chorus, the last of the tension slipped from my body. This was good. This was right. And whatever else might happen next, I had given Miles my truth.

I sang the chorus and the third verse, and as the melody transitioned toward the bridge, giving me a short break from vocals, I turned to beam at Jordan, so thankful he was backing me. I hoped he still felt good about giving me this chance.

But it wasn't Jordan at the piano. It was Miles.

He smiled at me, his expression soft and gentle. I stared at him, frozen, not noticing that I had missed the entrance for the final chorus until he sang it like he'd meant to do it all along.

"You make me new, I'm whole with you," he sang. "You're all I'll ever want or need…"

"We're the love story I want to read," I sang with him on the last line. Our voices blended as effortlessly as they had all the nights it had been the two of us in here, playing together like the rest of the world didn't exist.

He played an outro and let the last notes fade. I hadn't turned to face the audience since I'd realized he was there. It was quiet, as if they knew we were all holding our breaths together.

"Ladies and gentlemen," Miles said into the mic, never taking his eyes from me, "this is Miss Elle. My Ellie. And every song I've sung for the last three months has been to her, for her, and about her. But I've never actually said to her that I love her."

My heart starting kicking snare triplets.

"Ellie Jones, I love you."

A huge grin split my face, and he pushed back from the piano only to climb on top of the piano bench. He threw his head back and shouted, "I love Ellie Jones!"

The audience lost it. They broke into hoots and hollers and suddenly Jordan was onstage again, this time on the snare, tapping out a drumroll. The hoots grew louder, and then over them, Chloe's voice, clear as a bell. "Kiss her!"

Miles didn't need to be told twice. He jumped down from the bench, sweeping me into his arms and dipping me like an old-time sailor returning from sea. "I love you, Ellie Jones."

"Prove it," I said, grinning up at him.

His kiss made the whole world spin away, and when he set me back on my feet again, the audience was on theirs, catcalling and applauding.

"Now that's what I call a turnaround," I said, close to his ear.

"Better give them an encore," he said.

And we did.

ACKNOWLEDGMENTS

Thank you to the following people who helped me with story technicalities: Jimmy Hatch for the commercial real estate insights, Lefty at Euclid Records for explaining the Bywater vibe, and Alexis Simms for sharing your insight into the experience of being Black in New Orleans and your clear passion for the city. Thank you to Emily Poole at Midnight Owl Editors for her sharp copyediting, Raneé Clark for the formatting, and Karen Krieger for hunting out crutch words. Thank you to Camille Maynard for your supernatural proofreading abilities. Thank you to the Zoom sprinters who kept me accountable: Clarissa Kae, Jennifer Moore, Kaylee Baldwin, and Raneé Clark. Thank you to Jen Moore and Nancy Allen for reading this so fast for me. Thank you to Sarah Davis and Erin Olds for double-checking my tarot work. Thank you to my writing group, Teri Bailey Black, Aubrey Hartman, Brittany Larsen, Tiffany Odekirk, and Jen White for cheerleading and helping to shape these characters into almost real people. Thank you to Jenny Proctor for all the things. Thank you to my patient family, and especially to Kenny, who always gently interrupts if he needs something so as not to startle me when my head is in totally imagined places.